P9-CND-290

Praise for Zoe Whittall and
Holding Still For As Long As Possible

"With *Holding Still*, Whittall has established herself as a writer of immense vitality and courage; she stands as the voice of a lost, but thanks to her not forgotten generation: the boys and girls who will inherit the Earth." — *National Post*

"Whittall is a dexterous puppeteer, and the book is unput-downable." — *Globe and Mail*

"Whittall explores the very nature of intimacy and self-knowledge in an age of instant communication, mass exposure, and varying levels of chemical intervention . . . It's a harrowing, utterly compelling read." — *Edmonton Journal*

". . . a story that really speaks to the generation while offering some sage advice about living, and there are moments of genuine, understated authenticity, especially in Whittall's depiction of complex human dynamics." — *Fast Forward Weekly*

"In *Holding Still for as Long as Possible*, the awareness of mortality intersects with the romantic restlessness of youth. It makes for a story whose vital signs are fully present and robust." — *Toronto Star*

"Whittall is a writer of richly nuanced characters. There's not a flubbed note in any of the voices." — *Eye Weekly*

"All three characters are well crafted: at once unique, yet easily recognizable... Whittall never shies away from displaying their flaws or their problems..." — *Quill & Quire*

"*Holding Still* holds an astonishingly astute mirror to a generation still struggling to define itself. A fine sophomore novel by one of Canada's most promising young writers." — *The Westender*

"The opening chapter introduces dutiful Josh, a transgender paramedic, responding to a call from a delusional man who claims to have been stabbed in the groin by a ghost. Robustly etched, Josh's narrative is immediately—and consistently—engrossing. Not only does Whittall's depiction of his work and colleagues enthrall, but her expert and compassionate telling of his after-hours dilemmas and compulsions have a cinematic richness full of enticing textures and tones. The sure-footed promise evident in *Bottle Rocket Hearts*, Whittall's 2007 debut, is easily matched here." — *Vancouver Sun*

"Zoe Whittall is a championing voice of outsiders and outcasts, of surviving your twenties and all their hangovers." — *The Coast*

"Whittall's writing is vibrant, funny, and smart. She uses the power of the pop culture reference responsibly; rather than inundate, she picks her spots with effective mentions from a delectably oddball arsenal that ranges from *Waydowntown* to *Designing Women*... This novel firmly pigeonholes her as a kick-ass writer." — *Rover Arts*

Zoe Whittall

Holding Still For As Long As Possible

ANANSI

Copyright © 2009 Zoe Whittall

All rights reserved. No part of this publication may be reproduced or
transmitted in any form or by any means, electronic or mechanical,
including photocopying, recording, or any information storage
and retrieval system, without permission in writing from the publisher.

Hardcover edition first published in 2009 by House of Anansi Press Inc.

This edition published in 2010 by
House of Anansi Press Inc.
110 Spadina Avenue, Suite 801
Toronto, ON, M5V 2K4
Tel. 416-363-4343
Fax 416-363-1017
www.anansi.ca

Distributed in Canada by
HarperCollins Canada Ltd.
1995 Markham Road
Scarborough, ON, M1B 5M8
Toll free tel. 1-800-387-0117

House of Anansi Press is committed to protecting our natural environment.
As part of our efforts, this book is printed on paper that contains
100% post-consumer recycled fibres, is acid-free, and is processed chlorine-free.

14 13 12 11 10   1 2 3 4 5

Library and Archives Canada Cataloguing in Publication

Whittall, Zoe
Holding still for as long as possible / Zoe Whittall.

ISBN 978-0-88784-964-0

I. Title.

PS8595.H4975H64 2010   C813'.6   C2010-900098-6

Cover design: Ingrid Paulson
Text design and typesetting: Ingrid Paulson

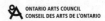

Canada Council   Conseil des Arts
for the Arts   du Canada

ONTARIO ARTS COUNCIL
CONSEIL DES ARTS DE L'ONTARIO

*We acknowledge for their financial support of our publishing program
the Canada Council for the Arts, the Ontario Arts Council, and the Government of Canada
through the Canada Book Fund.*

Printed and bound in Canada

For my parents.

"Though we live surrounded by evidence of our own importance... deep down we know that we are merely tiny particles in a vast interconnected chain of life, but for the sake of our immediate survival, we don't focus on that fact... In moments of relaxation, passion, joy, and fear or when we are confronted by death, injury or emergencies, this larger context is suddenly reopened for an instant, like a never healed wound."

— Allen Shawn, *Wish I Could Be There: Notes from a Phobic Life*

"The planes move in, the towers collapse, and people react with heartfelt shock and horror. You cry because you're sad and frightened. And then, before you know it, the images are repeated in slow motion with the Samuel Barber soundtrack and a close-up photograph of a singed teddy bear. Then you cry because somebody is making you and you wind up feeling confused and manipulated, like your own feelings weren't quite good enough and you needed professional help."

— David Sedaris, *This American Life*

[Contents]

Book One

[Life 1]

5:32:10 p.m. Delta unconscious. 92-yr.-old F.
Not alert.

You probably like to imagine your death the way it should be: You are old. By old, you mean ready to die. Resolved. You are in bed, with your mind intact and loved ones encircling you. Your regrets are few; your pain minimal. Your last words: golden.

Two medics were inside Martha Evanson's pale yellow room at Castleview Wychwood Towers nursing home. One of them, Mike, had been doing CPR for three minutes. "Sushi? Thai? Will there be a lineup at Foxley if we get there by eight?"

The second medic, Diane, grabbed the bag valve mask from the airway bag and whispered back, "I don't know. If we get a late call, we'll be screwed."

"What time is it?"

"Six."

The first rule of being a paramedic: People are going to die.

Mike broke the patient's ribs. That's how you know you're performing CPR properly. The first time Mike felt someone's broken bone poking against skin, he threw up in his mouth

3

some. Hyper-cognizant that he was making another being's heart beat for them, he had pumped so hard that his sweat dripped steadily onto the patient. Adrenaline had surged through his twenty-one-year-old body. When that patient died, Mike's gut felt like crumpled paper. He was wrecked for a week.

Seven years later, CPR was something he did so routinely, he rarely thought about it. Today he kept pumping as the nursing-home staff tried to find the papers saying whether or not the patient was a DNR. He was already getting tired.

He thought he'd understood it early on: that there was no such thing as a good life or a good death. Still, he used to be afraid of death, like everyone. The way his father taunted it; the way his mother tried but couldn't control it, or anything else, by making sure no one tracked mud on the carpet.

When people began to die around him, under his pumping hands, on his stretcher, Mike lost the cockiness of youth, and he stopped fearing death. He lost the will to understand the big picture but gained the wisdom to stop caring. Pump pump pump. Cardio.

Now Mike's biggest fear was being old and a resident in one of these homes. He'd rather take a bullet, be hit by a bus. If you were looking down at him right now, you would see his hair thinning on top. When he placed his hand on his lower back, massaging a repeated injury site, he leaned just like his father did.

Mike had attended to Martha Evanson before. She hadn't been lucid in years. Since her mid-eighties, she'd been barely alive. There were photos of her wedding day on the wall. Pin-curls, a corseted waist, a face in bloom. *She was one hot bitch in the 1930s,* Diane had noted last time she and Mike were called to the patient's room for a transfer.

Martha had been, for most of her life, the prettiest woman in any room. Her nickname was Beauty, even as a child. She had been happily married, in the truest sense, and lucky until the last decade, during which she had grown very afraid of everything. Her sister, Ann, had lived down the hall in the same nursing home until two weeks ago. At first, when she still had all her wits about her, Martha was confounded by nursing-home life. How do you make new friends at the age of eighty? She didn't know how. She had started to slip slowly. Didn't know who she was without her loved ones to remind her.

Mike and Diane didn't know any of this. They'd learned not to speculate.

Mike had expected to come across hideous things in this job. To kneel in human waste, to get spit on, to hold lifeless babies. He'd predicted repeated instances of having to wash vomit off his boots. But he had not anticipated the ugliness that eventually appeared inside him. The crystalline and more-than-occasional indifference to death.

Diane, on the other hand, for all her crass comments and tough exterior, was deeply religious, though she was private about it. Every time a patient didn't make it, she thought quietly to herself that it was God's will. Even though she could sometimes bring someone back to life with her hands, the decision was ultimately in His. She could compartmentalize, and make sense of, and feel content about all the good she managed to accomplish when fate allowed it.

One of the ALS medics on scene pronounced the patient dead. Mike peeled off his gloves while Diane packed up the equipment. Diane repeated a short prayer she always said when a patient died. As soon as she was finished, she thought about having a cigarette, and reminded herself to do a load of whites when she got home.

Mike splashed cold water on his face in the tiny bathroom adjacent to Martha Evanson's room. There were cards with inspirational sayings on the wall beside the mirror. One was by Goethe: *Nothing is worth more than this day.* Mike liked this one.

He and Diane took their time filling out the paperwork, lingering outside in the fresh afternoon sun, hoping this was the last call on their twelve-hour shift. Daycare toddlers walked by in linked pairs, bookended by weary guardians.

Diane lit a cigarette and leaned against the bumper of the truck. She rolled up her sleeves. Mike was briefly attracted to her, and surprised by this.

"Sushi, for sure. I'm craving tempura," she said, exhaling smoke. When she finished her cigarette, she and Mike got back in the truck and Dispatch sent them back to the station in time to book off.

Mike texted his girlfriend: *Eight should be fine after all. We'll come pick you up.*

September 2005

[1]

Josh

Our first call of the day: *"Bravo psych, 43-yr.-old Male. Groin pain. Says he was stabbed in groin by ghost."*

The phone call jolted Diane and me from our glaze-eyed slump at Station 34. We were lying on the long blue couches watching ER, mostly because the other option was persistent grey fuzz. "Okay, 10-4," Diane said, before hanging up and rolling her eyes. On the screen: gratuitous blood spilling off a gurney, sculpted cheekbones. I gulped from my Thermos of coffee, turned off the TV, and we headed out the door to the truck.

As the call details lit up on the screen between our seats, a light rain fell on the windshield. The call history displayed a myriad of psych-related incidents. Diane suppressed a giggle over the radio with Dispatch. "Do you know if the assailant is still at the scene?"

Diane's regular partner, Mike, was out sick, and I was still on swing with no regular partner or station. I hadn't worked with Diane much before, so I was happy to note she had a sense of humour. Nothing worse than working with someone too serious. Diane was one of those medics you can tell really loved Girl Guides and Cadets and anything requiring team spirit and leadership training and uniforms. Possibly a closet Dungeons and Dragons player; definitely walked old ladies across the street. What we called a Super-Medic. I couldn't picture her burning out, ever. Eighty percent of surviving the job is your partner. You wind up with someone boring as shit, who can't laugh at the ridiculousness, then you're screwed.

Have fun saving lives today, Amy had said, before kissing me over the lip of the window of our car. She stood and waved, chewing on a curl of red hair, in the driveway of her parents' house. Amy is such a visual person, it's like she stages those flashback memories in advance.

I had spent the afternoon in her parents' North York mansion for their thirtieth wedding anniversary. My mom's entire apartment could fit inside the carpeted parameters of the O'Hara family room. When Amy wanted to show me to her old bedroom, I swear we had to take the subway to get there. It's probably not possible for us to have been raised more differently than we were. Perhaps if one of us were raised by a cult, or a wolf pack or something. But in urban Canada, we were pretty much on opposite ends of things.

I was trying not to betray signs of obvious discomfort while slumped in a fern green armchair. I spit mouthfuls of smoked duck pâté into thick red cotton napkins and feigned good-natured nonchalance. Three hours and forty-five minutes of forced conversation passed—not boring, exactly, but I was restless.

I slipped out to the deck for a cigarette and was welcomed warmly by Amy's great-aunt Noreen, a plump lady in a loud purple fake-fur coat and matching hat. She was sitting on a wicker bench with a cigarette in one hand, a glass of wine in the other, and a very small dog in her lap that she introduced as Kitty Queen of All. I recognized Noreen immediately as the aging artist of the brood. Amy had told me she was a sculptor.

"So, you're the boyfriend, eh? Do you ever get to the casino?"

"Not much," I said, "though I'm told I'm quite lucky. I won five hundred bucks once." It's true I tended to win things whenever I gambled.

"Really, you'll have to come with me, then. Want to go now?"

"I've got to work, actually. And there's, you know, the dinner and everything."

"Yes, celebrating a marriage. How novel," Noreen said, inhaling.

I immediately loved her and her casual disdain for said rituals, her emphatic arm motions. Kitty Queen of All jumped into my lap. Noreen and I finished our cigarettes in silence, staring out at the garden in the expansive O'Hara backyard.

I hadn't spent much time with Amy's family all at once. Her mother and I knew each other well, since she and Amy were close and I'd been with Amy since 2001. We'd managed to avoid most large family gatherings because I usually work on Christmas and holidays. Sometimes we made Amy's mom brunch on Sundays if the two of them were going to go shopping in the afternoon or something like that. Amy's dad was a workaholic, so he basically just nodded at me from the front of the car whenever he picked up Amy's mom. But this was the first official family affair, and, well, I was pretty nervous.

When we arrived, Amy's mom had hugged me for about five minutes. She smelled like a vegetable garden. Fresh and wholesome. Her skin didn't betray her age but she didn't look like she'd had work done. She was kind of a miracle that way. She went to the fridge to offer me a small green bottle of Heineken, and gave me a thumbs-up sign after she handed it to me. I knew she'd bought them just for me, and I was touched by her thoughtfulness. Amy's father kept shaking my hand. It was like he kept meeting me all day for the first time. I could tell he didn't quite know what to make of me.

During dinner, Noreen winked at me from across the table and said, "This one's a keeper, Amy. No bullshit, this one. He's lucky. He's a lucky one. We're going to go to the casino together."

Amy's mother sighed. Amy's dad mumbled, "Why don't you just throw your money straight into the garbage, Noreen."

Noreen spoke mostly to Kitty Queen of All for the rest of the meal.

After a second cup of coffee, I got up to leave. "Well, thanks for the fantastic meal, Karen, and happy anniversary."

"Shame you couldn't stay longer, Josh."

"Yes, well, I have to go to work, unfortunately. Thanks so much, everyone." Those last four words sounded stilted, like individual sentences.

Amy walked me to the door, well aware of my plan to ditch the festivities before dessert for an evening shift I only pretended to be annoyed by. It was Labour Day, and that meant triple time.

I'd been working for Toronto EMS for just over two years. Amy and I had been together almost five. We first met when I was lying on my friend Roxy's couch in a medicated fog after chest surgery and Amy had nodded at me from across the room, where she was playing video games. Roxy's apartment at the time had only one room.

I thought I was imagining Amy. She looked exaggeratedly tall from where I lay, and her red hair fell in curls to just below her shoulders, kind of wisping off her face in that retro '70s way, a trend spurred by the *Charlie's Angels* remake.

On my nineteenth birthday a few days later, Amy brought me a pudding cup and a birthday balloon with streamers. She made me get up and walk outside. It was so quick, like getting shot, how we fell in love. I felt like you do when you're eight and a girl walks up to you in the playground and says, "You're mine." And you're kind of excited, but terrified, and glad she made the first move.

Getting comfortable with her extended family was a slow process. I'm very shy. I hate how shy I am, but you know what? Eventually you just have to accept who you are. I'm the shy guy. I don't get freaked out about it any more.

I was not shy at work, at all. I could look at your exposed tendons and then right into your eyes and tell you straight how things were. It was really only high-pressure social situations that got to me. Like today. I looked at the ground. I ate too fast and got a stomach ache. I'd been one of those kids who always had a stomach ache. I felt eight all day. But Amy looked beautiful.

"Baby, are you okay? Do you feel weird?" Amy had whispered to me as we stood by the front window in the living room of her parents' home. There was a blush in her cheeks, like she was kind of embarrassed by her family.

"No, I'm good. Your people are crazy nuts. I love them."

There was something incredibly moving about witnessing the person you love interact with their whole family. The project of determining similar features, the language they have for things, turns of phrase. Things you thought were only theirs turned out to be derived from generations of relatives sharing movement and intonation.

Amy and her mother had posed for the photographer, trying to make everyone else hold still and smile, looking nearly identical and as if they actually loved each other. As generations of Amy moved around the room, I was certain I'd never know anyone as well as I knew her.

Out of all the extended family, only Amy's mother knew the truth about me. To everyone else, I passed fine. It never came up any more. After years of hormones, surgery, I couldn't remember the last time anyone had questioned who I was.

Amy used to hate it, not being able to qualify *this is my boyfriend* with *he's trans*, especially with her queer friends, so she wouldn't seem like an ordinary straight girl. Amy was a little concerned sometimes that she was too conventional. I didn't really get it—I liked to blend, plus I thought she was like a fucking star in every room she walked into. But it was my life, and she got that. I guess I felt a similar way with friends who liked to introduce me with *This is Josh. He's a paramedic.* I had to tell people to stop doing it; it was my card to play. Because inevitably, you immediately got, *Wow, what's your craziest story? I could never do that!* But I doubt they really wanted to hear about the woman who jumped off her building last night, especially when all of us were sitting at the bar having a good time. But I got it. It was a weird job. I just didn't like to immediately be questioned about it.

Being trans rarely came up as a topic any more, because like everyone, Amy and I were complicated people with many challenges, and as Amy put it, "special gifts to offer the universe." Now we laughed about the ridiculous arguments over identity we used to have. But meeting all of Amy's family—I felt the familiar anxiety. I was relieved once I'd settled in and no one seemed to notice or care.

It was raining, and the sky was the colour of newly dead skin—a real Vancouver-like day. The kind of weather Torontonians felt really inconvenienced by but that reminded me of my childhood out West. I had huge memory gaps about most of the '80s, until I moved in with my grandmother, but things occasionally came back in waves. The weather reminded me of the month of December in 1988 that my mother, sister, and I spent in a shelter in Vancouver. A particularly un-stellar snapshot in the Lawlor family album. Judy had finally left Nick. I called her Judy because she was always the kind of mom who wanted to be a friend first and a mom second, and that really didn't ever make things much easier, but anyway, Judy finally left Nick, a.k.a. my father, who similarly hated any kind of parental moniker, when I was seven. Nick didn't relish the idea of being a husband or father, but very much enjoyed alcohol, CCR, and model trains. His three things.

I don't know where we were—somewhere near Kitsilano Beach, I think. In a house with a lot of beige carpeting, the kind that looks like overcooked oatmeal and feels scratchy like patches of old dog hair. The house was full of strange women and their confused kids. On Christmas Day, a lot of people cried. They would continue to have conversations about the cranberry sauce or who should set the table, all the while sobbing as though it were totally normal.

I remembered only flashes, certain objects and bits of scenery. That I had to share a bed with Judy and Heather, my ten-year-old sister, and eventually gave up the fight for space and slept on the floor. I kept expecting my dog, Smokey, to nudge me with his wet nose and curl up around me, but of course, he was at home with Nick, who had probably left him out all night. After we left Nick, I became more obsessed with the idea of finding Smokey than I was with seeing my father.

On Christmas Day Heather got the "For a Boy" present—trucks—because of her unfortunate bowl-cut, and I was grateful to exchange mine with hers. Heather grew into an adult who wore stilettos to the grocery store and acrylic nails with palm trees on them. You could tell when she was a kid that she'd turn out like that: she'd walk down the hall in Judy's only pair of semi-pumps and insist we call her Princess Heather the Magnificent.

Judy insisted on keeping my hair long in two braids, until I finally cut off the braids with my Snoopy scissors in the bathroom at school in second grade. It took a long time, but eventually I was able to flush each stringy twisted braid and I emerged victorious on the playground with uneven strands of dirty blonde.

So that Christmas, Princess Heather gave me trucks in exchange for my generic plastic baby doll. I can still see the trucks in their package, green and orange. I ran them along the floor between the feet of strangers, most of whom sobbed gently into Boxing Day. It was jarring to not spend the twenty-sixth with Nick, lining up to buy cassettes at Sam the Record Man.

I hadn't spoken to my dad since I was thirteen. Talk-show and self-help culture might insist I had some overwhelming find-my-father obsession. I didn't. That's how it was in the movies, you know, the kid with the quest. I had no such quest. My sister occasionally talked to him, mostly for guilt-money, but not me. I considered it a gift, being able to decide exactly who I wanted around.

You only have one life, my mother said. *Exactly my point*, was my response. Judy was convinced my seventh Christmas and ensuing traumas directly contributed to me being a paramedic. She used to insist I could have been a doctor, I was so smart, and that she'd failed me somehow, not giving me the self-confidence to go to med school. But I was happy not to stay in school for a decade and graduate owing the government fifty-thousand dollars in loans. My job was steady, and I got ample vacation time and experienced consistently inconsistent adventures on each shift. *Baby, I'm so proud of you*, my mom would say into the phone from her ugly grey house in Sault Ste. Marie. I never knew what to reply when she said that. It made me wish she could live closer, that we could have more of a relationship.

"Ready for another night?" Diane asked. Her long brown ponytail was slightly askew, and her eyes betrayed signs of sleep deprivation.

I muttered, "Uh-huh."

I had known I could do this job as soon as I did my first ride-out as a student. I just felt it. Capable. It was terrifying and exhilarating, and it felt right.

Tonight we pulled out onto Markham Street and Dispatch called in 10-26 for a higher priority closer by. It was an Echo, for a twenty-five-year-old VSA. Our pagers glared abbreviated details about a seven-year-old who'd called 911 for his father. While Diane sped down Dufferin, I ran through all the protocols in my head, making sure I knew what I was doing. Possible VSAs still got my adrenaline going.

"It's probably bullshit," said Diane, just as I was thinking the dude was dead. Dead for sure.

"I'm so sick of Alphas turning out to be Deltas and vice versa," Diane said, veering around a car that refused to move right, muttering "fucking moron" and laying on the angry-horn. Sometimes I wished I had a pocket-size angry-horn in everyday life, so I could just press it when people walked too slow in front of me or refused to give up their seat for an old lady on the bus.

The streets were mostly empty. Everyone walking alone looked exaggeratedly lonely. We pulled up in front of a high-rise on Jameson where I'd done a few calls before. In the building's front hall there was a small kid, with sprigs of brown curls jumping from his skull, wearing a Superman costume and no shoes. He was clutching a cordless phone and shaking violently, like he was really cold.

I crouched down to look at him and introduce myself. I hated talking to kids in situations like this. It was like two films started happening simultaneously in my head. The one starring attentive live-wire Josh, with the elevated heart rate and dilated pupils, body preparing itself to deal with the dad upstairs who might be dead already. The other one featuring calm, reassuring Josh, who could deal with the kid experiencing the most frightening moment of his life. It was always better to be calm, and not let the adrenaline cloud your judgement.

The kid identified himself as Kevin. I heard myself say, "You did the right thing calling 911, Kevin. Good job. Where's your dad? We're going to take care of him now."

Kevin led us to the elevator and pressed seven. He spoke with almost no pauses. "Mydadcameinfromsmoking and (gasp!) fellonthecouch! (gasp!) Hewastwitchingand (gasp!) thenIcouldn'twakehimup! (Gasp.)"

Diane and I rolled the stretcher down the hallway. Kevin ran ahead towards the open door of 7B, his cape flying behind him. I heard Diane stifle a giggle. That's another reason I liked her—the inappropriate laughter. We followed Kevin through the door, which opened into an L-shaped living room. A shirtless man who looked like an aging raver and wore threadbare track pants lay starfish on a couch. Still. I assumed, VSA. The room was furnished with a TV blaring the same ER episode we'd been watching at the station, and a coffee table strewn with glasses and ashtrays. This likely had happened fast but had felt really slow.

Kevin turned to me. "Can you just call my mom? Can I go to my mom's house now?" He was done playing this boring game of Dad Killing Himself.

Diane responded, "Go find your favourite toy in the other room, okay? I know you're scared but soon we'll call your mom." She was good with kids, and that was a plus. I could handle the crying families, she could talk "child."

I took the dad's radial pulse and found it full and bounding. Happy that he wasn't circling the drain entirely, I rubbed his sternum with a gloved fist, attempting to arouse him from unconsciousness. Just then, he opened his eyes. Screamed. We both jumped back as he kicked his muscled legs in the air.

The 10-2s and Fire arrived with movie-like timing. Calls were rarely this cinematic — I'd yet to witness a moment that could be punctuated with symphonic crescendos. It was just one of those days.

I asked the cops to restrain dad while I got the oxygen ready, and automatically repeated the same words we always do: "We're paramedics and we're here to help you. We're paramedics and we're trying to help you. Tell us what happened. What did you take?"

The guy continued to scream, and when the cops strapped him down he started muttering: "Mommy Mommy Mommy Mommy." Fire stood around like a circle of trees providing shade. Let me tell you, it was incredibly weird to have a huge tattooed guy gorked out of his head on drugs, probably capable of killing you without remorse, screaming for his mother.

Kevin poked at me with the antenna of a cordless phone. "Can you call my mom now? I want to go home."

I brought him over to one of the cops. At this point I tried to summon the detached exterior I'd cultivated in order to be a medic. There were calls you laughed about later, ones you learned not to care about despite the abject misery. There were only so many drunk guys you could pull out of their puke before you started to feel not much of anything besides annoyed. Like, *Stop fucking whining already and let's go get you a sandwich. Stop drinking the hand sanitizer and get in the truck already.*

But looking at Kevin, I felt the images begin to save themselves in my memory. Bouncing curls, hands shaking around the phone, tiny chapped lips. *Fuck this. This is fucked up.* My brain was a jumble of expletives and terrible thoughts about how so many people just shouldn't be allowed to have kids.

But I guess I wouldn't be here, if that were the case, right? My mom was barely seventeen when she had me. My dad was twenty and loved drugs more than anything else, and still did. They both still lived like they were twenty-five, just like this crackhead, who moaned on and on. I wanted to tell him to shut the fuck up, to kick him in the middle of his useless chest. I tried to summon compassion but came up dry.

Instead, I went back to asking questions. Getting him on the stretcher. Checking with Dispatch about where to take him. The practical, mundane motions of life-saving happen slowly. This job had taught me to be patient. There's so much standing around, waiting, because some things you can't rush.

My first call ever was a twenty-two-year-old male shot in the head. I was so brilliantly wide-eyed and determined, with empathy reserves likes a fat-cheeked squirrel, watching the city race by on the way to the call. We waited outside the high-rise building for the 10-2s, who arrived only to amble up the long concrete walk, bitching about how they were just about to book off shift when they got this call. A parade of cars following them, pulling up on the lawn, followed quickly by the TV cameras.

"You just starting?" the taller one asked us as we got into the elevator.

"Yeah, it's our first call." I didn't tell them it was my first call *ever*.

I felt as if my shoulders were attached by strings to the elevator wall, pulling me up straighter. The Canadian flags on our uniforms, the shiny yellow EMS stitches, letters aglow — it was as if we were action figures, hollowed out but purposeful. I felt proud, and totally, absolutely terrified.

At the door I stepped to the right while the cops knocked with their nightsticks. I'd been instructed to never stand right in front of the door, to avoid contact with fists, bottles, spit, bullets, a myriad of possible projectiles. My partner, Carl, a mid-thirties joker type, seemed completely relaxed. In my right pocket were a pair of pink panties Amy had folded in three. A good-luck charm. My mouth tasted like coffee whitener. The hallway of this particular high-rise smelled like cumin, paint, and mould. Carl shifted his weight from right to left and swore. He was not excited to be working with me. I was trying very hard to look like I knew exactly what I was doing. I put on my institutional green latex gloves that I carried in my left pocket. They felt inadequate.

After what seemed like five hours, the door opened slowly. Our patient was not, as anticipated, lying in a pool of his own blood next to a screaming girlfriend, but rather standing, facing us. A shining round black hole between his eyes.

"Holy fuck," I said, before I could stop myself.

"Holy fuck indeed," said Carl, sighing.

I heard the pound of more cops arriving, treading down the hall. I couldn't take my eyes away from the gunshot in the victim's forehead. I managed to bring into focus a girl behind him, who stood up from a bright red futon couch, reaching out her arms, as though about to cheerlead.

"Jesus!" she said to us. "It's Jesus. Jay-Jay is the second coming of Christ. It's the only possible explanation."

Jay-Jay/Jesus told her to shut the fuck up. She sat back down, spread her hands over her face, eyes popping between the Vs of two long fingers. The 10-2s talked to the girl, who seemed more shook up than the victim, while we boarded and collared Jay-Jay/Jesus. The bullet was somewhere unknown in his body, and we wanted to protect his spine.

Other cops sectioned off the area. I felt like the solid centre of a wasps' nest, tunnelling my sight to the victim. Carl attended, asking the patient what had happened, what his pain was like, his medical history. I attached a C-collar around his neck, and fastened him to a board with a series of complicated seatbelt straps. Jay-Jay was on a cell phone to his mother up until the very second I bookended his head with tightly rolled and taped salmon-coloured sheets. Jay-Jay/ Jesus spoke as lucidly as you or I, telling his mom to calm the fuck down, that he was all right, and answering Carl's questions.

I knew then, as Jay-Jay swore at me, at his girlfriend, at his mother on the phone, that I was going to have to cultivate a firm belief in something. That not believing in anything was going to be more of a hassle, every day of this job, than accepting things as they were in front of me.

Carl looked at me as we rolled the patient out of the lobby. "Get used to it, kid. You're gonna see some freaky shit."

Carl sat in the back of the ambulance monitoring Jay-Jay while I drove. I thought about how maybe I'd end up learning that sometimes the worst people got second chances, while some of the kindest dealt with humiliation only a body betraying you could provide. Or maybe it wouldn't be that black and white. I had to admit my reasons for wanting to do this job were related to a few wanting-to-be-a-hero daydreams from childhood. I imagined God telling me to lighten up, and I switched on the radio. "We Don't Need Another Hero." Carl sang along. *"Love and compassion, their day is coming."*

"Fucking cocksucker," Jay-Jay yelled at Carl, breaking through the song. "Anyone can do your fucking job."

"Oh yeah?" I yelled, slamming on the brakes too hard. "Seems to me if you were a better drug dealer you wouldn't have a bullet in your head right now. Eh? Huh?"

I looked back through the opening. Both Carl and Jay-Jay sort of smiled as a response.

"How old are you, babyface driver? Too young to wipe your own ass."

I told this story of my first call a lot, when people got curious. But that call didn't teach me anything, really. Except that a call has to be extraordinary to be remembered. And usually not in a good way. But I knew then that I could do the job. I'd been a squeamish little kid so I had thought I'd pass out the first time I saw a crushed limb, an eyeball hanging. But I didn't. While people fell apart, I could be there, helping. I could hack it. I might even get really good at it.

The rest of that first shift passed slowly—mostly transfer calls and minor bullshit. Gradually I started to feel less like an imposter. In the waiting room at Toronto Western I asked Carl to tell me about his weirdest call.

He ran his hand through his scruffy brown hair and chewed at the lip of his coffee cup. Then he placed the cup on a little table strewn with newspapers. "Oh, okay. Easy one. A 911 hang-up call out at Yonge and Summerhill. You know, I'm talking a big mansion. We had to go check it out. We got there before the cops, like tonight, right, and the door was wide open. We were young, you know, and curious and so we yelled, 'Ambulance!' No answer, so we went inside, and there was a pool of blood in the kitchen and a trail leading upstairs. So we followed

24

it up to the bathroom and there was a body all chopped up in the tub."

"No way!"

"Seriously! The weirdest thing, though, was that there was, like, Cheerios and Froot Loops and everything sprinkled in the blood on the floor. My partner was, like, do you think it's a serial killer?" Carl took a long drink from his Tim Hortons cup and shifted in the cold brown shell-chair. He looked over at the stretcher where our nursing-home patient was fast asleep and got up to check her vitals. He glanced back at me, smiling.

"Well…was it a serial killer? How come I never heard about it?"

"It was a *cereal* killer, get it? A *cereal* killer!"

I laughed, not because it was funny but because it was four-thirty in the morning.

"That's what I say whenever I get asked about my strangest call," Carl said, "'cause I'm fucking tired of answering that question."

"What was your first dead body?" I asked him.

"A twelve-year-old in Rosedale. Hung himself with a phone cord. The note said he hated his parents for ignoring him. They didn't find him for two weeks, because they'd gone away and left him alone. I'll never forget that." Carl paused and then glanced over at the pretty triage nurse. She nodded at him, politely, a red flush in her cheeks.

Shortly after that I fell asleep into my curled-up hand, and managed a twenty-minute nap.

The next afternoon, after a long sleep, I woke up with the smell of nursing home in my nose and what felt like a hangover. I held on to Amy. The smell of her skin calmed me. I nibbled between her shoulder blades. I told her Carl's joke. She turned over and looked at me. "I never heard about that case. Huh." She got up to make coffee, came back about ten minutes later holding out two mugs, eyes rolling. "You're an asshole. Cereal killer. Duh." She got back in bed and kicked playfully at my legs under the blanket. "That's such a *Dad* joke."

A few weeks after that, maybe a month, SARS happened. I was the new guy so I got all the shit jobs. I was a little nervous, sure. Okay, I was shitting my pants. The uniform was hot already and when I took all the proper precautions against SARS, I just sat there sweating. It was almost biblical, the amount of sweat. I lost about ten pounds. The heat made everyone even more nervous. It was definitely a test of my dedication.

Amy would make me take off all my clothes in the alcove where the coat rack was, and she'd stick a thermometer in my mouth and make me stand still not touching anything while she brought my clothes downstairs right away to wash, wearing latex gloves. Then I had to shower. It was pretty ridiculous, but I wanted to make her comfortable. No one wanted to hang out with me or come to our house, and I ended up getting a lot closer to my co-workers because they were the only ones who really understood.

I don't know how, but I got through that time—the protocols started to become normal. But a lot of the procedures that were put into place for SARS are no longer happening, now that the scare has come and gone. It's amazing how quickly we forgot. There should be staff scanning visitors before they enter the ER. The government promised thermal imaging scanners. But it all cost too much money. So you have a room full of people coughing and sneezing and bleeding; if anybody does have an infection and they come in, shit will spread like wild-fire. I'm surprised SARS didn't get a lot bigger.

I still wash my hands like crazy, wear gloves whenever I touch anything, especially in the trucks because they're so filthy. I try not to think about SARS, and mostly it never comes up. You can't spend your life worrying about shit you can't control. It's a waste of time.

Tonight, the triage nurse, Nina, looked about as happy to be at work as I felt.

"Twenty-five-year-old male, possible overdose of GHB. Found unconscious by his son approximately forty-five minutes ago. Rousable by painful stimulus. Immediately after gaining con-sciousness, patient was aggressive and violent and required restraining by police." I handed over his health card. In the photo he was smiling like it was Grade Two class-picture day. "Unknown medical history, unknown meds, unknown allergies. Blood sugar 5.8, heart rate tachy at 132, sats were 97% on room air, GCS of 12, not tolerating oxygen..."

I felt my phone vibrate in my shirt pocket. Nina was dis-tracted for a moment so I checked my texts. Amy. *Baby, Wish u didn't have 2 work 2night. Wish u were here right now. I miss yr gorgeous face. I'm loaded with Noreen. She wants me 2 drive her 2 Ngra Falls.*

I texted back, *Sorry, I Love You;* the tiny screen wasn't big enough to explain things like seniority and triple time to a girl who, until the age of twenty-three, had only ever held one job, as a summer camp counsellor. Every relationship has an obstacle, and money was ours. I came from a family that had struggled to get by; Amy didn't. It wasn't as if Amy didn't understand why I felt compelled to work so hard, but family, not work, was paramount to her. It was one of the reasons I loved her so much. She made me understand family in a way I'd never experienced. I clicked the phone shut.

Lately, though, for the last six months or so, it had felt like she and I were just going through the motions. Like someone had turned our lives greyscale. I didn't think it was just me that was feeling this way, but Amy seemed to be in denial whenever we actually tried to say it out loud. "Every relationship has ups and downs," she'd say. "We don't have to make everything a catastrophe, right?"

Back at the station, Diane and I moved around quietly because an ALS crew was asleep on the couches. Al Collins, the self-proclaimed laziest paramedic in the southwest quadrant, and one of those people who was always referred to by first and last name, slept on the navy blue sofa with the corner TV blaring *Weekend at Bernie's*. I pressed "mute."

Station 34 was originally a jail and it used to make me uneasy. It still looked like a jail. The bathroom doors had prison symbols on them. This seemed particularly meaningful on really long shifts.

On the second floor, an elevated block in the centre of the open-concept station, I checked my e-mail. Back downstairs, I grabbed one of the salmon-coloured less-than-comforting sheets from where they were generously strewn about the living room area.

Tracey and Rob came in, faces drawn from being on a two-to-two shift, with a story about an arterial bleed. "It looked like a murder scene. I've never seen that much blood when the patient wasn't VSA!" Rob said to me, eyes alight, as he rinsed out his travel coffee cup in the sink. "This security guard was running after a thief outside the Beer Store, and he tackled him and a bottle broke between them. I can't believe he made it." Rob took a swig from his water bottle and shook his head back and forth.

After he booked off, he tapped me on the shoulder to say goodbye. I nodded back. I liked Rob. I respected him. I hoped someday to be as good at my job as he was.

As I sank into the couch, the automatic slide show began involuntarily—a red Superman cape running down the hall. Tiny eyes with enlarged pupils.

Diane and I didn't talk about the call. When I was a student paramedic, one of the best pieces of advice I got was to cultivate an "I give a shit" on/off switch. For some reason, it didn't turn off tonight. My mind was spinning like that little aggravating icon that appears when your computer decides to not respond and just spins until you have to shut it down.

The sky was a pinky blue when I drove home at 7:30 a.m., and because I wanted to see Amy so badly, I hardly even noticed the delirium that accompanies not having slept for twenty-six hours. I found her asleep on the couch in the living room in bright green flannel pyjamas. The sun was starting to stream into the room at the front of the house. There was a half-full bottle of Maker's Mark she'd been pouring into cups of coffee, waiting for my return. I wanted to take a photo of her like that and carry it around in my wallet. She was so still. She looked like she had when we first met, before things started to get hard.

As I moved closer, I saw that a folded-up paperback copy of *The Places That Scare You* lay on the floor in front of her. She was always reading self-help and Buddhist books, trying to become a better person. I thought it was hilarious because to me Amy seemed like the most together person in the world. She could write one of these books, I was certain.

"How was work, baby?" she asked after stretching out and opening her eyes slowly. She turned to watch me in the doorway as I unbuttoned my shirt.

"Fine. Pretty busy."

She followed me up the stairs to our bedroom, helping me take off my clothes. Stopped and leaned against my back on the landing. We stood that way for a few moments before walking into the bedroom.

Amy fell asleep in minutes, and I stared at the ceiling. *Little eyes. Superman cape. Just call my mom.* My stomach felt like a pile of old sweaters. I pulled from the bottle of water on the night table. Two big swallows burned their way down.

I didn't understand this feeling. I'd scoured the side of the 401 to extract severed arms from roadside weeds to store on ice on the way to the hospital. I'd dealt with bodies after they fell twenty-eight stories, eighty-five-year-olds with broken surgery scars, or the result of what happens when a human hand meets an industrial saw. All of these things were fascinating. I'd lunged forward to watch and discover, curious, my heart pulsing. These didn't keep me up at night. It was amazing what I could deal with and immediately forget. You got used to peoples' sad lives. Mostly, I could see a dead guy, or transport a particularly pathetic case to the ER, and in an hour I'd have completely forgotten about it. It got to be routine. Sometimes I would text Amy in the morning about a VSA call, and when I got home at night she'd be concerned, saying, "Are you okay? How are you feeling?" and I wouldn't even remember what she was talking about. And you knew that it was someone's family member who'd just died, and it was a big deal, but really, when it happened all the time, you just stopped caring. You had to. I think that's why medics generally have a really sick sense of humour, that thin line between tragedy and comedy.

But today I couldn't sleep. I saw a child's enlarged pupils, hands around a dirty white phone, and the air became molasses and the day stretched infinite and there was nothing funny about it. Perhaps it was just my trigger—irresponsible, self-obsessed parents.

My gut swelling, wet yarn in my throat, I moved as close to Amy as I could, inhaling the smell of her hair, lavender and mint. She was like a little furnace. When I closed my eyes, even though my body was beyond exhausted, my brain felt like a buzz saw. I buried my nose in her hair and inhaled again.

After Judy and Nick had split for good, my mom and sister and I left British Columbia to live on my grandparents' farm outside of Guelph. Farms are a great place to be a kid. There's no one to watch you all the time making sure you're cool. You can stay a kid longer, just another part of the garden, because things grow when they grow. And it matters less if you're a girl or a boy. Everyone wears jeans and T-shirts and gets dirty and stays dirty, the adults and the kids. Spending hours in the hayloft, lying on my back against an empty feedbag, I listened to the wind whistle through the holes in the thin wood walls of the barn. All around me was packed earth and the smell of hay. No other smell had ever come close to conjuring in me such inner calm, until I caught the scent of Amy's shampoo.

I contemplated waking her up, explaining what had happened tonight. But she hadn't chosen my career. I didn't want to bring it all home to her and have her lying awake, thinking of abandoned kids or bloated corpses curled over two-week-old TV Dinner trays. Part of me didn't want her to know what I dealt with all the time. I used to tell her, when I first started out. But then I stopped. I'm not sure why. I guess I didn't want her to feel sorry, or to take on any of the stress. I took this job on. It was mine. I liked that the world hadn't let Amy down. I didn't want to be the first.

Besides, I thought, *when I wake up later today, I'll have forgotten about it anyway.* I had a pretty solid ability to appreciate the moments we have here on earth, 'cause God knows, it can all change in one second.

[2]

Billy

Have you ever been on fire? That's how I'd felt for the last year or so, like sparks were running around inside me. I looked at my skin and I couldn't believe it wasn't ablaze. Have you ever, like, really thought about your skin? We're pretty useless without it, right? But it's so insubstantial. Thin thin thin! *Breathe, Hilary, breathe. Good Will. Good Will. Good Will. It's just stressful. This is just a panic attack.*

I had my first panic attack on stage eight years ago. I didn't know what was happening. I passed out and woke up on a stretcher. This was not just the stage at a karaoke bar. It was the kind of stage that spurred headlines such as "Is She On Drugs?" And "Another Teen Anorexic?" Headlines on *E! News* and *MuchMusic*, sandwiched between the repeated playing of "Bitter Sweet Symphony." I can't hear that song without feeling nauseated.

The attacks happened a few times after that, and then I was fine for several years. As if I'd had an allergy that had abated. Until about a year ago. I was in my Major British Writers class

33

and my hands lit themselves on fire. My head turned inside out. I was afraid of everything, as suddenly as a sneeze. The only place I felt safe was at home.

Entertainment Tonight called panic disorder the new "It" disease of the stars. And I was a motherfucking star. Well, not any more. Yeah. I had felt fine that morning. I had hope for 2004. Four is a lucky number, easily divisible. Four is the only number in the English language with the number of letters in its name equal to itself. *Good! Will!*

I was at the dinner table a year after the panic attacks returned, vibrating legs skimming the hem of the off-white tablecloth. We'd taken the subway out to Scarborough, where my girlfriend Maria's mom had moved from Winnipeg last year.

"A steal, Hilary," she was telling me about the tablecloth. "You wouldn't believe it. I should take you to Winners with me."

Maria's mother appreciated a bargain. She was one of those ladies with a sensible short brown haircut and pants pulled too high up, just thrilled when she could buy a designer brand for less. I loved her.

"Mom, we don't need to do any more goddamn shopping," muttered Maria, filling up her wine glass. "The basement is like a bomb shelter already."

It was true — the amount of preserves, cases of drinks, bottled water, and multi-packs was almost impossible to take in with one glance. Maria's mom even had two fridges, full to capacity. She was prepared for disaster and mass hunger, binge eating for thousands. And what she could hold in the tiny duplex basement was nothing compared to what had been in her old house in Winnipeg.

Maria was no longer my girlfriend, as of 3:47 that morning, but we'd decided not to tell anyone about the breakup yet. It was too new, and it just seemed easier to play along for her mother's birthday. My voice was still hoarse from yelling, and things we'd said to each other with such finality echoed in my brain. An endless loop of *Why can't you just get it together* (her) and *When did you become such a paragon of sanity* (me) and *You drive me fucking nuts with your bullshit* (both) and *I'm so tired of you* (both).

We'd been dating since the end of high school — seven years. Succumbed to the cliché itch, I suppose. We had become like furniture to each other. But to be honest, we also didn't have a lot of other friends. Except for some brief threesomes and the odd crush, we'd never been with other people. The friends we had were mutual, except for Roxy, who I'd met at the café where I work. Last month Roxy had needed a room-mate, and Maria and I decided to move apart, to see if we could still date but have separate lives. That hadn't worked either. Looking back, it was really just a way to break up with-out saying it.

Maria and I had moved to Toronto together from Winnipeg in 2000. Her mother had moved to Scarborough a few years later to be with Maria's grandmother, who'd since passed away.

Maria and I were so familiar with each other's families that we no longer had to act polite. Maria's mother liked me because I got excited by girlie stuff, and Maria would rather poke out her own eye than go to a shopping mall or get her nails done. She got along great with my mother, who thought women who got manicures were betraying the sisterhood. My mother bought enough groceries that she could have lunch and maybe dinner. The only bulk items in our cupboards growing up were grains, flour, sugar, and coffee. Ingredients.

I think what was worse than a nervous breakdown was the route on the way to it. Everything is scarier when you anticipate it, right? I bet real crazy-town is actually not so bad. Maybe a little bit freeing. Still, I was trying to avoid it with every bit of my anxious, cautious self, and avoiding anxiety only makes it worse. It lurks in your periphery, taunting you with every doubt and possibility you could ever dream up.

Everything's okay. Right? On! Fire! Here we go again. Fuck.

I started thinking: *What if I just stand up right now and start yelling,* You can all go to hell! *What would Maria's mother do if I ruined her birthday dinner? Good Will.*

This was what I looked like: a little flush in my pale cheeks, gaunt from months of only being able to eat toast, soup, cup after cup of coffee. I appeared still, calm, smiling politely as if absolutely nothing was wrong. My short legs I'd neglected to shave, under apathetic black tights, holes in the knees. A mini-skirt cinched with a pin, because it kept falling down. Thick grey wool socks. My whole grown-up life I'd been a solid size eight, rounded-out 34 C-cup, and now I was in Maria's Clash T-shirt from high school. Maria, who people always try to feed. I kept thinking that I couldn't be as small as her, but apparently, I was. I fell out of my clothes, and didn't know why. I felt so unaware of my body. My hair, which had always fallen in thick dark brown waves, now a bleached blonde bob. My lips were always dry. I forgot to drink enough water.

I looked as if Toronto had beaten me up and neglected to feed me. But when I went back to Winnipeg over Christmas, all I got from old friends and relatives was compliments. Apparently I looked sophisticated. Thin. Stylishly unkempt.

It confounded me, that inside I felt too hot, then too cold, my heart racing, every light too bright, every sensation heightened. Invasive obsessive thoughts appeared without warning and refused to abate. But outside, glamorous? I watched everyone sitting around me, buttering their bread, slicing meat, so oblivious.

What makes someone do something violent and someone else refrain? What if I hurt someone? What if I just lost it? That would be the worst thing in the world. Oh my god, I could be the worst thing in the world. A reel of other thoughts followed. They said: *Oh my god, you're being irrational. Calm down. Things are fine.* But the obsessive thoughts were so much louder, so much more fierce. They were like a Pantera song blaring over the soft serenade of reason.

I thought: *Will Maria understand if I explain, if I have to leave? What if I have to leave right now, in the middle of dinner, because I'm afraid of what I might do? I can't eat. Food looks like stones, tastes too sharp.* I decided to go to the bathroom. I couldn't believe I had worn high heels. You had to have confidence to walk in shoes that high or else you couldn't stay standing. I tried to breathe.

"Excuse me, I'll be right back."

"You okay?"

"Yup, just gotta pee." *No, I'm okay. Listen to the soft song of reason, already.*

In the hallway I briefly leaned against the wall. During panic attacks, I searched out solidity in objects like support beams, sidewalk pavement, braced shelving units. I held on, keeping fingers flat, in case they ran off like baby spiders in all directions.

I inhaled slowly, opened the bathroom door and exhaled even more slowly, sitting on the fluffy lilac toilet-seat cover. I took off the black pumps. Ripped open the toes of my stockings. Stared ahead and inhaled again. *I am an emergency. I am not an emergency.* Reason and panic battled it out. I wished I smoked.

A bottle of yellow cleanser sat beside the sink. What if I drank it? *What. If.* I read the label. The entire label. I put the bottle back down on the counter. Put each shoe back on. Every sentence said to completion in my head started with *What if. Just go back. Go back to the kitchen. Walk down the hall. Everything is fine. Tap tap tap. I'm acting like a junkie. They're going to think I'm on drugs.* I almost wished I *were* on drugs. It would explain how I was feeling. *Good Will.*

These are your loved ones. These are the people who love you most in the whole world. You have never even so much as slapped anyone across the face. Seeing people in pain is horrifying to you. You are safe. The soft refrain played and I listened to it.

What makes someone evil? What makes them snap? *Good Will. Good Will.* What if I just went crazy? What if this was what crazy felt like?

I walked down the hall pretending to look closely at all the framed Sears portraits on the wall featuring the best of the mullet, the bowl cut, the high-bangs-and-braces combo.

"Hilary, you look so pretty. You've really lost weight. Toronto agrees with you," Maria's mom said, before biting into a dinner roll.

Bombs. Cracked skulls. Fire. I could light this table on fire, I thought. *Tip candles to tender cheeks, slam fist into gravy boat, pick shards out of skin.*

Maria grabbed my hand under the table, squeezed twice in a row and whispered, "Everything's fine. Just relax."

She was the only one who ever noticed my subtle unravelling. She promised me I was not dangerous. "It's a form of anxiety disorder," she would explain, highlighting lines in her psychology textbooks with lime green and calming blue. "Obsessive disorder. Repetitive bad thoughts. It doesn't mean you're a bad person."

Similar thoughts occurred to me whenever I stood on a high bridge or a balcony. *What if I jump? What makes someone jump?! What if I*... the thought ran around in my brain and didn't stop until I got back to the ground. In the past I've walked twenty blocks to avoid taking the subway, certain I would jump in front of the train. I used to press my palms to the pavement afterwards to stop the spinning, so grateful to be standing where there was nowhere to plummet from.

"Billy, I forgot you started using a nickname. I like it. It's spunky! I mean, I would think a short form of Hilary would be Hildy or Hilly. But Billy, huh?" Maria's mom said. "Is it so people will stop asking you about your music career? So you won't get recognized so much?"

"I just like it. I like girl names that could be boy names, I guess."

Holding up a glass of wine in a toast, Maria's mom said, "To getting older!"

Happy. Yes. Tap tap tap. When I was eight years old, I crossed my fingers for good luck for an entire year. My fingers grew curved. My index finger a half moon at the tip. Monster digits. I've never been right.

Good Will. Good Will. I repeated those two words. They were magical prescriptive words, meant to be said in careful combination so as to control the universe of uncertainty. The first time I said them, I was on the road and the tour bus had taken off without me.

I was presumed to be asleep in my little cot in the back of the bus, pink curtains pulled around me. Uncle Jonny had taken his drunken girlfriend's word that *the little one* was back there, when it was really Lou the sound guy and a music journalist from the Edmonton arts weekly. When Jonny's girlfriend heard make-out sounds she thought it best to leave it alone. Not tell Jonny and get him all riled up. Meanwhile I was dealing with a disgusting tampon emergency in the even more disgusting bathroom at the Irving station just outside of some small town in Saskatchewan. When I came out, I sat in the station restaurant for eight hours, smoking cigarettes and eating plates of fries, saying *fuck it* to the no-carbs diet.

After two hours I stopped looking out the window for the returning bus. I knew they'd be in Vancouver before the rest of the tour figured out I was gone. With a thin grey hoody and a five-dollar bill, I was undeniably *left*. Finally, I talked my way onto a truck going to Winnipeg that had stopped to fuel up. The driver said, "My daughter loves your music." I curled up in the front seat. The guy's T-shirt said *Good Will Trucking Service*. I repeated the slogan. My magical two words: *Good Will*.

What can I say about being famous? Why is it such a destination? Because you want to be liked, I suppose, in an exaggerated way. But what's underneath that, really? It's a fight against our eventual death. That's creativity in a nutshell. A messy tug-of-war with imagination to erase that feeling that nothing really matters anyway.

So I've been famous, the kind of famous where girls in grocery stores said to me, *You made me believe in myself/leave my abusive boyfriend/forgive myself for the abortion.* Sick kids wrote me letters. There were *Seventeen* magazine articles. Minor endorsement deals. And what did I feel? More scared to die than ever. Before I'd been scared to die, but also, really excited to live and make my dreams come true. My dreams came true. Then I became scared that this was the height of feeling: watching from the stage while crowds sang songs about my silly little feelings. You were not anything they wanted to be, but they believed you were. They believed being you would make such a difference in their lives. Their belief anchored them. Pacified them.

Therefore, you have no choice but to believe nothing. Because fame makes the whole world seem ridiculous. And stupid people love it. Are fuelled by it, get God complexes and forget how to eat and shit without their assistants. But have an ounce of intelligence and be famous, and you will be fucked in the head forever. Spiritual death. I promise.

This was why I counted everything. I put things in order. I made it all make sense, because ultimately, nothing did. It was a trick I played on myself and it worked. And even that thought, that nothing matters, was trite. Was no big revelation. But if you felt it in your chest, it hurt. It was a physical pain. A lack.

I lifted a spoonful of sweet potato to my lips and swallowed, thankful the conversation had shifted away from me. Maria's mother talked about her new business venture—candle parties. Like Tupperware, but with candles. My fingers stopped tingling. My throat stayed open. My heart slowed. I swallowed and tasted gasoline. My heart started up again and didn't slow until Maria and I were on the subway home.

It didn't matter that I understood what was going on physiologically in my body. My neural thermostat was fucked up. My body went into fight-or-flight response for no good reason. Blood rushed to my heart and legs, away from my fingers and face, causing my extremities to tingle. My stomach shut down, throat constricted. All these things are helpful when you're faced with an oncoming bus. Need to lift a car to save a baby? Awesome. Sitting at dinner? Absolutely incapacitating.

Afterwards, at Kennedy Station, Maria and I were a bit awkward with each other, overly polite. She ate one of the chocolate chip cookies her mother had wrapped in Saran for her, offering me one. I declined.

"I'm going to tell my mother about us," Maria said. "We need some independence. I mean, I know we have different houses now, but we need to spend some conscious time apart."

"Yes, definitely."

On August first, I had moved all of my possessions into Roxy's second-storey apartment on Gladstone. For just over a month, I'd had my first real bedroom alone since I was sixteen. Still, Maria and I continued to hang out a lot. It would have been unnatural for either of us to pretend the other didn't exist. And it was still easier to share a bed with Maria. The sounds she made while dreaming instantly pulled me into sleep. Alone, I dreamt about my teeth falling out, about getting shot fifty times.

When I got home, I dropped the remaining bit of Rescue Remedy, a flower-based tincture I'm certain is one hundred percent placebo, into a glass of water and spent the night watching *Designing Women* reruns on Roxy's TV in the living room. On a piece of paper, I wrote out a list of my shifts at the café, and the three classes I had registered for. So far independence wasn't my strong suit. I put my notebooks into my backpack with the two textbooks I'd managed to buy, and laid out my clothes on my bed, in hopes I might actually make it to class the next morning.

As I sipped at the Rescue Remedy, I knew the bitterness was probably a lie. I was an hysteric, a wandering womb. I might have made a great Victorian lady, dying in a tower somewhere, pinching my wrists until the wilting finally killed me.

[3]

Amy

This morning I woke up in a slug's casing of my own regret, pushing the duvet to the floor with my shoes. I had evidently fallen asleep fully clothed, heels and all. My mouth opened reluctantly and my extremities tingled. The clock read 7:15 a.m. Josh was due home soon. I managed to curl upwards only to fall back against the mattress with a moan. *I hate this day.* I cursed the sun with all its expectation.

I'd always been a morning person, one of those cliché bright-side-of-things people who drive normal folks crazy. At summer camp, I used to jump out of my sleeping bag at 6 a.m. for the polar bear swim, fuelled by the frigid temperatures and the euphoric calm of dawn light. Now I liked to jog around Trinity Bellwoods Park as the sun rose.

So it was unusual to feel this way, to wake up grumpy and disoriented.

On weekend mornings when Josh and I first fell in love, we would open our eyes around the same time, as if good timing had tapped us on the shoulders. Feeling the flutter of Josh's eyelashes across my back triggered instinctively the flutter of my own. One of us would press "play" on the stereo. We stubbornly played cassettes, even though we'd been raised on CDs and digital files. We made perfect mixed tapes. I made dozens of videos of him, followed him around with my camera asking him questions. I must have edited more than twenty short films that had my love for him as the only narrative thread. Pure beauty.

When we kissed too long in public, our friends would insert forefingers into open mouths with wrinkled gag-poised faces. Josh wrote e-mails home with subject headings such as *Bliss*, and opening sentences like *This is what everyone talks about. This is It. Amy is the One I never used to believe in.* He'd blind-copy me on them — we had no secrets. I knew all of his passwords. We shared a bank account.

Our elevated state of rapture lasted much longer than most and was therefore experienced not as a honeymoon phase but as a constant state of euphoria. We joked about getting a submissive houseboy for lazy Sunday mornings, so that we could have breakfast delivered in bed. We'd wrap around each other, ease into the day lazily, like melting ice cream cones accepting their liquid state.

When my mother met Josh she said, "Amy, I can see you with him for a very long time. He seems so solid, so good for you." She'd not been so supportive of my lovers before Josh, just quietly tolerant, making some efforts but nothing overwhelming. It wasn't a gender thing. She had liked my one girlfriend just fine. She had liked Jason, my high school boyfriend, all right. But she really took to Josh. She'd send us envelopes with clippings of anything in the news related to paramedicine or hospital issues, with *True Heroes!* written in coloured pencil crayon in the margins. She bragged about Josh to her book club when they read a book about the health care system. It felt as if Josh fit into all the areas of my life that had once felt separate.

I have a tattoo on my lower back that says *Hope*. When we got the tattoos, we were twenty, and in that stage where we still did things like have sex in cabs. Back when I felt somehow invincible, we got each other matching tattoos for Christmas. I still loved every inch of those letters, albeit a bit differently now.

I remember Josh pulling me out of the cab on our way to get the tattoos done and sitting me atop a bright green *Now* magazine box, and kissing me. If you've been kissed like this, you know what I mean. Heart-attack city, hair-ballad worthy, "throw all your money away for one more chance at love" kind of kissing.

The sun was going down and we hadn't left the apartment since Boxing Day, hadn't talked to anyone else, had turned off our phones, unplugged the computer. I was wearing a bright blue ball gown and he was in a '70s-style tux, and we didn't have anywhere fancy to go. We weren't high, just feeling momentous.

I'd been videotaping that whole day, watching through the camera lens the way Josh moved. At dawn, I had stood on a high stool in the corner of our bedroom, had caught him waking up from a beautiful angle, kicking the soft blue sheet down and stretching out his body. Our bed surrounded by Christmas paper and abandoned clothes. Usually he didn't let me record him so much, but his guard was down. "I like the way you see me," he'd said, "so I suppose I don't mind so much." You'd be hard-pressed to find much photographic evidence of Josh's existence, but on occasion he let me document *us*.

I met Josh when I was nineteen, through our mutual friend Roxy. She was teaching me how to edit movies on her computer, and there he was, asleep on her pullout couch.

"My friend Josh came to town to have chest surgery, so we have to be quiet."

"Where's he from?"

"Guelph."

"Huh. How do you know him?"

"We played in a band together last year. He used to come to the city to drum. Now he's moving here to go back to school and stuff."

"For what?"

"To be a paramedic."

"Weird."

"I know."

I was drawn to him immediately. Chemical.

When we first started dating, every once in a while we used to have this conversation:

Him: "You're going to leave me for a girl, right? 'Cause you're really queer?"

Me: "No. I date girls and guys. Are you going to leave me for a straight girl?"

Him: "No way, uh-uh. Why leave the perfect woman?"

It seems funny now, that we used to care about those things, be hung up on the politics and the way we were seen. But I suppose it's natural to question, given the hostility of the entire universe outside our safe bubble of progressive folks. Josh never, ever looked like a girl, even as a kid. He went on testosterone at seventeen. He's never not passed. He just looked a lot younger than he was, like a teenager. It bugged him.

47

He never really went back to Guelph, except to get his stuff and move in with me. We graduated the same year, he got a job with TEMS, and my internship at the film centre turned into a job. We were pseudo-married with careers while most of my friends were still dodging student loans and working at Starbucks.

By the time I had unzipped my dress on the second floor of the tattoo parlour, I was no longer concerned that the cooler-than-shit tattoo artist thought I was a tattoo-virgin wimp. She looked like a Suicide Girl, one of those online pin-up Goth vamps from the popular website of the same name. And like all those girls, underneath the red hair dye and sleeves of ink she had the body of your everyday prom queen. I stood there as she smeared my skin with Vaseline and placed the transfer sheet on a few different areas. I acted as if it was totally normal to have a stranger inches from my breasts.

"So, what do you do for a living?"

"I'm a student."

"She's a filmmaker. You should say you're a filmmaker," Josh said.

"I've made *two* short films. Hardly a filmmaker, yet."

The tattoo artist shrugged.

I had started out making experimental videos. Josh was the star of my first linear documentary, him having such a fascinating life story and all. The film was abstract, no actual talking heads, just text of his experiences and visuals taken from car windows and roller-coaster rides, the sky and the road blurring in patterns. He liked to plug it, pretend I was a few short credits away from Cannes.

I was mildly afraid of needles. I had an aversion, is more accurate. But that day I felt committed. I'd never been tattooed before because I'd watched my older sister, an early '90s hippy, get all the Grateful Dead bears down her back, a peace sign between her breasts, and a psychedelic *phish* on her ankle. Now she had to wear tights and long blouses to her law firm, even in the summer, and was considering laser removal.

I'm the youngest of four siblings: lawyer, surgeon, physics professor, and me, the artist who provides my parents with plenty of worry and lots of whispered speculation, the accidental baby twelve years younger than the rest. I am the beloved baby girl, the family pet, since lawyer and Dad are allergic to dogs.

Josh, tattooed since he was a teenager, grinned at me. "You don't have to do this, baby. But if you still want to, the pain isn't as bad as you might think. You can ask her to stop any time."

The tattoo girl nodded, examining the crumpled-up paper with our design on it.

"Why don't you go first?" I zipped my dress back up and sat on a grey office chair across from the tattoo bench. I pulled off my boots and rubbed the warmth back into my toes.

"Sure." Josh told the artist where he'd like it placed, and she pressed the transfer sheet down on his lower back.

I taped the whole process, watching as the letters appeared on Josh's skin, as blood was wiped away, the artist admiring her work at every step. She had a steady hand.

When I lay down and decided, finally, on the exact same spot on my lower back, Josh held my hand and kissed my shoulder.

"Brave, bravest girl," he whispered, buttoning up his tuxedo shirt.

The needle went in and I hardly felt it at first, I'd been expecting so much more pain.

Afterwards, we lay side by side on the tattoo parlour floor with our shirts off, our arms raised, and our heads turned to the left in faux sleep. The tattoo artist panned our bodies with my camera, lingering on the matching raised black letters. We were marked, and we had our whole lives ahead with this word. We were attached by it. I remember thinking that.

I always thought in terms of opening credits, and decided that scene would be ours.

That was years ago now, and eventually everyone becomes ordinary, right? Lately Josh had taken to waking up first, having a shower, eating a PowerBar, and checking his e-mail, all before I woke and felt the bed cold like a leftover pancake. He smoked in the backyard while I ran strawberry or eucalyptus bath gel over my body, sighing into the steam.

I'd channelled my restlessness into the acquisition of scented lotions, gels and powders, increasingly more expensive. I even built a new shelf to accommodate the bottles and jars, a nail between my teeth, hammering in a bright red rack beside the mirror. I got a little nutty and colour-coded them. Green apple facial scrub. Chocolate mousse shower gel. Cotton candy conditioner. Brown sugar exfoliant. Candy cane lotion. Martini cologne spray. Josh had watched me through a sliver-sized bite of the open door. "You look tough, like you used to," he muttered, claiming the muscles in my shoulders were more defined, sweat pooling in the divots.

I didn't feel my body much. I could smell it, watch my feet moving, but I didn't feel inside of it. Things that used to be seamless were now fraught with customs. I wanted things to feel good and normal. They didn't. Good and normal felt as far away as Whitehorse. But we were so clean. Skin brushing against each other in the hallway, plum scents and sparkle traces left behind.

I went to a psychic last night because my best friend Tina and I were drunk, arms linked and weaving down Queen Street. That afternoon, Tina, who is also my co-worker, stole my travel mug and returned it full of rum with a Post-it note on top reading, *This is to celebrate surviving the longest staff meeting in the history of the world. Love yr fav. drunken slut.* Tina liked to believe we were Patsy and Edina from *Ab Fab*.

At four we went from the office to Java House, a cheap coffee, beer, and spring-rolls joint. The place was crammed with back-to-school drinkers and the waiters seemed inconvenienced and our voices crept louder and louder up the walls with the cockroaches, curling around the amateurish Goth art. By the time most people were finishing dinner out on the patios along Queen Street, we were shit-faced.

The psychic had a storefront that promised answers, and I had just finished telling Tina how much I needed one. "How could a relationship that started out feeling like a religious conversion have turned into this?"

Tina didn't have the answer, other than to lead me through the garish door and into the incense-fumigated bachelor apartment where we paid the palm reader for some enlightenment.

So far, 2005 was not shaping up to be my year. I couldn't stand the *Sex and the City* conversations Tina and I kept having. I'd become the girl who needed to process her love life constantly, even with a psychic stranger. I didn't feel like myself. I'd always been able to keep it together. I was *Most Likely to Be Prime Minister* in my yearbook and until now had felt above this pandering to the heart. Oh love, the great leveller. Shouldn't

I have been calculating my carbon credits, organizing a benefit show, doing something worthwhile instead of this tedious inward search?

Tina wasn't a great help. Her longest relationship was an affair she'd had with her married lesbian doctor. Two years of clandestine hotel encounters, cell phones used only with each other, and neurotically safe sex. Tina thought I needed to cut Josh loose. "He was your first big-deal relationship. You're almost twenty-five now. Let him go and make some mistakes."

The psychic, a middle-aged lady with a thick French accent, took my hand and said, "I see an ending. You have been lucky, yes, so far in life. But you will be challenged."

I rolled my eyes. She sat back against her chair, satisfied with her vague and predictable assessment.

I reacted badly. "Why doesn't anyone have *good* news, eh?"

The rest of the night was sort of a blur.

I was piecing together some visuals, snippets of conversations, when Josh returned. My eyes brought him into focus, standing in the doorway pulling off his shirt. You could barely see the scars on his chest any more. He turned to set the alarm on the bedside table and I noticed his tattoo was starting to fade a little.

"Can you shut the blinds tightly, please?" Josh asked. "It was a really rough night."

I remained in a ball at the end of the bed for a few more seconds before I limped reluctantly to the window wearing one high-heeled sandal. "I'm just remembering taking a piss in full view of the Drake patio," I said.

Josh didn't seem surprised. I made a mental note not to drink for the rest of the week. I sealed away the offensive brightness with a few tugs of the thick, black drapes.

"Thanks, baby," Josh said, curling up under the blue sheet.

Pulling the remaining shoe off with one hand, I leaned onto the bed to touch Josh's forehead with the other. I pressed my palm against it, as though I were a mother checking for fever. He once told me this was the most comforting touch, someone's palm against your brow. But now he rolled away, covering his head with my pillow, irritated.

In the living room I made a couple of calls. I cancelled my brunch date with my mother, and my afternoon manicure. I fell back asleep until 1 p.m., and then set about watching an afternoon movie on the CBC. *Waydowntown*, one of my favourite Canadian films, where the characters lock themselves in an office building for a month on a dare.

When I pictured the movie version of my life, Tracy Wright played me, and Don McKellar, Tracy's real-life actor/director boyfriend, played Josh. Our banter would be witty. We wouldn't look pathetic when we spent days smoking joints and crafting from garbage. Somehow, at the end of our movie, you wouldn't feel ripped off even though nothing actually happens.

It would be like one of those Canadian art movies where the characters wear unconventional green jackets and don't have parents. They exist as though poured from the rusty taps of the local indie rock bar.

I had another daydream where I was Parker Posey and Josh was Jake Gyllenhaal, but we mostly just sat around looking pretty in that one. I saw them sometimes on their bicycles on Queen Street—I mean Tracy and Don, of course—and I always smiled, as if I knew them. And then when I got up close I remembered, *Oh, they are just Toronto-famous. They are not my friends.* I'd like to be famous in the same way most people would, but I think I'd get bored quickly. I'd rather hold the camera.

Not like Roxy's new roommate Hilary, who was so clearly a performer. When she walked into a room she didn't say much, but what she did say would be hilarious or just weird and memorable. Same with Roxy or Tina: they were always *on*. Josh and I *observed*. We might have been very different in most obvious ways, but there was a quiet relationship to the outside world that we shared.

It was hard to pinpoint exactly when I started to *expect* things. Recently I had heard myself say, in an offhand way, "I don't get out of bed for less than twenty-five dollars an hour."

Tina had nodded her head. "Oh yeah, fuck yeah, what's the point?"

When I said stuff like that, I sounded like the kind of artist my father could respect. My father was not one to understand the point of film if it wasn't comingling with commerce. He had tried to stop supporting me when I decided on art school. *I could cut off your money, you know. Your Mom and I have discussed it*, he had said on many occasions. I would say, *You do what you have to do, Dad*, knowing my mother would never allow it.

Now I no longer had to take anything from my parents and it felt good. And I'd stopped feeling guilty about the things stacked against Josh when he was growing up. We were both adults now, supporting ourselves, and as far as I was concerned, we were on even ground.

Whenever I said that to Josh, he'd point to the kitchen floor with his foot, like, *Uh, this house? Uneven ground*. But he made more than me now and was like a fucking rock of stability.

"Stop pulling that victim shit, Josh," I told him the last time it came up. "It's not attractive any more."

He told me I'd become colder. "You used to be the warmest feeling in any room," he'd said.

I looked at the date on an incoming text message from Tina that read, *You Alive?* I realized it was our four-year anniversary today, and both Josh and I had forgotten.

A week later, at Starbucks on Spadina, a jump below Queen, I saw my random crush. She was this little tomboy thing, blonde, messy-haired, always dropping something, always in a hurry. We'd progressed to nodding and smiling at each other, since we clearly had the same work schedule. She always ordered a tall green tea, and I was always two double soy lattes for Tina and me.

For some reason, seeing the random crush made me smile to myself as I walked across the street to work.

Tina noticed. "What's with the grin, goofy?" She rooted through her oversized purse for a pack of cigarettes while we stood on the polished wood floors of 401 Richmond, a beautiful building filled with galleries and offices for arts organizations, film festivals and magazines.

Tina and I worked on the fourth floor. We were waiting for Josh to bring the video projector down in the elevator. The lobby smelled like lemon, not in a Lemon Pledge way, but like the citronella lotion I used to wear at summer camp to ward off mosquitoes. The smell filled me with calm every morning when I came into work.

I was co-coordinating a project. Somehow my life had become a series of related *projects*. Tina and I were deciding who got grant money for a Super-8 film project, and we were watching the submissions at my house to narrow down the shortlist. The more I got involved in organizing festivals or teaching how-to-edit-film workshops, the less art I was actually making. But my inspiration had been dry anyway.

I rushed to the front door to prop it open as Josh marched through the lobby from the elevators, face eclipsed by the giant projector. He had come right from work, still in uniform, to help us out and drive us home. It could still make me feel something, that shade of blue.

I jumped ahead of him down the front steps of the building to our car, which was parked illegally outside the pizza joint. I popped the trunk and held it open so he could wedge the projector in between a bulk case of mineral water and the spare tire. Everyone stared at Josh when he was in his uniform. He'd learned not to care, but it weirded me out still.

We watched Tina bike through traffic ahead of us on Richmond Street, pounding her fist on the hood of a Beck taxi before darting through the intersection. Josh shook his head at her, drummed his fingers on the steering wheel, kept time with the Modest Mouse song. We sang the chorus while stopped at Bathurst behind a streetcar. For some reason being stopped behind a streetcar always seemed like some sort of divine injustice. Patience. I needed so much more of it.

Josh put his hand on my leg. I turned and for a moment saw him the way a stranger might. I tried to picture us together in five years. Who would we be?

After lighting a cigarette and narrowly avoiding collision with another Beck taxi, Josh told me he had got an additional job, that he'd been selected to be part of a national team of emergency personnel specially trained for disasters. You know those TV commercials that ask, "Do you have a 72-hour plan for your family should a disaster strike?" Well, Josh would be sent to the nerve centre of whatever disaster actually ensued.

A few months ago he'd worked like crazy on the application. "Can you believe it?" he said now. "The competition was really stiff."

"Congratulations, baby!" I said.

"We start training next week. I'll be gone for the weekend."

I pictured myself stretched out on the sofa, doing my nails and drinking cocktails, the whole house to myself.

I couldn't do his job; I wouldn't be able to handle all those final moments, the blood and panic. Josh is the perfect personality for it. He doesn't freak out. When he's at work, even if he is secretly bored or thinking about dinner or wishing his partner would fall into the centre of the earth, he appears to be concerned only about you and your welfare. I think he has something I'll never have, an inner calm, or some sort of perspective on life you have to be born with.

Josh looked at me clutching my BlackBerry. "We're so different," he said. "Sometimes it still confounds me that we fell in love."

"I know!" I said too loudly, like a hiccup.

"Although, when we first met, it seemed almost metaphysical, like we weren't in control of it."

"Otherworldly, for sure."

Pausing on a red, Josh took a final drag and dropped the butt into an old coffee cup between the seats, pulling his shirt untucked and unbuttoning the collar. "Did you know we missed our anniversary last week?"

"I remembered that day, but you were asleep and I didn't want to wake you."

Josh looked at me, and for a second I felt crushed under the weight of those lips, that familiar generous grin.

When we got home, he helped me set up the projector in the living room and he puttered around a bit before leaving for Roxy's.

Roxy and Josh had recently become close again. They had one of those long-term friendships where sometimes they didn't see each other for six months, but they were still family.

I suspected Josh had a crush on Billy. I could always tell. This made me feel simultaneously protective and jealous — affection laced with fear.

Mostly, after the door clicked shut, I was thankful for one hour of solitude before Tina arrived. I had time to correct the chips in my polish and watch some terribly entertaining tabloid TV show. If I wasn't working, I appreciated being able to shut myself off. I'd do anything to distract myself from contemplating these shifts between Josh and me, the uncertainty. Perhaps becoming this resistant to change was part of getting older. A depressing thought.

To be with someone in a healthy way, you had to be able to be alone in a healthy way. I believed this firmly. Right now the possibility of being alone made me hear horror-movie screaming. I hated that the universe seemed to be steering the wheel and I had no ability to get myself back on course.

[4]

Billy

Mid-September was unusually warm. The day I met Josh, I was hoping to do absolutely nothing, other than carry a bag of groceries from Price Chopper to my apartment. I planned to lay down on a towel on the back deck with a book and a cocktail and try to cultivate an easygoing personality. I wore a holding-onto-summer tank top. I was not expecting to meet someone who might alter the rest of my life. Or whatever.

While waiting in the checkout line, I covered Paris Hilton's face with my to-do list and marked a thick red satisfying line through *groceries*—accomplished! For an agoraphobic, shopping is sometimes a feat, although that day I wasn't so bad. The fluorescent lights didn't sear. The floor didn't sink. I remained a living body in a public space. Victory. I tucked the crumpled list into the back pocket of my faded, dirty jeans.

Most days, I would have had to rush to work at a café on Roncesvalles, or to school at the University of Toronto, where I was half-heartedly attempting a part-time English Lit degree. I'd been accruing an overwhelming number of sick days in both settings. And let me tell you, taxis owe much of their livelihood to the anxiety prone. I had spent most of my extra cash on cab-metre sums and bar tabs, prescriptions for Ativan, and, of course, coffee.

I'd been alone—sans Maria, totally friggen independent for the first time since the *Are You There God? It's Me Margaret* days—for seven weeks. Leaving my house was hard, because the panic attacks hit me at random, and I drank too much coffee and ate too few vitamin-enriched foods. Even though Maria and I had been alternately at each other's throats or completely bored with each another for the last two years of our relationship, I still felt like I needed her for simple tasks. Like, how do you make rice?

Yesterday she'd asked me via text—the main way we were communicating—*Have I ever had the measles?* We were each other's memory banks. I answered: *Yes, Grade Three. You also had mumps — twice.* When we were together, I would help her fill out whatever form she had on hand, because I wasn't scared of ticking boxes and had a freakishly good memory for detailed health histories. I also did all our budgeting and taxes. She made the rice, and fixed our bikes, and handled all the mechanical stuff. Without each other, we had a lot of learning to do. I was stumbling, splayed. Maria could always calm me down.

Now, I was learning to do everything alone. *Good Will, motherfucking Good Will.* Fifteen steps to the ground-floor landing. Three to the cement laneway. Five squares to the street. Gladstone. My new street. Maria and I had lived around the corner on Argyle for seven years, so I didn't have to break in a new neighbourhood. I hate new places and not knowing where I am. There was something about looking up at buildings for the first time, adjusting to a new skyline, that made me feel like I could just fade away by accident. I could fall into the street, and no one would know where to find me.

Maria had moved right downtown. She craved anonymity and an under-seven-minute subway ride to work. I never went east of St. George any more. Why bother? I'd rather get spit on in my own neighbourhood. If I was going to collapse, I'd want to do it near my house, so people would recognize me and tell the ambulance crew or police or whatever that if they just brought me back to my doorstep, I'd be fine.

Seventeen sidewalk squares to Price Chopper. I'd forgotten to count that morning, that's how triumphant I felt. For no reason, and that's the best thing. The possibility of stars colliding, chemicals balanced. Fucking right!

Despite my unafraid, totally happy mood, the air was wet and tragic—and making that pronouncement was factual, not pessimistic or overly poetic or whatever. Even in Toronto, 1,791 kilometres from New Orleans, people wore the after-effects of Hurricane Katrina on their faces like badly matched liquid foundation. Strangers with deep caverns under their eyes had conversations on the subway about whether or not the world was ending. The biblical people looked more purposeful, strutting confidently, clutching their pamphlets.

I was afraid that every surface I touched would be sticky, so I pulled my arms into my sleeves and opened things with my elbows. Trying to open my apartment door, I dropped my bag of groceries, but nothing broke. A head of iceberg lettuce, a bag of cherries, four yellow plums. One plum bounced down the concrete step and under a cedar bush. I accepted its release from my capture, picked up the bag, and walked inside. I closed my eyes walking up my apartment stairs, trying to see how long I could make it and still know where I was.

I started counting steps, then floor tiles. *I'm a Tilt-A-Whirl. Good Will.* I was waiting for a certain emergency. How quickly things can go from calm to freak-out.

When I was in primary school, I had a prayer ritual every night—a specific order of blessing people and keeping them safe: Mom, Dad, Grandma, sister, classmates, babysitter, mail carrier, school-bus driver. Then, in the same order, those people were to be guarded against cancer, car accidents, kidnapping, facial disfigurements. (It was the era of *Mask*, after all, the book and movie.) I had a big thing for kidnapping, probably because I had watched a made-for-TV movie about a girl who was kidnapped and didn't find her family again until she was fifteen, at which point she was a stranger to them all. If I forgot anyone, or forgot the order, I had to start over from scratch. Sometimes it took about an hour. I stopped doing it when Kimberly Actonvale was actually kidnapped in Grade Seven, and my grandfather died of cancer. *Fuck that,* I thought.

I opened my eyes, clutched my bag of bruised produce and double-jumped the splintery, wooden blue stairs, landing with two solid feet on the kitchen floor. Roxy sat at the table reading *The Globe and Mail.*

Her short black hair was a bird's nest. She was dressed in her work clothes for catering: white button-down men's shirt over her mostly flat chest, black dress pants and men's dress shoes, a sparkly pink Care Bear hoody overtop. Most people couldn't peg her as a girl or a boy, even from one foot away. Our cat, the adopted stray with one remaining piercing blue eye, was curled on a placemat opposite her, like a place setting. Her name was Joan Nestle, or Smoosh for short.

I ran one of the plums under the tap in the sink. *I'm fucking lucky!* I felt like yelling to whoever controlled my various mental disorders. We're all so lucky. Who cares if I was afraid of aneurisms, nosebleeds, spontaneous blindness? If I had a heart attack right now, and it was my time, then shouldn't I be happy I had lived such a struggle-free life? I took a bite. Sour. I threw the plum in the sink, where it landed in a bowl of half-eaten instant oatmeal.

Roxy smoothed out the newspaper on the kitchen table and started rolling tobacco on top of the Business section. We were just starting to have a roommate routine, something also entirely foreign to me. The exaggerated politeness, the am-I-in-your-way? feelings were fading. Roxy was fun to observe. She seemed to operate entirely in the present, with no obvious worries or preoccupations. She had a lot of friends, many hobbies, too many idiosyncrasies to mention.

I wished I were one of those "grateful for what I have, aren't we lucky to be alive today" people. I was without a doubt deeply terrified of the inevitability of death. And so I did what I could. I counted. I repeated. I breathed deeply. I distracted myself.

Despite Roxy's stripper name—the actual name on her birth certificate was Roxy Barbara Streisand Gillard, and I'm not even kidding—she was as far as possible from the way you'd expect a Roxy to look. Roxy was a connector—or was it a nucleus? At school I had always skipped biology, so I wasn't good with scientific metaphors. Anyway, she connected people.

She was pretty much how I made all my friends in Toronto. She made an effort to make plans with friends, and to introduce them to others, like a community hub. There—Roxy was a community hub. She was rarely alone. She was always up to something interesting.

We called our apartment—a second-storey two-bedroom number just north of Queen Street—the Parkdale Gem, after the area in Toronto where we lived. "A gem"—that's how it had been advertised in the local paper when Roxy found it a few years ago, a gem amongst the high-rise shit-holes, crumbling old Victorians, and rooming houses. The apartment's best feature was the large kitchen that opened out onto an expansive fenced-in balcony that could, if one wanted, fit a small yoga class. Our bedrooms were small, and the living room more of an idea squished between them in the long hallway of the house, but the kitchen made up for it and we spent most of our time there. Even though Roxy owned most of the furniture and had lived here for five years, I knew it would eventually feel like my home too. If I ever really unpacked.

Still, there was a new form of uncertainty in the air, and you could taste it in Parkdale. The west end of the city was experiencing a growth spurt along Queen Street west of Ossington Avenue. On the sidewalks I often kicked giant screws that had fallen from fast-rising construction sites. The area was definitely deep into adolescent tantrums, boisterous claims and lots of architectural posturing that hid massive insecurities.

A hotel that used to provide the neighbourhood a certain visible sketch factor had been rebuilt into a boutique hotspot called the Drake Hotel, with a hipster happy hour and over-priced entrees. The first Starbucks. Residents had reacted as if someone had taken a big shit on their front porch. The graffiti condemning it was witty. Roxy's friend Richard, a local multimedia artist, made pins that read *Blame the Drake*. Roxy wore one, somewhat ironically. Condos were sprouting like acne on every block. Rents were rising. Our landlord, who was old, usually drunk and lived in Mississauga, only remembered to cash the rent cheques half the time. We were lucky he probably wouldn't think to raise it. When Maria and I moved out of our place on Argyle, our landlord there said he was selling to a developer.

Roxy organized walks around the neighbourhood trying to mobilize residents against the encroaching virus of progress. She was full of historical tidbits, and she rallied against the takeover. Me, well, I secretly hoped they really would build the rumoured Loblaws or Shoppers Drug Mart. Then I wouldn't have to stand between peed-pants man and boob-touch guy at the 1–8 items aisle at Price Chopper. I was thankful for the occasional latte, sick of the syrupy swill from the doughnut shop next to the train tracks. I knew this made me a bad person, but whatever. You pick your battles. You do what you can. I was trying to cultivate some sense of balance.

Roxy stood up to reach for the sugar and pulled the white shirt out of her pants, her protruding beer belly sticking out slightly over her belt. "Listen to this, Barbara Bush is reported to have said this about the Superdome shelter: 'So many of the people in the arena here, you know, were underprivileged anyway, so this [chuckles] — this is working very well for them.'"

My coat halfway undone, I shoved the groceries into the crisper, checked the freezer, and found the coffee tin empty. Another cup. Doughnut shop.

"Coffee? I'm going back out."

Roxy poured a pink package of sugar substitute into her Diet Pepsi. She liked to drink things that taste like tinfoil. She preferred food with molecular properties akin to plastic bags. "Isn't that fucked up?" she asked, not waiting for me to nod my head or add anything.

Roxy liked to talk. I liked to listen. The roommate situation would probably work out well.

Roxy was raised in rural Quebec in a gay commune and didn't taste Coca-Cola until she was eighteen. Or not a commune, really. The way she explained its evolution, it seems that her two dads purchased a farm, and slowly their friends left the city to join them. They became an insular social movement, with solar-panel huts and organic gardens. Goats and pigs, donkeys and bunnies.

Needless to say, the time Roxy did spend in rural elementary school was hard on her, the only Jewish, ambiguously gendered kid raised by a group of men. Consequently, she grew an incredibly thick skin and uniquely independent disposition. Her dads (The Donalds: one Don, one Donnie) sent her care packages of home-made jam, photos of lambs, and an annual holiday letter like no other. She made meals out of Pixy Stix and hard yellow banana candy, chocolate sauce on microwave popcorn; she had an overgrown bubble-gum dispenser sitting between the toilet and the sink in the bathroom. Her teeth were a battleground.

Best of all, she hadn't had television in the 1990s. She never saw my music videos. She never went to any big concerts. I was just an ordinary fuck-up to her.

I zipped up my jacket and fished through a pint-glass of change on the shelf beside neglected vegan cookbooks, half-full bottles of vodka, and our near-finished collection of Smurfs figurines. I sorted the nickels from the quarters. "Want anything from the outside?"

"C'mon, Billy, this isn't really shocking, is it?" Roxy had that tone of voice like she wanted to debate something.

I didn't bite, just turned around and walked back down the stairs, kicking aside single dust-covered Converse sneakers, stiletto boots, orphaned mittens, and neglected Sports sections of the daily paper.

Outside the Gladstone Hotel, a few buildings south of our apartment, there was a bright pink BMX bike locked to a gas line. I wished I could steal it and give it to Maria. She needed some cheering up — she'd been working nineteen days straight. In the spring, she'd graduated from school and started working at a homeless shelter downtown.

She'd texted me earlier in the day to say, *Client threw bike at my head — wish I hdn't duckd so id b off on comp!*

The last time I saw Maria was two weeks ago. A few days after we had lunch with her mother, she showed up at my house in the middle of the night. Dating someone for seven years had its advantages when you needed comfort but couldn't talk about it. When Maria got stressed, she didn't eat. She took care of everyone except herself, and when she couldn't function any more, she called me. I was surprised by the randomness of her dropping in, but not put off. I held Maria the way I had hundreds of times before. After we finished eating, we sat on the couch in silence. I flipped channels, occasionally glancing sideways at her as she regained some colour in her face and her posture relaxed.

In the morning, I got up and scrubbed the pink and green bathroom tiles, then rearranged the canisters on the kitchen counter, while she kept sleeping. I sat in the living room with

Roxy, watching CNN footage from New Orleans, not talking. I was particularly comfortable lately when I was with someone but not talking to them. When Maria got up to take a shower, Roxy simply turned, raised one eyebrow, and ripped another string of red licorice from the pack on her lap.

"Walk me to the door?" asked Maria, wearing her shiny sky blue coat and courier sack.

Standing on the cement step, she placed a brief kiss on my neck before approaching my lips. Turning instead so her lips caught my cheek, I offered a hug. There was something final in it.

We agreed to stay close, eventually to become good friends, but for now to take some time for solitude, reinvention.

Even so, I hadn't counted on the reality of that agreement. I counted on things like the summer turning too quickly to fall, the healing power of repetitive words and motions. Maria grounded me in my history and my present. Have you ever met someone who was just *good*? Who, when you came across complicated moral questions, was programmed into your phone as "certain virtue"? This was Maria, exactly. Two weeks ago, when I watched her unlock her beat-up ten-speed, place her bag carefully in the ample front basket and ride away, I had no idea when I would see her again. Up the stairs I went, one leaden foot at a time.

Today I checked the lock on the pink BMX, and felt a wave of guilt for even contemplating stealing it. It was my day off. I had planned for the sweet, calming tedium of grocery shopping, perhaps a magazine read cover to cover while sipping a fourth cup of coffee, no random crimes. But there was something in the air: expectation.

I stood at the corner of Dufferin and Queen waiting for the light to change en route to the doughnut shop, the tight V-shaped pockets of my jacket weighed down with bacteria-coated pennies and dimes from the change jar. Coffee is easy to accomplish.

I was outside, breathing fine and elated by this normalcy. Jasper, one of the homeless people I see almost every day, said, "That's what I like to see! A smile on your worried face! What's the good news?"

"I don't feel like I'm being strangled today," I offered, in an uncharacteristic moment of complete honesty.

"I know what that's like," he said, pushing his shopping cart past me.

Good Will.

I spotted Amy and a guy walking two tiny black and white dogs that were bounding up the hill from under the bridge. Amy was one of Roxy's oldest friends, from the anti-poverty coalition in their teens. I'd only met her a few times, mostly when she dropped in at the café where Roxy and I used to work.

There were thirty-two squares of sidewalk between my front step and the doughnut shop. Some days Toronto still looked like it did the first day I arrived. Everyone was a stranger, all talk was small. When Amy called out my name, I was almost surprised at first that anyone knew me. I thought I might walk by them, unnoticed.

"Hey, Hilary!"

Amy approached while I stood frozen. *Do I nod or say hi?*

Amy and I offered each other overlapping staccato greetings. She looked amazing, as usual. I sometimes tried to glimpse imperfections on her — a scab on her arm or a yellowed bruise;

or I watched for her to lift up her arm and expose a ring of effort, the smell of exertion. Usually I scrounged up nothing but scrubbed, polished glory, a magazine page come to life. When Roxy used to work at the café, Amy would breeze in, her sunglasses on, her arms jangling with expensive bracelets while stirring Stevia into a tall iced soy latte. She'd sneak back into the kitchen to chat with Roxy and all the food orders would be late for about half an hour. But she grew on me, I suppose.

Together Amy and her boyfriend were attractive in an off-beat way. He was wearing a black T-shirt emblazoned with a silkscreen from a local band and long baggy Dickies shorts. He looked vibrantly, purposely unkempt, but clean. Amy wore a red-and-white '60s stewardess dress and vintage gold boots. Her hair looked as if it had been professionally styled that morning. Her skin was flawless, her purse a gorgeous hand-made number. She was thin like models are thin. But she had a slight cough. Excellent. She curled her fist to her lips and sputtered into it.

One of the dogs stopped to sniff me up and down and I fell in love with his scruffy lopsided head. "Oh, who's a good dog, who's a cute little piece of angelic perfection? Who's gorgeous? Oh, you are! You like your head scratched, don't you? Oh, cute boy!" Total retardation, the inane things that dog people who didn't have dogs mumbled intuitively.

Her boyfriend: "We're dog-sitting for a friend."

"We're thinking of getting our own," Amy said.

"He's an attention slut, this one," he said, pointing to the dog curled up around my leg.

"We can sniff out our own kind." Was that even funny?

He laughed.

"How are you doing, Billy?" asked Amy. "I suppose I'll see you a lot now that you've moved into the Parkdale Gem." Her white plastic bracelets jangled as she reached up to put her arm around Josh.

Dog #2 wanted some action, and nudged his big head towards my other leg.

"Oh, this is Josh, by the way. Do you two know each other?"

"No." I offered up my hand to Josh from where I was kneeling. "I'm Hilary, but I'm going by Billy now." My hands were dry. So dry. *Touch my sandpaper hands, cute boy. They're awesome! Shut up. Good Will.*

Josh chewed on his lower lip and cocked his head. "So you live with Roxy?"

"Yup."

"Roxy and I go way back," Josh said. "We were in a band together. She told me she had a new roommate."

"The Accident, right? Oh, that's cool." I successfully pulled off not looking like a total idiot.

"Well, kind of embarrassing in that heavy metal revival way."

"That's how we met, actually, through Roxy," said Amy.

"Small world. Roxy's how I meet everyone in Toronto."

Silence. I looked at Josh and he looked back at me, and I suddenly felt the way guys talk about feeling when they're fourteen and all they can think about is sex. This was unusual for me. It was his arms, I think. They were very defined and muscular, not in a beefcake way, but like he could have been a drummer. Drummer arms. Mmm. I was usually too concerned with potential danger, airborne viruses, sweaty handshakes, my breakup drama with Maria or possibly embarrassing blurt-outs to get this turned on by a stranger's arm.

I focused on giving the dogs love, hoping my face had returned to its usual pallid, anemic wash while I tried to secure a good exit line. A woman with an oversized purse and very small dog sighed heavily trying to push past me.

Amy piped up, "Billy used to be famous. She recorded under Hilary Stevenson. Remember that song…"

To my horror, Amy sang the chorus. Inwardly I raged, while trying to look humble. I felt like someone was choking me, or as if I'd swallowed a sock.

"Oh yeah, I remember that song. I was in Grade Eleven. My girlfriend at the time was a big fan."

So the whole story is this: When I was sixteen, I cut an album with my uncle, Jonny Brandon. Yeah, that Jonny, from the '70s Canadian super-group Epic Horizon. The kind of band that had one song everyone knew but no one remembers the name of the band. Except the CBC. The CBC still called Jonny at least twice a year to speak on the radio or be on a panel discussion about which small-town bar is the best for travelling musicians, or to judge their best new Canadian musicians. Anyway, my has-been uncle discovered me, and I had a year or so of experiencing some Canadian fame and one minor hit song in the States that got played during a Walmart commercial. Jonny got all the money for that one, 'cause he wrote it.

It happened like this. When I was about to turn sixteen, Jonny came to stay with us over the Christmas break, because he'd recently left his second wife and my mother usually stepped in to take care of him when he needed it. Christmas dinner in the afternoon with all extended family and any neighbours without family was a tradition my mother insisted on, even if on occasion she made everyone eat roast tempeh and avocado sushi instead of turkey. It was the kind of annoying ritual you don't get anything out of when you're in your late teens but are tethered to anyway.

After dinner, I sat cross-legged on the couch and practised my six-song repertoire with my mom's old acoustic guitar. I was deep into my Ani DiFranco–obsessed, goddess-pendant phase and Jonny was snoozing on the couch, arms resting on his sizable beer belly, exposed and hairy with his T-shirt riding up. By the time I was halfway through "My Little Pony Ran Away," a cynical tribute to childhood toys, his eyes were fixed on me. He said, "You have it all. You have what we want right now." Jonny had been one of *them* since the late '80s, writing songs for teens and easy-listening songstresses, rock bands and pop trios. "You're cute, you've got a pretty voice. You'll totally make it. Let's set up a meeting."

My mother rolled her eyes and said, "Jonny's an old drunk now, honey. Nothing he says is true. Don't you dare get your hopes up."

Except this time she was wrong. By spring I'd recorded seven songs—two of my own, five written for me—been given media training, teeth whitening, highlights, a padded bra, and a web site, and had scored an opening spot for a cross-Canada tour. I felt simultaneously lucky and ungrateful and self-important.

I didn't like talking about it any more. It was like one of those embarrassing things you did in high school that you can't help wanting to shed when you're in your twenties. I don't miss people knowing who I am. The more strangers think they know who you are, the less you feel you know yourself. Or worse, you might believe them. You might wake up every day feeling like King Shit of Fuck Mountain and the only thing to do after that is get high.

Josh, Amy, and I stared at one another. I didn't know what else to say. "Well, gotta run!" I blurted. Simple, direct, dishonest. "I'll see you at knitting group, Amy."

And Amy said, "Yes, can't wait! See ya!"

I'd recently joined Roxy's knitting group in an attempt to meet new people and expand my horizons. The cast of *CSI* had begun feeling like my only social group.

I watched Josh and Amy walk away and wondered how their day would unfold. Would they rush home to have sex all afternoon? Would they argue about whose turn it was to do the dishes? Now that I was single, couples looked like orangutans.

I pushed my fingers against the greasy sneeze-guard at the doughnut shop and ordered my coffee, thinking about my previous similar interactions with Amy. Short. Empty. I'd always thought we'd break through the cellophane of perfunctory greetings and friendly nodding and get closer. Sometimes you just have that feeling about someone. Like they're going to be important eventually, so you take note.

[5]

Amy

I'm not really a secret-keeper. I don't have any big whoppers to tell you. I never hit someone with my car and drove away. I never even shoplifted lipstick or gave an ill-advised drunken blow-job. Never had an STD or cheated on a test.

My secrets are just kind of weird. Like when I sit down to pee, I have to count down or I can't go. I don't know when I started doing this, but now, even if I've had seven beers or a quart of lemonade, I say, *5-4-3-2-1!* before I can relax enough to let it happen. I don't know why. I think it's kind of funny. I giggle to myself most times.

The other thing is that when I'm having sex I have to think about something totally mundane in order to get off. Sometimes I'll repeat a word to myself, like *yellow yellow yellow yellow* or *hand grenade hand grenade motorcycle pop-tart!* Anything completely nonsensical and without sexual connotation.

Okay, maybe here's something. Sometimes I daydream about terrible things happening to me. Like I'll imagine almost drowning and getting pulled onto the beach, or getting kicked in the face and having a black eye and a big scar, and having to tell people what happened. I'll imagine Josh leaving me for someone else, and our big showdown fight in public, my tearful exit. I don't know why. Most people probably daydream about winning an Academy Award, but I spend a lot of time imagining my funeral or how I'd look in a body cast. I don't even get scared. I just like to imagine them, all these potential emergencies.

Book Two

[Life 2]

*6:55 p.m. Delta F, 27, car accident,
head injury, confused speech.*

You would probably like Alison. Most people do. She has a way of putting people at ease. Her teachers call her a natural choice for nursing. They have an intuition about her.

Alison's mother was in Tuscon making jam. Alison's husband was wiping dust out of several champagne flutes at their house in Cambridge. Alison's twin brother was minutes away from pulling over to the side of Highway One, outside of Monterey, because he felt the breath go out of him.

Alison drew back her thick, black hair into a ponytail and adjusted it in the rearview mirror of Jam, her little Jeep. She named most of her beloved inanimate objects. A curl of bang escaped onto her forehead. She was listening to the radio, a story about a girl who was talking on her cell phone and accidentally walked in front of a turning truck. "Shame," Alison said out loud. When she got tired, she often spoke aloud to herself.

Key in the ignition, she traced the puffy dark surface under each eye in the rearview mirror, wishing she could be transported home magically. Jam was somewhat reluctant to start. Alison wished she didn't drive. She was a much better passenger. She liked to watch her husband drive out of the corner of her eye, observing how he seemed so sure of himself. She even loved his muttering at more incompetent drivers, his raised fist as he swore.

She still couldn't quite believe she had a husband, a house, all of these symbols of adulthood, when just two years ago she'd been in first year at nursing school, drinking at downtown clubs on the weekends, speculating about the future. The future was the present now, and it fit like a dress from her mother.

Alison's mother, in Tuscon, made a pot of green tea and let the cat back in. She was waiting to call her daughter at eight o'clock.

Alison reached back and inserted two fingers into the cage where Marmalade, a fat orange tabby, sat unfazed by his lack of freedom. Marmalade licked her fingers, and she purred at him in an effort to be comforting, although she didn't really need to. Whenever Alison got too neurotic, she thought about how Marmalade would handle things, and she just pretended to lick her palm and sigh and take a nap.

It started to rain; AM 640 announced high winds. Alison didn't like driving on the highway, but she'd started to get used to the daily route from Ryerson to her house in the suburbs of Toronto, a house she'd bought with John when they decided they had better start planning for the future. She wasn't used to it yet, the new renovations, the quiet at night, having to drive to get anywhere.

Alison's twenty-eighth birthday was tomorrow. She sent a text message to John saying that she'd be home soon, with a certifiably healthy cat and all the necessary ingredients for the most kick-ass guacamole ever. Earlier in the day, he'd sounded weird, excited, and this confirmed Alison's hunch that he was planning a surprise party for her that night. She was pleased, even though she'd rather relax on the couch, eat takeout, and watch terrible TV.

John read the text from Alison and grinned, happy that he was able to lie; it was not his strong suit. He finished blowing up twenty-eight pink balloons and went to pick up the cake.

Alison drove slowly beside St. Mike's hospital. She saw an ambulance unloading a patient, and said a little prayer that she'd get a job soon in a downtown hospital. She was experimenting with creative visualization, envisioning the things she wanted in life in specific detail. It had worked with the wedding, the good grades, even the house.

She pulled onto Lake Shore and considered a cigarette, rummaged in her small green purse on the passenger seat. Visualizing herself as a non-smoker wasn't quite working. Her own hand pulling out the pack of Belmonts was the last thing she saw.

In Big Sur, Alison's twin brother Alex stopped his camper van on the side of the road. He couldn't breathe. It was as though someone had punched him in the sternum. He'd parked on the side of a cliff on Highway One, overlooking the Pacific, and now he took a hit from his inhaler, watching the sun go down. Something was wrong, he could sense it. He woke up his wife, Susan, who had been asleep in the back seat, cradling their Border collie.

"It's nothing," she insisted.

"It's something."

"It's the full moon," she offered, letting the dog out the passenger door.

"No. It's Alison."

Jenny was on her first call as a student medic. Her preceptor was Alisha, a non-stop dance party. Alisha drove lights and sirens through traffic while Jenny tried to stay calm, keep her heart rate steady. On the radio was the new Britney Spears single, and Alisha knew all the words, was singing loudly as she pinballed through traffic.

Jenny recited silently, *If you keep a clear head, you will have the right instincts and be able to work fast.* She noted that Mark, Alisha's partner, seemed a little annoyed by her presence. She sat on the jump seat in the back, chewing her nails, trying not to get carsick as the ambulance wove at an impossibly high speed.

On the Lake Shore, the medics arrived right after the cops and found one female critically injured. She'd collided with a truck driven by an obvious drunk. Of course the drunk was totally fine, noted Alisha. *They're too relaxed to anticipate injury, and always walk away, stupid motherfuckers.*

"My cat is in the back seat," said the patient to Jenny, when they finally wedged her out of the mangled car after about half an hour of struggle. Even though she was in serious distress, the patient was able to talk as if they were sitting on a park bench, chatting strangers, her words clear as day. She went into cardiac arrest twice, and they managed to get her pulse back each time.

Jenny found herself praying for the woman, watching as Mark put her on the spinal board, noting her injuries. *She's so young. Please, God, c'mon.*

Later, at the hospital, Jenny sobbed into a coarse brown paper towel in the ER bathroom. She texted her mother: *I don't know that I can really handle this after all.*

She flushed her eyes with water, and tried hard to make it look like she hadn't been crying. She pushed through the Staff Only doors that led into the ER waiting area. Through the window, Jenny watched Mark and Alisha smoking and goofing around outside. Alisha handed Mark her smoke and spoke animatedly with her hands, then tried to do a cartwheel, half successfully. He clapped and laughed. Alisha then did a handstand, and Mark held her boots with both hands, a smoke in each. Another medic took a photo with her phone. Alisha's face turned red. Mark let go of her feet and she bounced into a standing position, took back her smoke, and bowed.

Jenny smiled a little to herself, but still couldn't shake her distress. Her phone buzzed again, her mother's number flashing. She pressed "silent," walked past Security, and joined the others outside.

"You cool?" Alisha asked, punching her playfully on the shoulder.

"Yup."

"Good, 'cause it's burrito time and there's no crying during burrito time."

October to December 2005

[6]

Josh

I woke up abruptly to a loud noise. A definite crash. A thumping from downstairs. Amy slept beside me on her back, head tipped back slightly, mascara drying under her eyes.

"Amy! Wake up, Amy. Did you hear that?"

"What? Hear what?"

"That?"

As soon as I spoke, there was another series of rhythmic thumps from below. Unmistakable.

Amy turned away from me and into the pillow: "It's nothing."

"No, it's totally something."

Whenever I thought someone was breaking into our apartment, I froze. My instinct was to just stay very still. Amy was the opposite. She would walk towards the sound, turn on lights, reach for the baseball bat, the frying pan, or the empty bottle of wine, and she'd walk right up to the door or window. I don't know where she got that kind of fearlessness.

"You *had* to have heard that."

"Fine." Amy was suddenly upright. "I'll go check it out. Relax."

"No! Stay here! Just stay quiet."

"Josh, relax. You're such a fucking pussy!" Amy teased, laughing.

She found it so ironic that my job was dangerous yet I was terrified of bumps in the night.

Amy stood up and her knees cracked. She was naked, but didn't reach for a robe, just flicked on the light and walked down the hallway with exaggerated annoyance. I heard her pad softly down the winding carpeted stairs towards the darkness and the noise. I plunged under the covers, one ear exposed. Amy narrated every move.

"Josh, I'm downstairs. I turned on all the lights. It's nothing. It's just the wind."

Crash.

I lifted my head. "What the fuck? What was *that*?"

Amy was silent for a few seconds. I was certain I'd find her pretzeled in the front alcove. Then I heard her laughing. This propelled me from paralysis. I ran downstairs.

Amy was standing in the front window of our living room, watching a family of raccoons going through our garbage, the crash having been the sound of them scattering the tin cans around. They looked up at us as if to say, *What? You want some?*

She took my hand and squeezed it, leading me back upstairs. "You okay, baby?"

"Yeah," I admitted, feeling foolish.

"I can't believe you're off to save the world next week from a fake terrorist attack or the bird flu, and cute little raccoons are making you shit your pants."

"Shut up!"

"C'mon. It's the only time I get to feel macho."

It's true, she did seem kind of tough. But the raccoons had been unaffected by our taps on the window, our stares. They were like brazen little masked pirates.

Until I met Amy, every time I had a conversation I would shut my eyes in protracted blinks. It was a symptom of excruciating shyness. The brief blips of darkness allowed me moments of repose when I could disappear from the agony of human interaction. As a kid I had thought this made me invisible. Amy was the only person ever to mention it. Everyone else politely ignored my propensity. We'd been dating for about two weeks when she asked, "Why do you keep doing that?"

"Doing what?"

"Closing your eyes when you talk?"

"I don't know. I never thought about it."

"You do it a lot. Maybe you have a tic. Are your eyes fucked up or something?"

The intense spotlight of Amy's gaze was so violently uncomfortable it almost felt like something of a relief. She was paying such close attention to my face, not letting me disappear into myself.

"It's just a habit, I guess."

"Huh. I like your eyes open. They're so beautiful."

I balked. But I felt a change, and from then on, tried to break the habit. She would put her hands on both sides of my face and look into my eyes. I couldn't help it. I shut them, laughed a little, then forced them open again.

"That's better," she'd say.

When I was a student and got stressed out about exams, she would run her hands through my hair, kiss my forehead, press her fingers into my clenched jaw and make small circles, listing off all the things she liked about me. *I like that you divide your food up into sections and eat them one at a time. I like that you remember all the actors' names on* Facts of Life. *I like that you have a phobia of touching wet paper products. I like that you're the smartest guy on earth. I like that you're the best kisser.* She had endless items on her list, and it made me feel beloved.

Now she turned away from me at night. Any cuddling was accidental. We'd decided it must be a phase. I wasn't sure, though. Something had changed, and I couldn't quite figure out how to change it back. For all my mechanical intelligence, my ability to take things apart and put them back together with ease, I couldn't see the plan ahead for us.

My alarm went off at 5:45 a.m. but I'd been lying in bed awake since the raccoon incident. I got up, dressed, and walked through the park and up towards the Annex, clutching my Thermos of coffee and trying not to think of the long day ahead.

I liked watching the neighbourhood wake up when the sun was rising. I saw a guy going up Beatrice Street on his motorized wheelchair. If I didn't see that guy, I knew I was late. We nodded. Well, he didn't nod, because he's half paralyzed from a stroke, but he looked at me when I nodded. Every once in a while I'd see a woman in a nightdress shuffling up Markham with slippers on, surveying the garbage on the street.

I'd walk past houses I'd been in, immaculate houses some of them, even though the elderly people inside could hardly move.

The best part of my job was the time between when you got the call and when you were inside the house, and you wondered what you were going to see. I liked meeting people and seeing where they lived and imagining why they lived that way. If people called for you, they were generally happy to see you. People who might have been hostile to you on the street treated you with respect. They got out of your way.

Right before I walked into someone's house, I wondered what kind of décor they'd have. Maybe they'd have a really cool painting, or a strange collection of stuff. One time I spent an hour talking to a famous artist in her late eighties, in her condo overlooking the lake. She was fascinating. Medics get to glimpse these random lives lived.

Our first call today was on my street, a woman I'd seen with her small red dog in Trinity Bellwoods Park. She was giving birth, and the midwife was late, and the woman was a potential high risk so she called us just in case. Her husband was a small man wearing a robe, who let us in, a kid of about six trailing behind him. We carried the stretcher in, and mom was in bed, aglow and panting, the size of a truck.

After the usual introductions, I asked, "So, how can we help you get to the ambulance?"

"Oh, I'm not going to the hospital," she said between exhalations.

My partner, a cute androgynous girl called Mandy, looked at me, brows furrowed. It was our second shift together. "But, uh, that's what we do. We're here to transport you."

"Nope," mom said, smiling. "I'm having the baby here. The midwife will be along shortly. She's just stuck in traffic."

Mandy and I stood awkwardly. I had the birth kit out, but I'd only ever used it in practice. I'd witnessed a birth in the ER when I was a student, and that was all.

"Have you ever helped with a birth before?" the mom asked, perhaps sensing our hesitation. The father curled up on the bed beside her.

"Um, no," I said, hoping Mandy had helped pop out a few.

"Me neither."

Mandy suddenly looked about four years old and terrified. The day before, I'd watched her pick up a drunk guy who'd been punched in the face and throw him on the stretcher. When he called her a fucking dyke, she just grinned and shoved him harder. She weighed maybe a buck twenty at most, and he was over six feet tall, but she managed to strap him down. We hadn't even really needed to call the cops. She was tough. It was kind of funny to see her whimper in the face of a birth.

The mother smiled warmly at us. She reached out and touched my arm. "Don't worry, it's going to be okay."

I laughed. "Awesome. So, what can I do to help you?"

The husband was telling his daughter what to expect from the birth. He looked up at me and motioned towards the dresser. "The olive oil, there's a bottle right there beside the mirror. Can you rub it on the perineum? To prevent tearing."

I tried hard not to burst out laughing. Mandy turned away from the parents, towards the front window, and bit her lip. I could tell she was trying to hold back too.

"Oh, sure!" I said, a little too eagerly, though in truth I was scared. I willed the midwife to hurry up and get there.

I poured the oil onto my gloved hand and tried to look like I knew what the fuck I was doing. A pregnant woman with her legs spread is probably one of the most intimidating sights to behold, let alone when you have to go in and help everything work smoothly, so to speak. I managed the task somehow, asking questions about the mother's medical history and the last birth.

Once the midwife arrived, the birth happened quickly.

Pregnancy calls were probably the best ones, I decided. Excitement and happiness were the predominant emotions.

For the rest of the shift Mandy called me Olive Oil Boy, making a circular rubbing motion with her hand.

I decided I definitely liked her.

After work, I met Roxy at Sneaky Dee's for some burritos and a pitcher of beer. She brought her new roommate, Billy, and I regaled them with stories of placenta mania and hippy Annex parents.

"They're not getting out of bed for a week. They're just staying with the baby constantly so it will be immediately used to love and comfort."

"That's fucking stupid," said Billy. "They clearly don't have jobs."

"It's called Attachment Parenting, and I think it's great. It makes sense," offered Roxy.

I could never be sure if she was disagreeing for the sake of a debate or if she really felt the way she purported to feel.

"Aren't we all woo-woo all of a sudden," Billy snorted.

"I don't know," I said. "I suppose it's good when parents want to be parents that bad. That kid is going to get the best of everything, be the centre of the world."

"He's going to think he's a little god, and be a total narcissist as an adult," Billy said, dipping a chip into some guacamole.

We sat at one of the booths on the side of the bar, and the noise of weekday drinkers insulated us from the cold outside.

Billy ordered three rounds of shots, and when she talked it was like she was half mad, speedy and hilarious and self-conscious all at once. It looked like she hadn't brushed her hair in weeks, but her eyes were lined expertly in black and her skin looked as if she was still thirteen, dewy and perfect. She was wearing tiny jeans and gold flats, a V-neck black T-shirt.

"I hear Julia and Jamie are having a baby," Roxy offered. "It really does seem like the year for long-term couples to have babies."

"Julia and Jamie break up every five seconds! I can't believe that," Billy said.

"Well, couples often have babies or get new puppies right when they're about to break up, like grabbing for something else to focus on when they're panicking about losing each other," Roxy said.

"Yeah, totally, I've noticed that too."

Across from us, a really drunk girl fell off her bar stool. Billy dug her nails into my arm and we laughed so hard we almost threw up.

Roxy giggled and said, "Oh god, you guys are perfectly sick in the same way." She got up to see if the drunk girl was okay, and helped her stumble to her feet.

"Wait, wait. Wanna hear my favourite joke?" asked Billy.

I nodded.

"Why'd the monkey fall out of the tree?" she asked.

Roxy rolled her eyes as she arrived back at the table.

"Why?" I said.

"'Cause he was DEAD!" Billy took her shot of Jäger and slammed it down with a grin. "Josh, I think you and I are going to know each other for a long time," she said, stealing a few of my nachos.

When she reached out her arm, I saw a criss-cross pattern of cuts above her elbow. They were white, so probably old.

Billy noticed me noticing them, but looked at me like, *So what?* She rested her chin on the edge of the table like a cat might, mostly because she was too short for the booths. She'd spent most of the night with her knees curled under her to stay at eye level. She looked up at me and grinned.

I felt like I'd been shot in the gut.

[7]
Billy

What I think while having a panic attack:

My mouth is dissolving. My eyes take in too much light. My eyes are open wider than any eyes have ever been. I no longer have eyelids. They were cut off. I should touch them. I can't uncurl my fingers. Uncurl your fingers, asshole. God, I'm a fucking loser. LOSER. Maybe I should just punch myself with this fucking fist I can't uncurl. I'm going to jump out of this cab. It's 3 a.m. but I'm still just going to jump. Breathe, just breathe. Take a deep breath. Inhale. What is wrong with me? What is wrong with me? This is it. This is a sign. That lady is a sign. My hands are shaking. I'm having a stroke. Who has a stroke at twenty-four? People who live in toxic cities. Maybe I should move home. I don't have a skeleton. No, I have one, and it's going to break through my skin. When I get home I'll be able to gauge if I am really dying or if I am just panicking. It's probably just panic. But it might be the flesh-eating disease. It might be meningitis. It's an aneurism! ANEURISM. Stop it. Of course it's an aneurism. It's a sign. Everything about today makes sense now. The day will end with an exploding blood clot. Of course! They will play the wrong song at my funeral and only people I hate will talk. Dad will go on and on. He will show off my track and field trophies. Okay. Shut up. SHUT UP. I've been through this before and lived. You're going to live. What did that fucking book say? Change your thoughts. Change your thoughts. I am Fine. I am Fine. I am Totally Fine.

[8]

Josh

"Kids show up either dead or alive, and there's not much we can do about it." This is what the ER nurse said to me at 7:30 a.m. in the Toronto General Hospital Atrium. Starbucks was open, filled with the early-morning dreary. I nodded. I was trying not to say the nurse's name because I wasn't sure if it was Anna or Angela.

She spoke so matter-of-factly. Wearily. She could have been anywhere between thirty and fifty. Smoker's lines, night-shift skin, but still young in her eyes. She had taken a liking to me a few weeks ago. I wasn't sure why.

"Adults can fight, but sometimes with kids they just can or they can't and there's not much of a grey area. But it was your first dead baby?"

"Yup."

"Are you okay?"

"I'll have a double espresso. What do you want?"

"Tall mild."

The baby was dead when we got there. Dispatch would've sent an ALS crew, but Mandy and I happened to be on standby two blocks away. Mom fell asleep breastfeeding. Must have rolled over onto Baby. Fire got there first, and one of them looked like he had no blood left in his face. He was about twenty years old, the body of a linebacker. I told him to go outside and get some air. His eyes were out of focus.

Sometimes I liked it when other people reacted, so I didn't have to.

Mandy said, "Maybe we should book off on stress."

We contemplated it, sitting in the truck after the coroner arrived. We stared ahead through the window at absolutely nothing. No radio, no late-night joking. Our phones didn't buzz. Eventually, I heard Mandy unwrap one of her many vegan green-veggie energy bars. I usually made fun of them, but this time I just listened to her chew and swallow, fold up the wrapper. She leaned her jacket up against the passenger-side window, and cradled her head against it. She looked like she was a tired eight-year-old on a family drive.

We cleared with Dispatch and had started driving back to the station when we got another call. *Delta chest pain; female 52.* We took it, and now we'd been waiting on offload for four hours at Toronto General.

The baby call felt like it had happened years ago. The nurse and I were chatting in the atrium to stay awake. I paid for her tall mild and my double shot, and walked slowly down University Avenue and back towards the ER. I was practising nonchalance. It occurred to me that if Amy and I did break up, I really would have no idea how to start dating. It made me sad to think I'd even want a new girlfriend. I kept feeling surprised that we'd got to a place where we were even contemplating it.

Driving back to the station, I saw Billy paused at a red light on Bathurst, leaning against her handlebars, smoking. I leaned out the window and whistled like a jerk. She scowled and looked up, and then smiled. Winked.

"Hey, hottie!" she yelled.

"You're blushing," said Mandy.

"Shut up."

When I got home, I sat on the back porch. The autumn sun warmed my face and I could hear the sound of kids playing in Trinity Bellwoods Park on the other side of the fence. I drank from a glass of whiskey and smoked a cigarette, and played around with all the possible things I might have said to Billy, actual words that would've been better than a cat-call.

Inside on the fridge, I found a note: *Your mom called, said to remind you it's your dad's birthday tomorrow.* I hadn't called my dad on his birthday for about five years, but my mom still tried. Her capacity for forgiveness was nothing short of astounding.

Amy slid open the porch door, dressed for work in a long blue jacket over a brown dress, and high-heeled boots. Her red hair curled perfectly. When she reached out to hug me, I cringed slightly. She smelled like strawberry oil.

"Nice to see you for at least forty-five seconds today."

Amy took a drag from my cigarette, exhaled. She was able to smoke sometimes and not become addicted. It made me really jealous, her ability to abuse substances for about five minutes, without them taking their toll on her. We sat side by side on the picnic table, and watched the tall red wooden fence that squares off our yard, as if it were a TV. The sound of the children playing on the other side rose and fell.

The sound reminded me of how we'd been living together for just over a week when September 11th happened. We'd been out of high school for three months. We were both revelling in first-time independence and playing adult. I'd woken up with a fever and hadn't gone to school. Amy was getting over a similar flu, so we threw back capfuls of NyQuil, stayed in bed, and unplugged the phone. We didn't know anything had happened until the evening, when we stumbled downstairs to the living room and turned on the TV to watch our 6 p.m. *Law & Order* rerun. We were aghast at what we'd missed.

We watched the news until we couldn't bear it, then opened the windows and stared outside at the ordinary day. Switched channels and watched the fires, the people walking across the Brooklyn Bridge, the horrified faces. Amy tried in vain to call friends in New York, flipped from news story to news story to try to catch every angle. She reacted by pacing, exclaiming, seeking out more information.

I reacted with calm. I'm sure it's something about the way I'm programmed, but when something shocking happens I tend not to dwell anxiously on it. I sliced up a long loaf of bread, and reheated the chicken soup Amy's mom had dropped off. I placed a pot of ginger tea and mugs of soup on the coffee table while Amy made phone calls, cold cloth on her head. When I called my grandmother in Guelph she said, "If it gets bad in the city, come here. Bring all your friends." The sound of fear in her voice shook my calm.

Amy and I both suddenly felt hollow, and through the haze of my fever and our combined disbelief we took off our clothes and grabbed at each other, passion fuelled by sorrow. Sex didn't really make sense, but nothing else did either. Like when you laugh out of shock at a funeral, or grasp towards joy after someone you know dies.

Roxy called and left conspiracy messages on the voice mail. "Bush did it himself. It's so obvious. His approval rating is going to skyrocket."

As the sun went down, we watched TV again as the emergency workers laboured in the rubble, their faces dusty and sometimes caked in blood.

"I worry sometimes, what if something happened here? You'd have to be right in the middle of it. What if we lived in New York? That would be you," Amy said, eyes wide, rocking back and forth under the white wool blanket.

"Well, you can't spend your whole life worrying," I said.

But we were both shaken by what we'd seen. It was as though someone had peeled the mask off certainty and our first-world assumptions about safety. Bombs happened halfway around the globe, not nearby. We were used to abstract faraway injustices and violence. We'd been cushioned our whole lives, had no idea how to act or what to think when faced with this disaster.

Today that episode felt like ten years ago, not four. I felt so much older, drinking whiskey in the morning so I could sleep. The things I'd seen since then. The gnawing in my bones of a kind of tired I knew wasn't healthy. But I was so used to it, it didn't matter any more.

"I guess I'd better get going. I wish I could call in sick and sleep next to you all day," Amy said.

"Do it," I said, and poked her in the side, then yanked at her skirt like a child.

"Can't. Grants due tomorrow." She pulled my face into her breasts and kissed the top of my head.

I turned my head to breathe, and felt calm and sunny, and ready to sleep. It was the most affection we'd shared in weeks.

"What are you doing tonight?" Amy asked.

"I don't know. Might hang out with Roxy and Billy again."

"Oh yeah?" she said.

I couldn't be sure, but I thought I saw her roll her eyes. I shrugged.

"Okay, well, I have to go. I love you," Amy said.

We'd agreed long ago always to leave each other with love, because you never know, right? But her face looked different when she said it, as if she were actually saying *cooked green beans* or *don't forget to buy milk.*

"I love you, too," I said back to her, rotating my glass and watching the syrup swirl and wave.

[9]

Billy

On Halloween I was dressed like a zombified French maid.

My body, still mine and moving when I told it to, was splayed like a thrown jack on the kitchen floor of the Parkdale Gem. My left foot on a polished black square and my right foot on the adjacent white tile. Two of thirty-eight tiles. My toes pointed ballerina straight like, *yes yes yes*. I sat up partway, spine flat against a cupboard. I closed my eyes like, *no way*.

Between the open scissors of my legs: an upside-down plate of spaghetti. Sauce seeped out from under the bright blue dish. I brought my knees up to my elbows and placed my head in my hands, fingers messing up the gory makeup Roxy had worked so hard on. Roxy was going through a special-effects phase, making her own fake blood and scar tissue in the kitchen sink.

Good Will? More like: no will. Anxiety had turned into deep sad. Boring, awful sad.

Something had been broken, something that connected my body and brain. I had read somewhere that most human problems come down to the fact that we are living beings made up of non-living chemicals. I was just tired of being afraid all the time. My fears had become so pronounced, and there were so many of them, it made the most sense just to stay at home. Fewer fears here. Comfort. The floor, grounded.

Roxy had gone out and I'd lost track of how long I'd been lying on the floor. Smoosh was curled around me, looking almost accusatory, as if I'd taken her spot on the floor. She licked at my feet and fell over on her back.

I could have blamed my mother. On the phone the day before, she'd asked about Maria.

"Why don't you get back together? I saw her sister at the store the other day. She tells me Maria got a full-time job at a crisis centre. Such a hard worker, that Maria."

My mother liked to pretend that she had taught her kids to have a strong work ethic, but in truth she taught us to follow our whims and not settle for something we didn't really want to do. Hence my waitressing and telemarketing career, and my plan to fail out of university. The last time I sat through class was two weeks ago.

"Maria and I broke up three months ago. We are not reuniting anytime soon."

Lately the anxiety had slowed, to be replaced with a colourless glaze over both eyes. I didn't even bother with *Good Will* or counting things. My heart was still beating, but never fast enough to cause alarm. "I am having a quarter-life crisis," I announced to my mother.

"My generation never had those, we just had babies and thought about killing them from time to time."

"Gee, thanks."

"Oh, not you, Hilary. You were an angel. I meant your sister. I left her at the mall one day when you were in kindergarten and I almost didn't try to find her. I went crazy. She wouldn't stop crying."

"Well, none of my friends are giving birth. I don't think any of us could quit smoking long enough to have a kid."

"That's true. You're all chimneys, angry little chimneys."

That was my cue to light another cigarette off the one I'd just finished. I heard my mother do the same. She could cut out sugar, dairy, wheat, emotionally withholding men, but she couldn't quit the smokes.

"Not to mention, gay." My mother was one of those people who thought gay people just didn't ever have children, as if it wasn't possible.

"That doesn't make it biologically impossible, just a little harder, logistically." I heard my mother start to chop vegetables fast against a wooden cutting board. "And stop labelling me. How's the weather in Winnipeg?"

"Stinky. Toronto?"

"Today the sky could best be described as vomit-coloured."

"Move home."

"No."

"Have you been writing songs?"

"I've been trying to write corporate jingles on the ukulele. Make some cash."

"You know, mail still comes here for you. Your uncle calls once a week, wants to know when you're going to write again. He won't ever just call you, though. Still mad."

"Tell Jonny that I peaked at sixteen and now I'm living an adult life of mediocrity. I've embraced it. Besides, I'm the one who should be mad. He's the one who made money off of me."

Whenever I thought about how much money I could actually have if, I don't know, I had understood one thing about business at sixteen, or had had a mother who understood a thing about business, I got so angry I could hardly breathe. So I just chose not to think about it.

I received a text message from my sister while on the land line with my mother. *Uncle Jonny is going to be a judge on Canadian Idol. CHEESY.*

I texted back: *Buy some crackers.*

Later that night, I had a sick feeling in my stomach. It was confirmed by an e-mail from Jonny Brandon Enterprises dot com. *They want you to come on the show and teach the kids how to perform. It will be billed as your comeback.*

I e-mailed a subject heading message: *I am 25. Too young to come back. Plus, reality shows are the new opiate for a nation of narcissistic morons.*

He sent back: *You should go to AA, Billy. Find your higher power. I can tell you're drinking too much.*

The blue plate sat so still, the sauce hardening. The cat's paw prints were red where they dotted across the tiles and out onto the patio. Smoosh sat licking herself clean on one of the tall wooden stools beside the barbecue. My feet were tingling, the right one numb. Still, I didn't move.

I had got up early that morning to work an opening shift at the café, the dreaded 7 a.m. to 1 p.m. shift. I'd burned my hand on the espresso-machine steamer and couldn't concentrate. My manager, Marla, who had something against me for some reason, kept making jokes that I drink too much, which was kind of funny considering how obsessed I was with being sober and in control lately. I couldn't deal with the hangovers. So I'd taken to having two drinks and watching everyone around me get drunk while I pulled at loose threads in my clothes.

I drank three double lattes and walked home, clutching my heart. In the apartment, I was promptly zombified by Roxy. When Roxy went out, I warmed up the leftover pasta, turned to walk out onto the patio and somehow dropped the plate. That's when time stopped working for me again.

In about an hour, I was supposed to be hosting the punk knitters' group. It was true what those cheesy mags said: knitting is a soothing activity. I officially did not care what this said about me. I could barely put a sentence together most days and now I'd completed a pot holder, half a mitten, and five pairs of leg-warmers, all pink and red. Roxy was knitting tiny finger-puppet monsters. The Gem was peppered with balls of wool and potentially stabby knitting needles. At night my dreams of gun-toting psychopaths and teeth falling out had been replaced by simple repetitive scenes of *knit one, purl two*, a collection of unconscious body memories. Sometimes Paul Simon sat beside me in these dreams singing songs from the *Graceland* album that reminds me of childhood. It was a nice break from the galvanic reality of my body trying to eat itself with fear.

I jumped up when I heard the door click and Roxy bounding up the stairs. Feigning normalcy, I clutched the plate and scooped up the noodle mess with a paper towel. The accident was easy to remedy. I felt silly for having stared at it for half an hour, making it some overdetermined metaphor for all my recent failures.

Roxy kissed my forehead. "I have to redo your black eye, doll. It looks like you smudged it." She put both hands on my head and tipped it back to examine the extensive fake gash across my neck. "Still slit beautifully! I'm really improving."

Roxy poured two glasses of beet and ginger juice and reapplied my bruised eye. While she cleaned the kitchen, I scrubbed the tile grout in the bathroom with a toothbrush, dusted the windowsills, then vacuumed the stairs. The domestic details in my life were incredibly spotless, if nothing else. One square inch in front of another—this was how I was determined to see the world.

I took out the *Knitter's Handbook* and placed it on a side table. Clicked on the TV to *CityNews* in time for an alarmist feature on bird flu. I turned it off right away. I already suspected I'd be patient zero. Bird zero. I was imagining the plans for my funeral and surmising who'd play my character in the Toronto bird flu made-for-TV movie when the doorbell rang.

Amy walked up the stairs holding a Tupperware container of cookies, her shoulder bag overflowing with yarn and knitting needles. "Hey, Billy! I have a terrific pattern for a hat with stars on it." She'd made her wool hoody herself. Black with a skull-and-crossbones design on the back. She wasn't wearing a costume.

She hugged me awkwardly. "You look so freaky!" she said, her voice a few decibels higher than normal.

I felt like a kid in a cardboard robot outfit.

Amy offered me a cookie from her container, which she had placed on the kitchen table. The cookie was soft and chewy, still a little bit warm. "There's no wheat or gluten in them, and they're fruit sweetened."

Of course they were. They tasted like sawdust. She leaned against the wall in faux repose, looking as if she could be standing in a magazine, advertising her outfit. Her skirt was a patchwork pattern from vintage T-shirts. I'd seen it in a boutique on Queen Street for $175.

Roxy walked into the kitchen and whistled at Amy. "You sure are prettying up the place," she said, and kissed Amy on the cheek.

I wondered if they'd ever slept together. Probably. Roxy pretty much slept with everyone when she first met them. She had tried to hit on me, but I was with Maria so we had quickly slid into sibling roles.

Roxy had always appeared odd to other people, so she never really experienced angst about it. Never belonging had given her the strongest sense of self-esteem of anyone I knew. At least, this was how it came across to others. Not conventionally attractive, but undeniably sexy, she appeared weird to just about everyone, even the punk rockers and art kids who tried their best to stand out. Roxy had never been able to change the fact that she stood out, so her authenticity was alluring. I bet that was what Amy was drawn to. No matter how many skull-and-crossbones sweaters Amy knitted, she always looked undeniably approachable, clean, normal.

"I'm going out to the liquor store," Roxy said. "The freezer is oddly lacking in vodka. Want anything?"

We both declined. I gathered up my spool of red wool, wondering how it would ever turn into an object like a hat. I was just hoping it would become a square of some sort. An ugly square, but whatever.

Amy half smiled at me the way you do when the conversation has died but you still want to appear to be attempting a connection. I dropped a stitch and laughed for no reason. The CD that was playing in the background — the Detroit Cobras — paused between tracks. The room stopped being sexy and soulful, and started feeling empty and too clean. Amy and I had always been a little awkward, but now I had a crush on Josh and I felt that she could somehow sense this.

I glanced around at the room at the plain IKEA coffee table, the TV and DVD player on top of an old credenza Roxy and I had dragged home from a roadside goldmine. On the ivory walls hung two canvases of Roxy's — comic-book style paintings — and a shelf with DVDs: two complete seasons of *The OC*, all of *Twin Peaks*, and a bunch of John Waters' films. A small bookshelf contained a few hardcover Taschen art books.

Finally, I stared down at my lap and thought: *If I glance up and across the coffee table, Amy will be a corpse, killed by boredom.* This silence was my fault. "I think I hear the door," I lied.

I went downstairs, nervously surveying the street for other punk knitters. Tina, Tara, and Lisa were arriving en masse, a frenzied bundle, locking their bikes to the railing outside. Soon after, a tiny gay guy named Phil who was obsessed with knitting pink bunnies with insect legs showed up and settled into the armchair.

It was Tina who got the evening going. She could launch into a stand-up routine for no reason at all. If you got a call in the middle of the night with a slurred yet emphatic voice urging you to come out and help her steal cars, it was likely Tina. If you brought a camera out to a party, half of the photos were likely to show Tina, shirtless, with a lime in her mouth and playing air guitar on the edge of the DJ booth. I'd only known Tina a month or two, through Roxy, but felt as if she was the human embodiment of show business: a manic attention-seeking cut-up everyone was drawn to. I had decided to keep her at arm's length, and she responded by looking right through me most of the time.

As everyone settled into the living room, I backed into the kitchen, nearly tripping over the cat dish, and busied myself with a giant plastic bowl of pink icing for the cupcakes. I decorated the tops with red and orange sparkles. I never followed recipes; baking was mostly science and intuition anyway. If you understood the basics and had a keen sense of pleasure, you were pretty much set. Like with sex.

I overheard snippets of conversations from the other room, the sounds of PhD dissertation prep, publishing contracts, auditions, and promotions. Toronto was everybody's lucky horseshoe, the place where accomplishments came quickly. I said a quick prayer of thanks for Roxy, who besides having some vague film aspirations was still as stuck as I, doomed to say *Hi, how may I help you?* until the scratch cards uncovered three matching numbers. *Come on, triple cherries*, we said on Sunday mornings, which was scratch card and latte time.

Roxy slammed the outside door and clomped up the stairs two at a time. She twisted around the banister, dropped her coat on a kitchen chair, and did a fast U-turn past the bathroom and went in through the living room. The knitting crew stopped purling and knitting to absorb her.

I handed out the cupcakes. Amy didn't take one. She doesn't eat sugar. Of course.

While everyone knitted and discussed their lives, I couldn't stop thinking about the lump in my throat. How I felt as if I were being choked. I swallowed over and over, but still felt it, as if someone was pressing into my neck.

Later, after everyone left, Roxy and I washed the dishes together. I dried the cups and plates, and she washed, careful not to get her new arm tattoo wet. The tattoo was a bunny, softly drawn in brown ink. Roxy was starting a woodland-creature tattoo theme on her arms.

"Amy's so hot for you," I whispered, handing Roxy three tiny ice-blue espresso cups laced through my fingers. They were shaking. I tried to hide it.

"No, that was over years ago." Roxy's ears turned bright red. "Plus, I've known her forever. It would be weird, too familial at this point. And she's still with Josh. Josh and I have a rule about not dating the same girl."

"Really?" I felt curves of disappointment show around my lips.

"Well, it's unofficial, but the relationship is pretty much, like, over. You know. They just won't break up and be done with it. Personally, I think Josh has a bit of a thing for you, Hil-ah-ry!"

"No he doesn't," I asserted in a voice that said *Tell me more*.

Lately, Josh had been showing up around the house a lot. I didn't know why I was drawn to Josh, really. He appeared very ordinary. His socks always matched. His teeth were always clean. He exuded a kind of polished humanity I could never accomplish. His hair was brown in a uniform way, no variations. I'd never seen him freaked out about anything. He was my polar opposite. Except when we laughed. And I was fascinated by his job. My life was populated with waiter/singers, cashier/actors, student/poets. I regarded anyone science-minded with curiosity. Plus, I was obsessed with random accidents and freak aneurisms, and he dealt with this every day. His work-life terrified me. ·

Oddly, despite our differences, we appeared to see eye to eye on a lot of things. "I'm going to be your new best friend," I had said to him on a night when the three of us—me and Josh and Roxy—sat up watching a *Kids in the Hall* marathon and speaking in British accents. By this time, Roxy had passed out in the armchair.

"Okay," he'd said. "I'm okay with that."

But afterwards, I had decided to put away my attraction for him so as not to interfere in his relationship with Amy. Plus, why would he want to date a crazy lady?

"Don't worry, I didn't tell Josh how crazy you are," Roxy said, pelting me with dish soap. It was as if she could read my mind.

"I'm not crazy!"

Roxy went over the stove, mimed turning it on and off, on and off. "Really? Totally normal?"

"A lot of famous and smart people have OCD."

"A lot of crazy people have OCD too." Roxy kissed me on the cheek. "Anyway," she leaned in, whispering, "apparently Amy is jealous of you. Like, Josh comes home and your name comes up in the Google history on their computer. She's been checking you out. He asked her about it and she said she was just curious. You know, about your fans, your music career."

"And you think that's, like, impossible? That my career was so embarrassing that no one would want to read about esoteric moments in Canadian celebrity?"

Roxy opened the back balcony and placed a cigarette in her lips. She didn't want to hurt my feelings, I'm sure, but that didn't stop her from launching into an emphatic mocking chorus of "Building a Mystery" by Sarah McLachlan. When I ignored her as I would an obnoxious four-year-old, she stopped.

"Of course, it's possible Josh is just an egomaniac and thinks everything Amy does is related to him. But I think he's been honest with her about wanting to ask you out."

"Huh. Maybe Amy likes me instead. Maybe it has nothing to do with Josh. What do you think of that?"

Roxy shrugged. "Femme-femme couples are the new fag couple, I s'pose."

I knew this wasn't the case.

I went into my room and took off the zombie outfit, pulled on my red slip, and turned around in front of the mirror a few times, then lined my lips with a red pencil. I threw on a hip-hop playlist and danced around to Ol' Dirty Bastard. Then I made the bed and reordered my bookshelf by author. I felt as though I'd been offered a brief respite from the anxiety that had been plaguing me for months.

[10]

Josh

On the coffee table sat an information pamphlet I'd already read three times. It was early November, the night before our first training session, and I was unable to fall asleep. The pamphlet read:

The Goal of COHERT:
To organize Health Emergency Response Teams across the country, ensure that they are ready to be deployed on a continual basis to assist provincial and local authorities in providing emergency medical care during a natural disaster, explosion or major chemical, biological or radio-nuclear incident. Each team will have expertise in triage, stabilization, evacuation and patient management.

Hours later, I woke up to Amy straddling me on the couch, her legs like a wishbone.

"Instead of breaking up, maybe we should get a dog," she suggested, one freshly manicured hand wrestling with the elastic band on my drawstring pants, the other holding a cigarette to her lips. She looked like a truck coming at me. Smirking.

"Uh. I dunno. I didn't think we were breaking up. Are we breaking up?" It's true we'd been tabling the possibility lately, but I didn't think we'd made a firm decision. "You know I love dogs."

"I went on the Humane Society web site yesterday. I found a few adorable little pups! Or we could go to a breeder."

"Yeah. Okay. I'm not sure it's a good time. We're both so busy."

Amy shrugged. Exhaled smoke over her right shoulder. The curves of her clavicle were so prominent lately. Instead of looking like a sculpture, a fancy art model, she looked drawn, her skin pulled tight against bone.

"Why are you smoking in the house?" I asked. "I can't get sick right now."

The clock on the DVD player read 5:05 a.m. Amy clearly had not been to bed. I had been sleeping fitfully on the couch. The plan to sleep alone, and therefore sleep, hadn't worked. From 3 to 5 a.m. I had fallen into a tumble of dense dreaming.

Amy continued to straddle me, grinding her teeth like a teenaged meth freak, red-eyed. It was still dark outside.

"I have to be in a field by the airport by quarter to seven for COHERT, Amy."

"I know. I remember. God, Josh, it's not like I don't listen to you."

Amy started jerking me off. I didn't want to give in but we hadn't had sex in weeks. These days she looked at me like I was a maggot, when she looked at me at all. The sex was hot. It was terrible that it was hot. I didn't know how to understand my responses any more. Amy could be a scary top when she wanted to be.

"Disaster training, Do you even care that *we're* a disaster, Josh?"

"Amy." Repeat the patient's name. Look in their eyes. "Fucking relax."

"Relax? Oh, *that's* my favourite thing to hear."

This whole interaction mightn't have seemed like a turn-on, but Amy knew me too well. I closed my eyes, and I saw Billy's tits in my mind. I pictured her hand, her face. I got off with my eyes shut tight. My body took over. Amy pulled her hand away, looking at me like she'd just given me a balloon at the county fair and I should be grateful. Kissed me aggressively on the forehead.

She got up and dropped her smoke into an empty Steam Whistle bottle on the coffee table and marched down the hall to the kitchen. Her legs, her arms, mechanical. Metal eyes. In her voice I heard her mood change, from bitter and frantic to conciliatory, as she asked Tina if she wanted breakfast. Why are people always so much nicer to their friends than their partners? It doesn't make sense.

It didn't surprise me that Tina was there, and that Amy hadn't even bothered to mention it. Tina was around all the time now, as though Amy needed a constant distraction. The two of them went out at night and didn't stop until ten in the morning. It was like they were still seventeen and didn't have jobs or lives.

After a good minute-long stare into the still darkness of our street, I made my way to the kitchen, hoping Amy had calmed down a little. I felt guilty for picturing Billy during sex, but what are you gonna do? It was either Billy or one of the many celebrities usually reserved for daydream bit-parts.

Tina had her legs up on the kitchen table. She scratched at her left nipple as if she were trying to erase it through her thin white T-shirt. She was one of those people who'd be completely comfortable answering the door stark naked and carrying on a conversation with a courier. Like, *what's your problem?* I thought she might be a sociopath. She could be hilarious but not quite present at the same time. It was creepy.

I slammed the coffee-filter holder into the machine and it popped back out. I slammed it again. While I was in the shower, the kitchen expanded with the smell of Ethiopian dark roast.

After drying myself I took my new uniform off the hook behind the bedroom door and dressed hurriedly. The uniform felt like a cracker, so stiff and new, and it fit a little awkwardly.

Tina watched me walk to the kitchen counter to fill up my travel mug. She was smirking at nothing. "You're going to play fake terrorist-attack today for the department of public health, I hear. Boy, I bet there's some fucked-up politics going on there."

I didn't answer, and focused instead on the perfect cream-to-coffee ratio, the heaping spoon of sugar. I stuck the spoon in my mouth and sucked on the raw crystals. Sitting on the wicker bench by the porch door, I did up my boots. I had shined them last night, the way I used to when I started at EMS and felt proud. I hadn't stopped feeling that way necessarily, but now everything was a little more laid-back — my posture, my seams. Now I was lucky if my shirt was tucked in properly. When you're a student and you ride out with paramedics, all you want is to get a call. After about six months of working for real, all you want is to sit around the station avoiding calls. It was amazing how quickly you could shift like that.

Tina took my silence for another opening. She hated having no attention paid to her. "Don't you think it will be fucked up politically, though, Josh? Don't you feel weird being around all those military people?" Tina's long, thin fingers shook as she flipped through a magazine.

Amy selected two unnaturally blue bottles of Gatorade from the fridge, blew her hair out of her face, and sighed before handing one to Tina. I knew she was high then, without a doubt. Refined sugar ingestion was a major tip-off.

"Josh doesn't talk politics at work, Tina. He doesn't rock the boat."

"You don't think there are fucked-up politics at *Vogue*?" I said, picking up the magazine Tina was leafing through, pointing at the pursed lips on an anorexic-looking model.

"God, Josh. Relax. We're all friends here," Tina said, the way a boss might make a vain attempt at corporate team building. "I just wanted to make sure you're still on our side, right?"

I glanced over at Amy, who had her back to me as she wiped down the counter. She was making exaggerated motions with the cloth around the coffee machine because she hated how I left drips and dregs to dry and crust over.

"What are you guys on?" I asked.

Tina just smiled. Amy didn't answer.

I tried to remember if it was someone's birthday, if there'd been some art opening, if there was any reason why they'd still be awake and grinding on a Tuesday morning. Then again, Tina didn't usually need a reason to indulge.

I left through the back patio door, walking around the side of the house to my car. I hadn't said goodbye.

It was 6 a.m. when I stopped at the 7-Eleven on Dundas to get gas. I ran into Rob, one of Amy's film friends, at the pumps outside. He was an indie-rock white guy with messy brown hair and cowboy shirts, the kind of guy who said things like *I like Alice*

Coltrane, and belonged to bands with twenty-three members, half of whom played the accordion or a single oversized cymbal.

"What are you doing up so early?" he asked.

"I'm going out to train for a fake disaster." It was in moments like these that I realized how different my life was from that of almost everyone else I knew. Rob nodded. I wondered if he'd heard me or just didn't care. He looked burnt-out. "I've been up all night shooting a zombie movie," he said. "Gotta crash. Say hi to Amy."

I was almost at the 427 by the time I stopped picturing Tina in various states of humiliation.

Our training session was out in Etobicoke, near the airport. The organizers emphasized repeatedly that during a real emergency the only thing you could really know for sure was that everything would be unpredictable and the environment would be totally uncontrolled. You had to roll with what happened.

It was odd to park the car, carry my heavy pack past the gates, and have no idea what I would be walking into. I checked in with a coordinator, Dave, who was dressed like a soldier. Even before we got started the site had been set up with actual debris and fake dead bodies.

I had understood from our initial training sessions in the classroom that this would be how the exercise would look, but I hadn't really imagined the detail. There were over a thousand participants, including rescue dogs and a HUSAR team going through a fake bomb blast, complete with real rubble and student actors preparing to be stuck under beams. One had a ripped-open head. "Does this look real?" he was asking his buddy, who stood beside him adjusting his fake broken leg.

Like most things organized by government teams, there were glitches and things yet to be set up. I was led into a warehouse where a bunch of nurses I recognized were sitting on fold-out chairs playing cards. While the Mission Support team set up the remaining triage tents, I kicked ass at euchre and drank terrible coffee. Everything was pretty disorganized. It was freezing. Amy kept texting me with notes such as *Arf! Meow! I talked to the cats. They're ok with it.* I ignored her.

I was holding a grudge, stemming from last week when Amy qualified our relationship as her "learning" marriage—meaning that eventually she'd have a real one. The comment was hurtful, and she had made it almost casually as I was leaving for work. I hadn't responded in depth to her question, *What can we do to make things better? I need to hear how you feel. What do you feel?* Apparently *I can't get into this now* wasn't a good answer. Later that day, I had called her from work and she had apologized.

"I wanted to hurt your feelings."

"Accomplished."

"I'm flailing."

I wanted to say something that could save the conversation. Remind us that we actually liked each other. Something sweet such as *Me, too. I can't even picture myself without you.*

Instead I said, "We're getting a call. Have to go," and hung up. In reality I had been waiting with a patient on OLD for hours at Humber Church. I wouldn't even take my cat to that hospital. I had been standing outside the doors, trying to list off concrete things I could do to save our relationship. I came up short. I had been deep into feeling terribly sorry for myself.

After I hung up on Amy, I had watched a man who'd just been discharged walk towards his car. I turned around to light my smoke when I heard some yelling. At first, I couldn't figure out what was happening. I supposed the man had fallen down. A few other medics by the trucks ran over to him. "He's bleeding out!" yelled Anna. "Get a stretcher!" I ran to get one, but by the time I got back the stretcher was no help. The man died right there. Just fell. Blood everywhere. Everyone ran out to help, but there wasn't anything we could do.

Back in the crowded emergency room, a medic I didn't know and a nurse yelled at each other, brazenly unprofessional. "You shouldn't have discharged him! I can't believe this bullshit! He walked out and DIED!"

"We don't have time for this!" the nurse yelled back.

The medic was keyed up. He looked at me and said, "I can't believe how many people die from total carelessness! I knew that guy was really sick, and they didn't take it seriously." It was the kind of statement that didn't require an answer. I nodded, though, and understood his frustration. Outside, he kicked a telephone booth. I wanted to suggest he book off on stress, but I hardly knew the guy so I just watched him for a second and then looked away. Then I asked my patient how she was doing.

There's something about watching someone die right in front of you that makes your petty relationship problems seem of little importance.

That was the kind of shift that made me thankful for opportunities such as COHERT. Today was a break from the routine and a chance at something outside EMS. I was afraid that my regular job was starting to fuck with my perception of the world and my place in it.

Now I emerged from the tent and blinked into the sun. It was 8:30 a.m. I watched a few airplanes land, and for a couple of minutes got sucked into the rhythm of watching rush-hour cars on the highway. The gutted and bloodied actors playing patients walked by in a team, their make-up artists trailing them, clutching giant black lunch boxes. I just wanted to get started.

Finally, our director, an emergency medicine specialist, instructed the staff to gather in the main tent. I met fellow members of Team C, which included two doctors, several nurses, and one other medic. We walked to our tent and I felt something reminiscent of the first day of elementary school. I was nervous, excited. We arranged the equipment how we wanted it. Then people started bringing in patients.

The Heavy Urban Search and Rescue Unit combed a blasted-out building, looking for survivors. The actors were triaged according to the severity of their injuries. Our first patient was an evisceration, organs falling out of a gash across his gut. The next few patients were eye protrusions, various blast injuries, and then there was a series of patients you would normally see on the road, heart attacks and psych patients.

Eight hours passed quickly. I didn't notice how hungry I was until I was physically in pain. I was shocked to see the time on my phone along with eight bursts of blue light. Texts from Amy, first playful, then needy. The last one just kind of sad. *Maybe we need some space. Maybe I should take a trip?* I hated it when she forgot that I was at work, not tied to my text-message icon.

At dinnertime in the main tent, I found myself sitting among a bunch of medics and nurses talking about divorce. "Shift workers," a guy with a red moustache said, "have a high rate of divorce, right?"

"I'm just tired of coming home and having to deal with more bullshit. I want to relax. My wife doesn't really understand it," said his friend. "She tries, though. I'll give her that. She's got a lot of patience."

"I need to space out sometimes, just watch TV. I don't want to think about anything."

"I dunno what you're talking about," said another guy. "Shelley and I are fine."

"Isn't she an ER nurse?"

"Yeah."

"So, she understands, right?"

I turned off my phone, tried to rub some feeling into my frozen feet, wished I could have a beer. One of the actors sat next to me and offered me a coffee. She had two mugs under the makeshift blanket poncho she was using for extra warmth. "I stole it from the HUSAR tent. They get real coffee, not this bullshit." She pointed to the instant swill the other medics were drinking. "So, what are you guys talking about?"

"Marriage."

"Ah. Fuck it. I'm never getting married," she said.

"What's your name?"

"Head Trauma 1, Lost Child 2, and Hysterical Amputee 4. Or you can call me Jenny. I'm a student paramedic." Jenny had wide blue eyes, and freckles across her nose.

"What do you think so far?"

"Well, it just got a lot more interesting." She winked at me. Winks. I wasn't used to someone being so blatant. I had forgotten about this part—the moment when a new girl became interesting. She stood up suddenly. "Well, I gotta go make it look like my head's half caved-in. Another day, another dollar."

I slept for maybe four hours that night, on a tiny cot inside a tent with the other paramedics. I had an awkward phone call with Amy, full of long silent pauses rather than words. The next morning, my first patient was Jenny, as Internal Bleeding Woman. After she fake threw up into the pail beside her cot, she looked up at me and winked with the one eye not covered in imitation gushing. Maybe she just winked at everyone. After an exquisite fake death, we tagged her VSA, and she took a bow. The nurse and doctor weren't impressed with her theatrics, but Jenny saw me blushing.

We shared a cigarette behind the HUSAR tent on our break. I halved a dried fruit bar Amy had stuck into my knapsack pocket, and offered it to her. Jenny accepted it and chewed it with her mouth open, pausing to smoke and pick dried blood out of her hair. I pegged her as one of those girls who just did not give a shit about decorum, a tomboy who had grown into a woman other people probably pegged as a dyke.

"So, why a medic?" I asked her.

"Well, I was going to join the army, right? My whole family is in the military. But I suppose I wanted to do something a little different, and I'd never lived in a city before, right? I wanted to come here, and I wanted to help people."

I smiled and nodded, though I felt like telling her the "wanting to help people" wish was going to fade fast.

"Plus, when I was a kid I was always wanting to perform surgery on animals or when people got hurt. I was totally fascinated by it. It just seemed natural." Jenny put her cigarette out on a rock, and looked at me. "I hope I get hired in Toronto. I'd love to be right in the action, you know?"

"It's definitely not all action," I said. "It's lots of bullshit." We got up, straightened up our clothes.

"What do you mean?"

"Oh, nothing. It's all madness, all the time. You'll love it."

After we had debriefed and packed up our stuff, I stood in the parking lot in front of the car for a moment, unsure if I had the energy to drive. Jenny appeared in a blink. "Wow, I guess you make a lot of money," she said, leaning her knapsack against the back window of Amy's parents' old BMW. They had given it to us after my shitbox Toyota died. "Mind giving me a ride?"

"It's my girlfriend's parents' car. They gave it to us."

"Girlfriend, huh?"

In regular clothes, Jenny looked like the kind of girl I used to work with at a campground in Guelph when I was a teenager. Roots sweatshirt, hiking boots, navy blue tuque, no make-up, kind of a jock. Tough. She threw her knapsack in the back seat before I could answer her.

She didn't ask me if it was okay to change the radio station. She selected some classic rock and sang along, terribly, to "Rock You Like a Hurricane." She still had some fake blood on her face. "I live really close to Humber, not too far from here."

Even though I had to take a winding, annoying detour and was so tired I was probably as dangerous as a drunk, I felt quite happy to be taking Jenny home. Her apartment was in a tacky suburban Etobicoke townhouse.

"I live in the basement," she explained. "The family upstairs is all right. Quiet." She gave me her number, scrawled in blue pen across a triage toe tag. "Call me," she said. "I hardly know anyone in Toronto, and I guess I need to make some friends. So, you know, I hope you'll hang out with me some time."

I knew I probably wouldn't call her, but I folded the toe tag and placed it in my wallet anyway.

[11]

Billy

I can remember the exact moment I stopped believing in the afterlife. I was on vacation with my best friend, Emmy-Lou Fielding, at her parents' camp north of Brandon. After four days of popsicles on the dock, canoeing, sleeping on thin mattresses, and whispering about Donnie and Dave, our respective crushes, I stepped on a wasp. I looked at my foot curiously and then I passed out. When I came to, Emmy's mother's face was hovering over me. "What on earth? Are you okay, Hilary?"

It occurred to me that in those ten or so seconds, I hadn't existed. Everything went on and I simply wasn't there. I can't describe what I felt exactly, but the next time I saw my grandmother, I asked her, "How do you know Heaven exists?" Her answer was not satisfying. "I have faith."

After that, anytime someone asked if I believed in God, I felt the emptiness of those ten seconds.

[12]

Josh

I was walking towards him when he struck the match. He was standing in the middle of an alley, the one between Bathurst subway station and the back doors of the Bloor Street Theatre. There were kids bundled in snowsuits playing in the parkette to our right. The sun was going down. There were crowds of rush-hour commuters everywhere, still happy about the first December snow.

We headed towards one another like two cowboys about to square off. The 10-2s blocked the entrance behind him. Fire trucks bookended us. People gathered, curious, leaning over the barriers.

The gas can made a hollow sound when it hit the pavement. The match was struck. I watched.

Then I turned to yell at the 10-2s and Fire, and turned back. He laughed and flailed. This was one big show. This was the jacket sleeve of *Wish You Were Here*. Cops and Fire ran towards him. I didn't. I don't run towards flames. Instinct. I walked slowly.

Only when I got up close did I realize it was my father. I could pick out his features in the charred skin. My eyes. His eyes. The tear-drop tattoo on his face. I couldn't smell a thing but all around me the other medics, Fire and cops were gagging from the smell of his rot.

I smelled just like him. I was used to it. I realized then that my feet were bare and it was dark, a new moon above. I reached out to touch him...

My head hit the steering wheel. Close by: honking.

Dispatch: "3434, what's your 20?"

Diane's voice came from the back of the truck: "JOSH, the LIGHT IS GREEN, buddy! Wake up!" She laughed.

"We're 10-9, approaching Toronto Western." My voice cracked. My watch read 5:30 a.m.—the time for silence, occasional hysterical laughter, and involuntary napping at intersections. We were five blocks from the hospital with a patient in the back, a senior needing a G-tube reinsertion. Foot to gas, blink blink blink. Honest Ed's lit up on my right as I passed. Jarring. *Wake up, buddy, wake up. Wake up.*

At the hospital, Diane sat with the patient on OLD while I ran to Tim Hortons. I ordered one double double, one black. The lady behind the cash looked like my father's sister, except that her name-tag read *Anita*, which was not my aunt's name. Still, she looked at me longer than you usually would. My aunt's name was Betty. She's probably dead now, I thought. Raised next to a paper mill. Cancer got the ones who weren't in prison. *The ones in prison have cockroach genes*, my mother used to say. *They'll never fucking die.*

Oddly, our patient got a bed right away. Our coffees were still warm when Dispatch said the magical number combination: *10-19*. I made sure Diane drove back to 34 instead of me. I kept seeing my father on fire whenever I blinked.

Diane and I had been temped in together again, and were starting to get into a rhythm. It was the last day of our C-shift, lovingly referred to as *the shaft*. Five 12-hour days in a row, and this particular rotation was all night shifts.

I'm not kidding when I say we hadn't had a single life-or-death emergency that entire week. In fact, we'd had repeated calls from a woman who liked to use us as a taxi service no matter how many times we explained what 911 is for. She would just complain that she hurt "all over" but that she never got any help from the ER docs. They would send her home, and she'd call again the next day. It made me want to bang my head against the dashboard. Plus, this was the beginning of the Christmas season, so psych calls were up. Diane talked about her Christmas vacation plans, and I told her I was bummed about having to work. But really, I was relieved. Working over Christmas meant I didn't have to go to Amy's family party and pretend things were totally fine between us. The pressure of the holiday was starting to get to me.

We'd taken a call from someone who'd broken a nail and passed out. We'd taken calls to deal with a few drunks. And then there'd been a guy who got punched in the face at the Brunswick House on Bloor Street and had fallen down. The bartender had called us, which made things difficult. When injured people called us themselves, they wanted us there. When other people stepped in, we were like the meddling much-resented presence of evil authority.

Let me tell you, most guys who get punched in the face deserve it. I would say maybe eighty percent of them fully deserve what's coming to them. Maybe the other ten percent could've used a good tongue lashing instead. This guy was one of those people I wished I could've taken out myself. Every second word out of his mouth was *faggot* and he'd uttered a variety of rotating racial slurs. He smelled like a decomposing liver.

When Diane and I had walked into the pub, which was full of university students, the crowd parted for us. People waved us through, pointing towards the punched guy. If I'd walked through this room wearing a jeans and T-shirt, people might have been hostile, but when I was in uniform it was a whole different story. I'd be lying if I didn't admit this was empowering, especially at first. A power trip.

I told Amy my statistical assumptions re: punched out guys yesterday morning and she said, *No one deserves to be hit, Josh.* She didn't catch that I was commenting on my job, the absurdity of it, the way it sometimes made me hate people. When I dropped in at Roxy's place later and told Billy the same thing, she said, "Yeah, fucking totally. I see what you mean. I totally wanted to punch a guy at work today who made me redo his latte three times before I told him to get a fucking hobby."

"Have you ever hit anyone?" I asked. I half-expected either answer. I could see Billy just losing it on someone. I could see her as a person who'd had a scrappy childhood—an older-sister type who'd punch a bully in the playground for picking on her younger sibling. I could also picture her as being too aloof to get into it with anyone.

"No," Billy said. "I actually don't even know how."

So I taught her some basic moves. She practised on my forearms.

This morning Diane and I were back at the station at 6:00 a.m., and praying for the phone not to ring. FYI, it's best not to have an emergency at 6:45 — a.m. or p.m. If you do, you're guaranteed to get some grumpy, exhausted medic.

Of course, at 6:28 we got an Echo. A guy found his uncle not breathing, was doing CPR on him. The uncle was seventy years old, and lived a few blocks away in a two-storey apartment above a restaurant on Bloor.

"I just talked to him on the phone twenty minutes ago!" swore the nephew, who looked to be about forty, as he ran up the dank staircase and into a nearly empty apartment. "I came to check on him and make sure he was eating breakfast!"

It was clear by the position of the body that the uncle had been dead for a few hours already. He was lying on the couch, limbs extended like a crab, stiff. The smell was telltale. The apartment was filthy; I thought it was perhaps the perfect visual representation of loneliness. The man owned hardly any objects, so there wasn't much clutter. A line of brownish dirt was smeared around the baseboards, and beyond the smell of death was something else vile. The 10-2s arrived, and then the coroner. There was crying. I think that's what makes me most uncomfortable — family members crying. I know how to talk to them now and not appear uncomfortable, but it's difficult. The nephew continued to insist he'd spoken to the uncle on the phone only twenty minutes earlier.

It was clear that the only thing this man had loved was his cats. I could see and count about fifteen, all grey and white. Eight of them sat on the stairs to the second floor, each in the same upright position, as if a sculptor had made vases in a cat shape. The animals peered at us with huge yellow eyes, their faces betraying concern. As I got closer, a dozen or so kittens, maybe six months old, poked their heads through the upstairs banister, surveying us, one after the other, as if their moves were synchronized.

While one cop talked to the nephew, who slowly sobbed while he spoke, another stood beside me at the window we'd pried open. We looked over Bloor Street as the sun rose, gasping for cleaner air. A flatbed truck piled with Christmas trees was stopped, blocking traffic, trying to rescue a fallen clump of wired-up trees from the road.

"Good he came by, it's always the worst when the cats start snacking on 'em," the cop said.

A cat jumped up on the windowsill, and rubbed against me. I hoped the cop was joking.

[13]

Amy

After a few teasing snows that melted right away, the drifts were now ankle-deep and stubborn. I'd never before felt that wintry dread most Canadians speak of, but this year I wanted to tunnel inside warm places and stay there until March.

I was sorting laundry in the basement. Stacks of black, green, and blue. One stack of argyle plaid, a couple of hoodies with pink stars and rockets. To either side of my head hung EMS uniform shirts suspended from pipes on plastic hangers. I was ignoring the blinking of my phone, which sat next to me on top of the detergent box.

I folded with so much care, stacking shirts then pants, creating perfect fists of matching socks. I love doing laundry. Maybe because I had a maid growing up, and never had to do it. I find laundry relaxing. It makes me feel accomplished.

I heard the door open and saw Josh standing at the top of the stairs, holding two glasses. He looked like he was rehearsing what he might say.

"Hey," he said.

"Hey."

He looked at me. The land-line began to ring and he turned.

Above the washing machine was a calendar. I tried to remember the last time Josh and I had had sex. Besides the quickie on the couch a month ago, I noted it was probably the time we both got drunk at a dinner party and afterwards had the laziest sex in the world, as if we had happened to bump into each other while masturbating. We might as well have been in separate rooms.

Yesterday a man at the Whole Foods salad bar caught my eye. He was picking single green beans out of a corn, cabbage, and green bean mix. He had one of those indie-rock near-beards, an old Descendants T-shirt, and faded designer jeans. He passed me the balsamic vinegar and when I said thank-you, he replied, "I'd do anything for the most beautiful woman in the world."

I blushed. Normally, I would have shrugged, rolled my eyes, had a snappy come-back. But I felt all bones as he kept looking at me. I walked away and pretended to look at cheese, all the while contemplating something else to say to him, imagining doing something impulsive such as suggesting he come down to my car in the parking garage to make out. But when I turned away from the aged cheddars, he was gone.

Now I looked up at the doorway, and Josh was gone. I heard him cackling with laughter on the phone. I leaned against the dryer, and tried to picture having sex with Descendants man. I moved the stacks of carefully folded colours onto the washing machine and perched on top of the warm buzz. This usually did the trick. I imagined taking off the salad-bar man's shirt.

Put a girl in the picture, watching us. Nothing. Made Descendants man watch, and put the girl on a motorcycle. Still nothing. I jumped off the dryer, and twisted my ankle upon landing. Hopped on one foot and whipped my head back into one of the many blue shirts, pushed at it with my hand and sent the folded laundry tumbling to the floor. *Fuck. Motherfuck.*

Josh clomped heavy-footed down the uneven wooden stairs. "You okay?"

His concern was infuriating. I pulled each blue shirt down, one by one, until there were eight on the cold, dirty, cement floor. I kept my eyes locked on him.

"I'm fine, Josh. I just wish you would for once actually take your shirts upstairs once they are dry instead of dressing down here in the mornings."

"Drink?"

"Your shirts. Pick them up."

Josh handed me a drink.

I sniffed it. I tried to stand on the twisted ankle. The pain faded. "It's 10 a.m.," I said.

"I'm on nights. Come upstairs. I think we should talk on the porch."

"Why?"

"'Cause it's sunny out finally."

"But why the talk?"

"Well, when was the last time we talked?"

I didn't answer. Josh started up the stairs, and I picked up the shirts, rolling them into a ball. At the top of the stairs I reached my right hand out to place the drink on the kitchen counter and I let the shirts drop on top of the closed garbage can. Josh was already outside, smoking.

When he first became a paramedic, he was supposed to quit. How can you see so much cancer and not quit? But now he smoked more than ever.

The last time we fought I'd yelled at him, "What do you actually give a fuck about, Josh? Like, besides getting drunk on your days off?"

"Oh, you're so precious. Your life is so full of meaning," he'd sneered.

I sat hunched on top of the picnic table, close to where Josh had carved our initials inside a heart when we first moved in. Josh took off his bulky ski jacket and draped it over my shoulders.

We drank and smoked and stared at each other. Then Josh stood.

"It's over."

"Yup."

Josh went inside, kicked off his boots in a snowy mess, took two Gravol from the canister beside the coffee machine, and climbed upstairs to bed.

I mopped up the slush on the floor and walked his boots to the front alcove. I took a bottle of Maker's Mark into the living room, sat at the computer, and tried to buy two tickets to a Cuban resort for Tina and me. The computer kept stalling. I gave up.

I retrieved Josh's shirts from the kitchen, and folded them again in front of the TV. On MuchMoreMusic they were showing videos from the '90s on *Where Are They Now?* Hilary Stevenson's "Bottom of My Ocean Heart" came up. "I wonder whatever happened to her," said the male VJ. "She was really hot."

The female VJ punched him on the arm. "For god's sake! She was sixteen."

[14]

Billy

Walking towards Toronto Western Hospital, I flipped the bird at a guy in a minivan who yelled, *Nice ass!* I noted the empty car-seats in the back, sighed, and said a quick prayer for his children's welfare. Onlookers would've surmised, *Confident.* I walked liked I used to walk, full of attitude, shoulders back as if they held wings, smirking, making eye contact. As though I was playing the part of myself in my younger years.

It was a good show, except for the fact that I was certain my organs were grey. Standing at the light at Dundas and Bathurst, I squished a half-smoked cigarette beneath the pointed arrow of my red shoe and stretched òut my hand, revealing the thin layer of skin wrapping my wrists. It appeared yellow in the harsh smoggy grey of downtown Toronto. I imagined the skin simply tiring out and eventually tearing, like the rubber of a worn-out balloon. I stared at the blueness of my veins. *Good Will.* I pulled my mittens out of my coat pocket and put them on.

I was not alive. I hadn't thrived in months. The business of my body continued on without my brain. I was a passenger in my own body, driven recklessly around the city by anxiety. And anxiety nearly got me hit by a cab because I was staring at my wrist and the mess inside it. The driver screamed at me in a language I didn't understand. Even though I was in the wrong, I gave him the finger.

I was on my way to see my therapist, Dr. Harris, for a one-on-one. I usually go to her office concerned that I have poor life skills and leave an hour later absolutely sure of it. This time, after two minutes, during which I was certain she couldn't remember who I was from my last session, Dr. Harris tried to convince me to take pills.

"Take some samples, Hilary."

"No. I need some perspective is all."

Then we started over again. I'm not entirely sure why I bothered.

"So, when you're having a panic attack, what are you afraid of?" Dr. Harris asked.

"It depends."

"Describe the last one you had."

"I was afraid the subway was going to stop underground."

"What if it did?"

I tried to picture it. The scenario didn't seem as scary in my imagination as it had when I was standing inside the subway car, palming the smeared windows. "I'd freak out. I might faint. We might run out of air."

"What do you think would happen if you fainted?"

I knew what she was doing. She was trying to trace the fear to its origin so I could understand what the real issue was. Always the real fear is death, lack of control. The usual cocktail.

"You would regain consciousness eventually," Dr. Harris prompted. "Everyone does."

"Okay, then, I'm afraid of dying. But isn't everyone?"

"Yes, you are afraid of dying."

"Aren't you?"

"No. And we're here to discuss *your* feelings."

"So how do I fix this?"

"You don't. You accept it."

I knew this. It was obvious. It was like my brain was stuck and I couldn't move forward. Maybe I was emotionally retarded. Still, I thought, I might as well talk about it.

"How does anyone accept it?"

"Are you religious? Do you believe in anything?"

"Not really."

There was an uncomfortable silence. I bit my nails. Dr. Harris scanned the clipboard in her lap. I thought about telling her that lately I'd become concerned whenever I saw elderly people or babies, people on crutches or very small dogs. I thought about what would happen if I suddenly snapped and stuck my foot out in front of them, caused their brittle bones to break. What if I poked a soft baby skull with my thumb, by accident? Even the thought of doing these things made me sick.

In this book I own, *Understanding Your Obsessive Thoughts*, it says these thoughts are signs of a type of obsessive compulsive disorder, only without the compulsions. According to the handy quiz section, I am a pure obsessive. People have upwards of four thousand thoughts a day, and a normal person can filter out the ones that seem absurd. Pure obsessives fixate, worried that having the thought in the first place proves they are bad people. The obsessive brain becomes preoccupied with these thoughts, like someone who is so afraid of being sacrilegious they pray ninety-five times a day. *That's me. This is me*, is what I had said to myself when I was sitting on the floor of the self-help bookstore on Harbord Street, taking the quiz in the back of the book.

"What if I did suddenly lose my mind?" I asked Dr. Harris.

"Hilary, I really think you should consider medication. Think about the quality of your life."

"No. Do you know how over-prescribed SSRIS are today? I just read an article about it."

"I understand you're frustrated, Hilary. This time of year is hard on most people."

Back at the apartment, Roxy was hanging up our stockings and making invitations to our annual Christmas Eve dinner party for friends who don't visit family for the holidays. She'd rented a deep fryer and *Guitar Hero*, and had a Charlie Brown tree in every room. The holiday season fuelled Roxy, filled her with kindness for all the local orphaned twenty-something misfits. I just wished the holiday was over. *In January, I can start over*, I thought, *along with everyone else*.

Dr. Harris took notes, filling in the silence. She wore a ridiculous Christmas sweater. I visualized stealing it and dipping it in the deep fryer. I felt annoyance that Dr. Harris had probably never been afraid of death, never been afraid of going outside; that she could be happy and healthy and just freakin' fine. I felt the kind of self-pity endemic to the depressed and anxious, where you're absolutely certain that the fear and sadness you're currently experiencing is the most that any one person has ever felt. I realized this was insane, but that's the way it felt.

"What do you want right now, Hilary?"

"If I could just pause for a few weeks. Be where no one expects anything from me, like rehab."

"Do you have a problem with drinking right now?"

It was questions like these that made me suspect Dr. Harris wished my problems were easier to label, like alcoholism. During our first session she had asked me if I'd been abused, if my anxiety was post-traumatic, from childhood. My somewhat unusual but otherwise loving family seemed to confound her.

"No, I wish I did. I mean, I wish it were that simple."

"You should know it's not simple. Your father is one such example."

Aha; she remembered me. She probably had DRUNK DAD, USED TO BE FAMOUS, TOTALLY NUTS scrawled on her notepad to differentiate me from the other patients.

"If I had a drinking problem, the solution would be simple: Stop drinking."

"Billy, I think you might depressed. It is common for people with anxiety disorder to also develop depressive symptoms."

"No, I don't think so. I'm just tired of being anxious."

"Billy. I think you should—"

"I don't believe in the goodness of the pharmaceutical industry. Besides, I tried it once and it didn't work." Paxil had made me forget how to spell basic words. I left out consonants. I would put on my shoes, walk into another room and completely forget where I was going. I had dreamt every night that I was standing in line at the bank machine.

But it wasn't only that. I had pretty sane friends, on the whole. I was probably the most crazy of them, in the traditional sense. Yet almost everyone I knew had at some point been prescribed these drugs, whether it was to quit smoking or get over a job loss or a breakup. It was astounding, how commonplace it was. It reeked of conspiracy, according to Roxy. Perhaps I was starting to listen to Roxy's conspiracies too closely.

Dr. Harris looked at the clock, wished me a Merry Christmas, and told me to remember to breathe. She gave me a piece of paper for a new medication that I ripped into little sweaty pieces in the hallway, like I always did.

I took the elevator down nine floors and tried not to notice how many greasy fingerprints peppered the large metal doors, or think about how many of those fingers had touched the numbers outlined in orange glow on the keypad, or the horizontal metal banister that split the wall of the elevator in two.

There were four other people in the elevator, standing straight and looking forward. I was definitely looking like the healthiest, upright in a tidy black dress, red boots, and matching clutch purse, a leather coat across my right arm. When I caught my reflection, I realized I actually had a glow in my cheeks, a thin sheen of gloss on my lips. This was the look I had perfected. Fearless. But I felt grey. I pressed G with certainty.

The person beside me was a fat man in a polyester suit with a cast on his arm. He reminded me of Uncle Jonny and I felt comforted by his display of solid masculinity. A thin woman with a salt and pepper mullet and teeth that had lost a battle with coffee and nicotine stood beside him. A silver-haired nurse who appeared to be on the 24th hour of a shift and resented my perky demeanour was next. An elderly man in a wheelchair drooling rivers made me saddest of all.

I pressed G again, and continued to press it after the doors closed on every floor, just in case. I was trying to be prepared for anything. I had very little faith in technology and lots of experience with human error. The elevator emptied completely on six and then stopped between floors five and four. Paused. Black.

Good Will. Good Will!!!

I moved my hands around to where I remembered seeing the alarm button and the phone, but in the end I wasn't sure about any of the buttons except for the familiar G. I pressed it again. Nothing. No comforting orange light around the tiny circle. No sound.

I found the phone, picked it up, but couldn't hear a tone, connection or voice. I let it drop.

The darkness and silence illustrated my options. Even my cell couldn't get a signal. I was waiting for the magician to cut my legs off in this box. I couldn't do anything. I could only stand there and breathe.

Oddly, I started to feel calm. Acceptance. The tingling in my feet stopped. I took a deep breath and my throat opened.

The elevator jumped slightly, and the lights flickered back on.

"You okay in there?" said a voice.

"Yes!" I said, a little too loudly, almost chipper. The doors opened again on the ground floor. Walking home, I felt as if the panic was miraculously gone. At least for a while. It was freeing. Why bother focusing on the panic when I was finally calm? Calm moments shouldn't be wasted.

When I got home I found a note from Roxy on a ripped cigarette pack. "Your boss called. You missed work again. She said not to bother to come in tomorrow. Sorry, my lovely. You'll find something else soon. xox rox."

I couldn't believe I had mixed up my shift times again. They were written in red on the calendar on the fridge. I stared at the numbers: 4 p.m., which I had interpreted as 9 p.m., for no reason at all. The details always failed me. I fell into bed.

When I woke up three hours later, it was because Roxy burst through the house and pushed open my door, which I had shut earlier with a pile of discarded laundry long overdue for a wash.

"Billy. I'm making you get up."

"Why?"

"Because you've been asleep forever, and Josh is here and we're going to play Risk. We found the whole game in the neighbour's garbage and it's time for world domination."

"No."

"C'mon! Don't you remember the Cold War?" When in pursuit of immediate fun and pleasure, Roxy stopped at nothing. She jumped on the bottom of my bed. There was plenty of room because I sleep like a snail.

"BILLY! BILLY! There's plenty of time to sleep when you're dead!" Roxy used this excuse for everything: plenty of time to be skinny, sober, well-behaved, when dead.

"Fuck off."

Roxy jumped off the bed, pulled a sweater off my laptop and pressed play on my Gym mix. A '90s house song came on. Roxy clicked the volume up as high as it could go and began to sing along with words she made up. "Billy loves me, she loves me so much! I'm her best friend in the wooooorld. If we were at all attracted to each other, we'd make the best couple ever! Oh, Billy, Billy, Billy!"

I surrendered, sitting bolt upright. "You'd better have brought home beer."

"Even better. Josh is in the kitchen making hot toddies. Fuck winter!" she yelled.

"Fuck winter!" Josh replied from down the hall.

A few minutes later, I sat at the kitchen table, rubbing the sleep from my eyes and staring at Josh, a blurry animal who smelled really good. Like cookies and man cologne. In the middle of the game, Roxy's phone sang the chorus to "The Humpty Dance." It was a call from her fathers; she took it out on the balcony. Josh and I paused to refill the mugs of rum. Warmth filled my whole body.

"How was work today?" I asked.

"Some guy stabbed in the gut by his brother."

I laughed. I couldn't help it. "Oh yeah, I heard about that on the news. I wonder what would make someone do something like that?" What if *I* could do something like that, I thought suddenly. I felt unable to swallow. I moved my glass up and down to taunt myself, testing to make sure I wouldn't hurl it across the room. *See? I'm okay. Change the subject.* "So, how's Amy?"

"We, uh, just broke up, actually. So I'm not sure how she is." Josh looked down at the table.

"I'm sorry to hear that. How long were you guys together?"

"Almost five years."

"Oh yeah. I just broke up with my girlfriend not too long ago. We were together seven years. I have to say, it's the hardest thing I've ever had to go through, really. Losing her."

"Me too. I think I'm still in denial. I mean, we're still living together. Who did you break up with?"

"My high school sweetheart, Maria." Quick*, say something that indicates you also date boys*. I decided on a look instead of words—an unavoidable flirty come-hither look I perfected long ago. It worked. Josh blushed.

"When I first met her," I said, "I would've thrown myself in front of a bus if she'd said it was a good idea. Now we're working on being good friends." When you said these kinds of things out loud, they sounded so much simpler than they felt. "So, what's it like to be single? What are you going to do for the holidays?"

"I have no idea!" Josh said, laughing. He took a long sip. "Work, I suppose. Triple time." He smiled warmly. I smiled back.

"So, I hear you need another job. I heard about this telephone research place that my friend Jenny was working at while she was in school. It's crappy but good money."

This always happened: As soon as I quit or got fired from one service job, another one fell into my lap within twelve hours. And while I excelled at letting my anxiety render me unreliable, my ability to interview enthusiastically and convincingly allowed me to recoup.

Josh wrote a number on a piece of paper. "Here. I'll tell Jenny you're calling the place, and she'll tell her friend to make sure you get the job. I mean, a monkey could do this job. As long as you're not a criminal, it's pretty much a sure thing. She was doing it during school, and she just graduated."

"Thanks." I'd always wanted to get a job with such low expectations.

"But," continued Josh, "I've always wanted to ask you this. It's kind of invasive, but don't you, like, have tons of money from your songs?"

I hated this question above all questions, but was used to answering it. "Well, I didn't write the one that was really popular. My uncle gets the royalties. And he's been really stingy with me since I quit the business. And I spent almost everything I did have during my first two years in Toronto. I paid for Maria's tuition and mine, paid for our apartment. I took us on vacation twice in the wintertime. I bought fancy groceries and $400 jeans. It went fast. It's really amazing how fast it can go. I don't have anything to show for it, really. Pisses me off."

"Yeah, I guess it would."

I sounded like a wash-up. I don't like to talk about money. Someone careful and not eighteen might have lived on that money for a decade. I spent and spent like the money was a burden, a glass I had to empty as fast as possible. It panicked me. Maria always said, *You should be more careful*, tried to reign in my spending. I didn't listen.

In my bedroom I had the remnants of that bank account: two laptops, some home recording equipment, two vintage Gibson guitars, Seven jeans, sheets softer than rabbits. If you looked closely around our apartment, which mostly looked like the apartment of every slightly trashy artist-kid in the neighbourhood, there were some expensive objects amongst the dollar-store dishes and collection of kitsch.

Josh was eyeing me.

"What? Why are you looking at me like that?"

"Like what?"

"That!" I squinted my eyes, smiled a half-smile.

"I guess I just really want to know you, Billy. You intrigue me."

I swallowed the last of the hot, sweet rum. It stung the back of my throat. "Well, Mr. Medic, the feeling is quite mutual." I reached under the table and touched his knee, pulling it back fast. *Good Will.* When Roxy came back in the room, I gained control of Australia and fortified my troops. By the time we'd emptied the bottle of Malibu, I had won the game.

I took my guitar out of its case and tuned it while Josh and Roxy cleaned up the game and split the last beer in the fridge. "Play us a song!" Roxy said. "I haven't heard you sing in so long."

"Only if we all sing."

I started in with "All Along the Watchtower" and by the time the sun rose we'd covered every song for which we knew more than two verses. My fingers hurt from lack of practice, but it was good to play again. A little bit of myself had come back.

[15]

Amy

I could feel it looming, like the day of aches you get before the flu hits. This was acceptance, I supposed. I was dropping things. First, a wet filter full of coffee grinds. Then I swept a glass of wine into the air with a swing of my wrist, and it crashed onto the floor of the bar in the Gladstone Hotel, where I'd been trying to work on my laptop.

I wasn't even trying to illustrate a point. My arm just took flight. I'd been avoiding home. Drinking in the afternoon. I kept tapping away at my table, watching the red wine stain seep into my skirt, and I didn't even bother dabbing it away. It set in the shape of a running leg on thick blue cotton.

The waitress with computer-screen tattoos said, "It's okay, honey. It's just gravity." She swept the glass shards into the dustbin while a line of sweat formed on her hairline. I was tearing up, trying to help her with some half-hearted mops of my cloth napkin. My fingers dry-stained with house red. I cried softly, shading my eyes with my right hand, wishing myself invisible. I don't think I'd ever cried in public before.

The bright Google notifier in the right-hand corner of my screen lit up. A tiny box of text indicated a new e-mail, an unfamiliar address. The subject heading: *AMY AMY AMY, it's Jay. Your One True Love!* And as though eight years had not passed, my heart pounded at the mere sight of his name.

We'd been alone on the dock at summer camp in upstate New York. Jason McAuslan and me, pushing a canoe out into the water. Across our feet were sandal tans that wouldn't fade until the following March. Sixty-one sleeps on thin plastic mattresses in simple wood cabins, bright-coloured plastic friendship bracelets making tiny cubes on our wrists.

The week before I left for camp, my grandmother had died. I'd stayed with her every night in the hospital. I turned sixteen holding her hand, telling her terrible jokes. The funeral was the day before camp started.

For the first time, my mother didn't monitor my packing. My father didn't drive me up the laneway awkwardly talking to the other fathers pulling large knapsacks out of their expensive cars. I drove myself in my grandmother's navy Oldsmobile, smoking American Spirits, listening to The Counting Crows. I didn't cry.

Every night from midnight to 5 a.m., Jason and I slept in the same slim cot. Before sunrise, his watch would beep and he'd cross the rugged dirt path to the boy's CIT cabin and sleep until the wake-up bell. From the age of thirteen, six of us had returned every year. There was a religious quality to our connection; we would have trusted our lives to each other. Jason and I had those two months together from ages thirteen to sixteen.

That night, the sun was going down over the hills above the lake. We were in love. Back then, you knew the difference between *in love* and *not in love* because the first time you felt something monumental, you could name it. Throughout the previous year I'd go through the mail Nanny would leave on the front table by the door, scanning desperately for a New York City postmark. Our two best friends, Kat and Alex, were already out in the middle of the lake and we paddled towards them with packages of hot chocolate powder, stolen from the kitchen, in the pockets of our hooded sweatshirts. The water was so still that dropping our chocolate-coated fingers into the cold blackness made tiny circles. No waves. Kat said, "I can't believe how calm it is. It's like we're the only ones on earth."

"Let's lie down and look at the stars," suggested Alex. We stripped off our bulky orange lifejackets and stuffed them in the bow and stern as pillows, and shimmied our legs and hips under the wooden seats. Jason and I extended an arm on either side to hold onto the side of the girls' canoes. They liked to paddle alone and do things like swim across the lake every year. The only sound from the three canoes, the water, the surrounding forest, was our breath and the occasional loon. The water was a polished floor. We closed our eyes.

I could hear my grandmother's voice in my head, telling me between delusional mumblings that I shouldn't do anything in my life just to please my parents, that I had privileges she'd never had. I felt weightless. "Maybe this is why people meditate," Jason said, breaking the silence. I came up to look around, and all the blues had turned to black. The moon was an eyelash curl of white. We'd drifted nearly half a mile down the lake. We could see the campfire on the beach and we knew we were in some sort of trouble. We giggled to each other, then paddled like mad towards the light. Exhilarated. Sat down on a log in the middle of fifty-six youngsters singing a song about greasy grimy gopher guts, holding hands.

Later that night, Jason and I had sex in the boathouse. I told him it was my first time, but it wasn't. He told me he wasn't a virgin, but I could tell he was.

That summer, a seventeen-year-old girl from Michigan showed up as a replacement counsellor after Bette McFadden was carried away for her eating disorder. Her name was Star. She had a shaved head and a nose-ring. She talked about things I'd never thought to think of before. She had a tattoo on her shoulder of a cat and a T-shirt that said "Vegans Taste Better." I didn't know how to talk to her. When the summer was over she wrote "I Love You, Amy" in my autograph book and I stared at it all the way home. I was so tired I asked Jason to drive. He was visiting me in Toronto over the Labour Day weekend. My parents were in Florida golfing and we pretended the house was ours.

The first night at home, Jason shaved my head in the upstairs bathroom. Red curls in the oversized marble sink. All we could talk about was Star.

"Star hitchhiked across the country. Did she tell you about that? She told me about it that time we took Tyler to the nurses' station together."

"Star is in love with an older guy named River who lives in a lighthouse. She told me that the day we went canoeing together."

We were oddly competitive about Star's attention. I was a little jealous when it became clear that Jason had a crush on her, but at the same time, who could blame him? I certainly had a crush—at least, what I understood to be a crush at that time. Maybe it was awe. We agreed she was the most original person we'd ever met.

I looked at myself in the bathroom mirror, opening the two mirrored medicine cabinet doors on either side so I could see the back of my head in the reflection of the one behind it. Fingering the soft stubble, I felt a shift. Jason kissed my head. I shaved his head too, and we sat delirious in the backyard under the stars smoking joints and rubbing our shaved skulls together.

When I kissed Jason at the airport it was with longing and sadness. I felt this every year when we had to part, but the feeling was all the more tragic because I knew somehow this year would change us. People grow a lot between sixteen and seventeen. Jason said, "Don't worry so much, Amy. We won't be apart for much longer. We'll go to the same university. We'll get an apartment together."

Jason moved to California the following summer and didn't go to camp. We lost touch, fell in love with others. Star and I became best friends, the twin weirdos who returned to camp faithfully every summer until we were eighteen and nineteen. We took a solo canoe adventure for three days, pitched a tent in a wooded area down the beach and spent the whole time having sex and eating s'mores. I was in love and she was experimenting. When we got back to camp she hooked up with a older guy who worked in the kitchen and I never went back to camp again. Last I heard, Star was in South America building a school.

After Josh and I had been together just over two years, I took him to meet my high school friends. We were all twenty-two, and we met in Yorkville at a café. After our lunch, he named each girl after characters from *90210*. I felt awkward. I am conventional amongst my non-conventional friends. Roxy calls me "Gateway" because when she got interested in the stock market, she asked if I could hook her up with my dad. Like, I am "Gateway Girl to the Man." When any of my friends gets into legal trouble, they call me, because they're pretty sure I know a lawyer. But sitting next to Jenny, Valerie, Amanda, and Amanda's new baby, talking yoga classes and jewellery and the perfect spot to vacation in Cancun, I realized my high school pals still regarded me as their wayward friend. They said, "Oh, Amy. Really? Wow. You're so...unusual!" Josh couldn't believe anyone considered me unusual—*except unusually brilliant and pretty*, he said hurriedly, to save himself.

I had to stop myself from returning Jason's e-mail too quickly, using all caps. I had often thought of him, too, wondered who he'd grown up to be. His message told me that he was back in New York City, had started a PhD in history. He'd heard that Star had married an older man who led a cult somewhere in Colorado. He'd heard that I was gay now, or something like that. I laughed. I laughed because Jason had such a *husband* appeal—the *I'll take care of you* machismo that, sometimes, on days like this, I found so attractive.

I started to write back to Jason with details of Amy's Life as an Adult, but stopped halfway through the second paragraph, aware that I sounded like someone trying to write a fake Christmas letter, trying to prove to myself, more than to him, that I'd grown into a successful and happy person.

I could see it all so blatantly on the screen in front of me. I didn't know what I was doing. Probably for the first time ever,

I didn't have any answers, or any hilarious bright summations for a long-ago lover. I was in danger of memorializing, giving in to nostalgia. I stopped myself just short of suggesting a clandestine getaway, a reunion of teenaged passion.

I pressed "save draft" and decided to wait until later to respond in an honest way. I could feel Desperation's presence in the room, hanging around me like a stifling, wet wool sweater. I was not going to let that bitch get the better of me.

Josh

It's always the quietest people who are experiencing the real emergency. For example, the woman I drove to the hospital who didn't even know she had sliced her arm off until I was relaying her condition to the trauma team at Sunnybrook. She talked quietly about her dog the whole time, about whether or not she'd get home in time to walk him.

The people who are about to die often walk themselves to the hospital, or don't call 911 because they don't want to seem like they are over-reacting. There's a look in the eyes. They usually say something vaguely psychic, such as *I feel as though I'm about to die.* Heart-attack patients usually know. They tell you. If they don't tell you, you can usually see it.

I can't remember the last time I was seriously thrown by a call. Most days, it's tedium express. Our first call today was a woman with a headache. Seriously. *Marty*, she kept whining. *Someone call my husband. I'm dying!* Marty wasn't picking up his phone. Gee, I wonder why.

The headache woman occupied our stretcher for four straight hours in the waiting room at Toronto Western. I hadn't wanted time to think because I knew all I'd do was obsess about Amy, the breakup, and what it meant. I wanted car accidents and overtime calls and constant epi shots. Instead I got the glare of the twenty-four-hour newsreel in the waiting room, and taking turns with Dave, my partner for the day, napping in the ambulance. I smoked way too much, and my voice got hoarse.

In the middle of a conversation about some ridiculous reality show, all the male medics rubbernecked towards triage: a blonde ponytail, a new medic. "What is she? Like, fourteen?" Mike laughed, but didn't stop looking. Diane rolled her eyes.

The new medic pushed her patient into the offload delay room beside the vending machine while her partner talked to the triage nurse. It took me a second, but I recognized her from her snorting laugh—it was Jenny, the student medic-actor from COHERT. "Hey—Josh!" she said, nodding at me. I felt the other guys immediately begin to like me better. I gave the introductions.

Just as I was finishing, my phone beeped. *Thinking bout going 2 NYC 2 c Jason, my X? Let me know if u'r not okay w this, or need 2 talk.*

I concentrated on my hands, trying to relax through the surge of anger and jealousy rising up my throat. I suggested to Jenny we go get coffees for everyone. Offload delay meant there were about ten of us sitting around and this gave us something to do, right? Right.

By the time Jenny and I hit Bathurst Street, I'd learned a little more about her. Recently broken up with a guy from back home. Moved from Sault Ste. Marie to go to Humber College two years back. I suddenly remembered she was new in Toronto, and felt bad I hadn't called her. In the couple of months since we'd last seen each other, she'd moved out of Etobicoke into a bachelor apartment on St. Clair. Hadn't made a lot of friends at school because she'd been studying too hard and living in Etobicoke. Jenny was the only medic from her class hired on in Toronto.

She had to stop at the Scotiabank ATM machine to get some cash. It was only when the ATM spit out her card and began to beep that she pulled her tongue out of my mouth. "I want to take you home," she said. I was seriously drawing a blank about how to form a sentence, let alone tell her that I was not some ordinary straight guy, not in the least. This might turn out to be my first attempt at *that* conversation and I was not looking forward to it. Another consequence of leaving the comfort of Amy.

Luckily my pager went off right at that moment. My patient had been off-loaded and there was a Delta down the street for a kid seizing. I had to forget coffee runs and cute forward girls and get going.

As soon as I left Jenny, the burning, angry, fist-through-a-wall feeling in my stomach returned. I pictured Amy with her idyllic academic boy, walking through New York City over the Christmas holidays while I stayed here with the depression calls and overdoses. Instantly I saw their baby, their dog, their brownstone in Brooklyn and fancy cottage upstate. I had imagined it all as soon as Amy told me he'd been back in touch, that she was thinking of connecting with him. She had said it with such fake lack of concern, I knew it had to be a big deal for her.

When a day starts going to shit, it just keeps going that way. Dave and I got a call involving a twenty-four-year-old woman, short of breath, feeling anxious. Shortness of breath automatically means a Delta.

The only calls that annoy me more than panic attacks are the ones that people make because they assume they'll be seen quicker if they arrive in an ambulance. Or Dial-a-Nurse tells them to call. Dial-a-Nurse always suggests calling 911 so as to cover their asses legally even though the caller is clearly suffering from the flu. Unless you're ninety-two, the flu isn't an emergency. Go to bed. Call your doctor.

I'd been awake for two days straight. Amy wouldn't let me sleep for more than three hours without waking me to process the end of our relationship. She'd been reading books about grief. She was underlining passages. As a result, I was not entirely pleasant to be around. My circadian rhythms were all fucked up from working too many nights in a row, and I felt crazed. And now I had to deal with her new boyfriend, or her old boyfriend, or whatever.

I felt lucky that I'd been teamed up with Dave. He was one of the younger guys — a slow mover, a wisecracker, no bullshit. I didn't have to make small talk or listen to him bitch about something stupid. "Some chick freaking out again," Dave mumbled, looking at his pager and taking the driver's seat. Most of the time I alternated half the shift driving, half in the passenger seat. Not with Dave. When we were together, Dave drove. I didn't mind, really. I was tired. It seemed as if I always got panic-attack calls when I was on the fourth night shift in a cycle and feeling as if I wanted to punch people when they breathed too loud.

People always think they're having a heart attack, not a panic attack, but heart attacks are easy to spot. You don't have the energy to hyperventilate when you're having a heart attack. If I had to go to one more panic-attack or backache call, I was going to blow my head off. In school they made it seem as if every call was a real emergency, that you were helping people and saving lives. Truth is, most calls were bullshit. When I told this to Billy she said, "Isn't that a good thing? Do you want more people to be dying all the time? Besides, even if they're not dying, you're still helping someone." I hadn't thought of it that way. I just didn't feel as if I was making a difference any more.

The girl with the panic attack was living in a dorm at the University of Toronto. We went through all the questions: *Why are we here today? When did your symptoms start? What were you doing when they started? Any pain, how much pain, for how long?* She was stressing out, hyperventilating, but ultimately did not want us there. Her roommate had called: *I thought she was dying.*

We took the girl's vitals, assured her they were all within normal parameters, and she started to look fine. I wanted to feel compassion, but I couldn't muster it. I was hungry, tired, and I couldn't help thinking we were taking up so much time here, and there must be a real emergency somewhere else. I ranted inside my head while talking to the girl in a calm voice, listening, asking the right questions. She smiled at me, though her face was puffed up red and her pupils were darting. "Thanks," she said. "It's ridiculous, I know, but it feels so real. Like a truck is coming at me all the time and I can't stop it. I really thought I was dying. God, I feel so ridiculous now."

Just for a moment, I felt good about being there.

Dave and I got back in the truck and I began to think a miracle might occur: we might get a lunch break before eleven hours had gone by. I had never needed a half-hour more than I did in that moment. And that's when we got another call.

"Josh, buddy," said Dave gently, taking the last bite of a 7-Eleven taquito before scrunching up the wrapper, "there's another person dying to meet us." I slammed my fists on the dash as he started up the lights. "You gotta relax, Josh. What's with you today?"

"Nothing. Just girlfriend trouble."

"Ah, that's why I do not date girls."

I looked at him more closely. "You're gay?"

"Yeah."

He looked at me, just as close, and all of a sudden I saw that he knew about me. "My family has the queer gene, I guess. My sister is, at the moment, turning into my brother."

I nodded at him, wishing the subject away.

"I don't know, man. I think that's pretty fucking cool, you know. She's always wanted it. I mean *he*. I'm always fucking that up: *he's* always wanted to be a guy. If there's anything this job has taught me, it's that life is too short to live a lie, right?"

"Amen," I answered, lighting a smoke.

"I mean, I don't talk about it at work 'cause, like, all these assholes and stuff."

"Yeah," I said. "That makes sense."

"But you only get one life to be happy, and you may as well fucking be happy!"

"I hear that."

After work I went to Roxy's house to drink beer instead of going home. We sat at her computer and finished all our Christmas shopping, then played video games. I couldn't bring myself to think about Amy. I didn't tell Roxy about Jenny and the bank machine.

"Where's Billy?" I asked.

"She's in her room."

"She's been in her room this whole time? Even though she knew I was here?"

Roxy laughed. "Imagine, you're not the centre of her universe..."

My surprise about Billy not paying attention to me had nothing to do with arrogance. Rather, I felt an exaggerated sense of rejection before anything had even happened between us. I suppose this was part of Billy's allure, the fact that she seemed into me one moment, but dismissive the next.

In the kitchen I took another beer out of the fridge. Looking out through the glass patio door onto the back deck, I made out the moon and some stars. When I looked more closely I saw Billy curled up in her parka on a lawn chair, cigarette dangling from one shaking hand, rocking back and forth. She looked manic, head tucked into her shoulder, cradling a cell phone.

"What's wrong with Billy?" I asked Roxy. "Did she get some bad news or something?"

Roxy, immersed in the video game, took a few moments to answer. "I dunno, nothing. Same old."

"Same old what?"

"I dunno. She gets panic attacks and stuff. Really bad. She doesn't talk about it with me but a lot of times Maria comes over and I can hear them talking about it. Or sometimes, she'll ask me strange questions over and over again about things."

"What kind of things?"

"I don't know. I probably shouldn't be telling you this. It would embarrass her."

Billy stuck her head into the living room. "Hey. Going to bed. See you later."

She didn't seem to register that I was there. Her face was red and blotchy, and she was clutching a pillow in her arms. She was gorgeous when she was dishevelled.

Earlier today I had decided to finally ask her on a date, as an emphatic movement away from Amy. Now, something about the way she was walking made me refrain. Maybe it's not the right time to start something new, I thought. What do I even have to offer? I can bandage you up, but who knows what else I can do for a girl. If Amy and I couldn't make it, maybe I was meant to be single. I would sleep with random people—Jenny; the nurse from St. Joe's. Single guy. Uh-huh.

But I had no idea how to be that person. I was *such* a marrying type. Maybe there was some sort of book on how to not be a lap-dog, I thought. Maybe Amy was already highlighting sections of it to leave on the table when I got home.

I knocked on Billy's door anyway. She was wearing a bra and panties but standing as if she were fully clothed. I tried to look at her face. It was really difficult.

"You want to go for drinks next week, or maybe the weekend after New Year's?"

"Sure, yeah." She shrugged, pulling at a string of her hair and twirling it. She looked at me as if to say, *Is that it?* All over her bedroom floor were art supplies, spilled glitter, cardboard, and drying holiday cards.

"I mean, like, a date. Do you want to go on a date?"

Billy raised her eyebrows, and I thought: *For the first time in my life, I'm going to get shot down.*

I have never been so relieved to see Billy's trademark smirk emerge. She reached up and put her hand on my face, rubbing the stubble on my cheek. "I'm gonna have to get used to stubble, I suppose." With that she kissed me softly, biting my lower lip and then pulling her hand away to slap me gently. "Sure, baby. I'll go out with you."

I stood there, grinning like a moron.

She looked at me. "I'm going to finish these cards. Call me next week, then."

"Okay, sure."

Billy closed the door and for a while I just stood there, legless, armless, in the hallway.

Book Three

[Life 3]

11:30:05 p.m. Delta seizure, M, 40, hx of same.

11:30:20 p.m. Fell from standing, active seizure,
hx of possible brain tumour.

It was a party like a lot of parties held in loft apartments rented by couples in their mid-thirties before they have kids. Looking down on it from above, you'd see some confident poses and some insecure hovering, hear a burst of too-loud voices, see the blink of a laptop screen displaying the cover art of the album that's playing. Music by a band from somewhere in the Midwest.

The host, Carla, was standing by the Ficus tree in the front window, pretending to talk to her boss, a mid-fifties pothead and publisher of the magazine where most of the attendees worked. He was so repetitive she wanted to gouge her eyes out, but was compelled to stay by the good view she had of Christyn, the leggy blonde her boyfriend Jim had fucked a few months back when they went through a brief "open relationship" phase. Carla was obsessed with keeping Jim and Christyn at opposite ends of the loft. She would never have invited Christyn but for the fact that Christyn was now dating Ted, the music editor, and Carla had felt obligated.

Christyn, meanwhile, was pulling at her thumb with her teeth. She liked to bite the skin all the way around the nail. Ted called it vile, so she tried not to do it around him, but he wasn't paying attention. He was talking wine with the twenty-something girl in brown corduroys who had given everyone at the party a flyer for her "improvised sound poetry installation and social experiment." The flyer had a photo of the girl with her top off. Christyn thought she vaguely recognized her as one of the waitresses at a coffee shop on Queen Street she frequented on Sunday mornings. Christyn stood by Ted and the intern, occasionally feigning interest or nodding, but not really paying attention.

Nothing is more boring than talking about wine, Christyn thought. Wine all tasted the same to her, and only functioned as a way to get her clothes off. She liked wine's transformative quality, but that was it. She continued to chew at her thumb, and covertly slipped her pinky finger into her ear and then smelled it. This was also one of her gross but very satisfying habits.

Besides Ted, whom she'd been dating for three months, Christyn knew one other person at this gathering: Jim, the boyfriend of the host, Carla. Most attendees worked at *Yes Magazine*, the city's biggest arts weekly, as journalists, editors, or designers. Except for Jim, who was a bartender, and Christyn, who ran her own jewellery business. The corduroy girl was the new intern, and she wore thick-rimmed glasses and a tight Journey baseball shirt, although Christyn knew that Journey had been popular way before said intern was born.

The intern was having, possibly, the most exciting night of her twenty-year-old life, drinking free Pabst Blue Ribbon from a can, and talking wine and David Byrne with Ted, the music critic she'd been reading since junior high.

Ted had just turned forty, and Christyn knew he didn't think he had many years left of fawning interns and impressive indie-rock credential carry-over. If Christyn weren't present, she surmised, he'd have put a move on the intern for sure.

Carla crossed the room and, smiling, offered Christyn a refill on her glass of wine.

Christyn was blissfully unaware that Carla knew about her and Jim; Ted certainly didn't know about her and Jim — their one-nighter had happened a week before Ted had asked Christyn out for the first time. Christyn assumed the invitation to Carla's meant that all was fine.

All around Christyn was talk of ironic viewings of the R. Kelly "Trapped in the Closet" video, ironic love of hair metal, eye-rolling obsessions with Kelly Clarkson and *Laguna Beach*. Christyn often wondered what this crowd sincerely enjoyed, besides pretending to like low-brow culture, going to yoga class, and watching *The Wire* or *The Daily Show*. She was bored, and so she walked to the kitchen to get another drink. She thought about how a few lines of coke might make this party fun, if only she hadn't given up the drug, with firm resolve, last year when she'd turned thirty-five. She missed it, though, the feeling of being interesting and interested and unaware of time.

The door to the loft opened, and Jim walked in with a case of beer. Christyn went to greet him by the kitchen island. This was the first time they had seen each other since the night they'd slept together.

Jim worked at a bar down the street from where she lived, and she used to notice him when she ordered drinks. His cute scruffy face, the way he looked in faded vintage cowboy shirts. How grumpy he was. She liked it. He was a challenge.

And now, here he was in his kitchen, putting bottles away and preparing to slice up limes at the counter.

"Hey, honey," he said over his shoulder.

Christyn put her empty glass down and placed her hands on his hips. He dropped the knife and turned around to look at her. They hugged the way people do when they still want to sleep together, and kissed lazily on the mouth a few seconds longer than friendly. Christyn wanted nothing more than to drag him outside and make out covertly, as if they were still in high school.

"You smell great," she said. "How are you?"

"Bored to death."

He smiled. But he had a strange look in his eye, an absence. He steadied himself against the counter. His face grew pale.

"Are you okay?" asked Christyn, as Jim's right arm began to twitch, then his left.

At first, she thought he was kidding her. She had a hard time understanding what was happening. When it sunk in, she yelled, "Carla! Jim is having a seizure!" But Carla was there, kneeling beside Jim, before she'd even finished her sentence.

Christyn had no idea what to do. *Aren't you supposed to put something in their mouths so they don't bite their tongues?* she thought, calling 911 on her cell.

Carla tried to keep Jim from injuring himself while his limbs flew here and there. It was over in moments, and then he just lay on the kitchen floor. Christyn brought pillows from the couch.

A small group of friends had gathered in the kitchen area, while others had moved farther away to give Jim some privacy.

Finally, Jim looked at Carla.

"How you feeling, Jim?" she asked.

"Well, I'd like to grow some cauliflower in the backyard," he said.

"He's had these before," Carla said to Christyn and Ted, who were leaning against the kitchen counter. "It takes him a while to make sense. I think it's best if everyone just leaves, guys. I'm sorry."

When the paramedics arrived, Christyn and Ted put their coats on and walked to the car, not talking. Christyn wished she had a reason to stay, but it seemed invasive.

"I wouldn't want people around if it was me," Ted said when they reached the car. "We'll call in a few hours and make sure he's okay. Just give him some privacy. Apparently he's been having seizures a lot." Ted rubbed his cold hands together. "Rumour is he has some sort of brain tumour. It doesn't look good."

Christyn chewed and chewed at her thumb, and realized that in their haste to leave, she had left her purse inside.

When she went back into the loft and extracted the purse from under the side table in the living room, she heard Jim telling the paramedics, "This is a really good soundtrack, right?"

"Do you know where you are, Jim?"

"Yes, I am at the carnival, and this is the best party of our lives."

Christyn was at the age where she was starting to lose friends. Breast cancer, overdoses, freak aneurisms, suicides, and car accidents. In her twenties it had seemed as if only grandparents died. Now there were fewer and fewer peers with both parents alive, few who hadn't had a personal cancer scare or a serious injury. She didn't like those odds. She shivered on her way back to Ted, who was sitting in the car, listening to Yo La Tengo on the stereo.

Inside, one of the paramedics — Dave — listened as Carla tried to convince Jim to go to the hospital. Jim didn't want to go. Still postictal, he moved in and out of lucidity.

"What are they going to be able to do anyway, the doctors? They won't know what's wrong any more than they did last time."

"What happened last time?" asked Dave. He was taking Jim's blood pressure again.

"This music is for spring. Don't you think? Spring," Jim said, "and I thank you for making the awesome soundtrack."

Dave liked seizure calls for their absurdity, but it was frustrating that the patients were usually reluctant to go to the hospital. So Dave and his partner, Josh, made themselves comfortable in the kitchen, wanting to stick around and make sure Jim was back to normal before he signed the papers refusing service.

Carla looked at Josh a little closer. "Amy's boyfriend!" she announced.

"Uh-huh."

"Film-fest stuff," Carla half explained. "I know Amy from the festival."

"Small world."

The three of them talked until Jim came around completely. As the medics prepared to leave, Carla assured them she'd watch Jim closely.

Josh repeated three times that Carla should take Jim to the hospital if anything else happened. He felt odd being on a call that involved proximity to people he knew in his non-work life, a party filled with familiar faces from the neighbourhood.

As Dave and Josh walked down the hall towards the front door of the building, Jim stood in the doorway of his loft and waved.

January to May 2006

[17]

Billy

My New Year's resolution was to stop being afraid.

It was January second, and the resolution wasn't working.

The leader of the Morning Meditation! group was urging me to picture my lungs and give them a colour. I pictured both, hanging like socks on a line, disembodied, floating in front of me. I saw my hand reach out and grab them. I imagined they'd feel like those stress balls you squeeze to relieve tension. It was a long way down to the alveoli. *C'mon, oxygen!*

I sat cross-legged on my mat, a dusty thin carpet sample that smelled of mould. *I'll go home unenlightened and with bedbugs.*

Both the group and my resolution now seemed ludicrous. We were a dozen stressed-out Toronto residents sitting around in a church basement like checkerboard pieces with no game plan.

Okay, start paying attention. The leader is noticing you're far from centred. Breathe. I inhaled and held my breath. Then I exhaled fast and gulped, which made me dizzy, which made me panic. I thought about how having a panic attack in the middle of a meditation group would be a little embarrassing. Then I giggled because I was being competitive about meditation. I made it through the next forty-five minutes by taking about seventeen successful deep breaths, and decided that was good enough.

On the streetcar later, I felt like a frantic hummingbird, a starling with a half-wing walking around itself in circles. I willed myself to feel like a stone on the red-upholstered seat, solid, but my brain kept chirping. I caught my reflection in the window. Starling-faced. Panicked.

Having a panic disorder means you're way too alive, as if someone has turned up your volume button to deafening. Somewhere inside, the real you lies dormant, asleep for fear of having to live like an electric current, a lightning bolt, a bottle breaking into shards. I'm a jack-in-the-box that won't stop jumping out, an uncontrollable, hiccuping heart.

I noticed the snow piled up on the sidewalks. The world was carrying on, even without me noticing. Depression and anxiety made people — me — so self-centred. *Good Will. Good Will. Good Will.*

I texted Maria. *Want 2 come over later?*

She must have been drunk. Her response: *Just thnking bout u, how we belong 2gethr, the way it's sposed to be.*

I turned off my phone. Later, at home, I texted her back: *This is something we should talk about in person. I'll call you tomorrow.*

Sometimes I did want to go back in time and fix it all with Maria. But in calmer, stronger moments, being single was a kind of freedom I'd never felt before. It was really good when it wasn't catastrophically terrifying.

If we were able to select our moods from a menu every morning, I'd pick "Four Drinks In" every time. After four beers on my first date with Josh, I started feeling fine. We were at a pool hall on Queen Street near Bathurst populated by suburban commuters and the occasional table of tired tourists. It was January third, one of Josh's few days off in weeks. I was so tired of the holidays, having spent mine between the house my dad lived in with my grandmother in Hamilton and Roxy's week-long holiday festival at the apartment.

I looked at myself in the pool hall's bathroom mirror and smiled wide, swallowing the small fluorescent room. My teeth were calming white jewels. I lined my lips in a sheer gloss with tiny sparkles. I looked good. The anxiety was thinning out my face. I felt great. GREAT. *God, maybe I should just drink more.*

Back outside I sidled up to Josh at the table, pushed my hip into him. I placed my hand on the small of his back while he tried to sink the eight ball, distracting him so he missed. "Some shark," I said.

Josh had been talking to me about his job. Earlier in the day a woman had made naked snow-angels in front of a day-care. Then a thirty-year-old guy had told the paramedics that he had a bad headache, and they thought he was a bullshit call, but then he started speaking nonsense, projectile vomited, and died before they could do anything. Aneurism, Josh supposed.

"Every single day you deal with things I spend a lot of my time worrying about happening to me," I told him. "Do you know how often I worry about getting meningitis or an aneurism?"

Josh laughed. "Well, you can't dwell on it, right?"

"I do the neck-check constantly," I continued, pressing my chin to my chest as an example.

"You can't control what fate has in mind."

I laughed and shrugged, took a sip of my drink. If only he knew how much it consumed me. All those random variables. The pointlessness of being human.

"Billy, you scare the shit out of me," Josh said, all of a sudden.

"As if," I said. As if *as if* was a response!

Right before he kissed me he blinked his eyes, and I noticed his hands shaking. With a few drinks, his shyness had almost faded.

After the kiss, I asked him, "What are you most afraid of, Josh, for real, besides scary ol' me?"

"I don't know." He paused. "I guess I get really afraid of social situations sometimes. Like, even though I see you quite often just hanging around your place, I was really freaked out about this date. I changed my shirt about eleven times."

I was wearing the dress I'd had on all day. Other than washing yesterday's mascara off my face, I hadn't stressed out about meeting him. My biggest fear had been whether or not I'd catch whatever had made Roxy puke all yesterday. I'd checked for signs of nausea all the way to the pool hall.

The game paused. I touched Josh's arms, the taut cluster of muscles. Suddenly I wanted to know all about his childhood. When he knew he was a boy, or that he wanted to be a boy. I was shy to ask. I wondered if it was too typical a question. Was it offensive? I didn't get a chance to ask anything, though, because Josh kissed me again, hard against where the table jutted up to the edge of the sofa.

Over the next couple of hours the bar emptied of most people except the bartenders, but Josh and I continued to drink as if we were navigating a river of apprehension. One minute I was playing pool, and the next I was making out against the pinball machine in the back corner. I felt like I was on a new planet, a strange paradise. Josh's breath quickened and I bit his neck. I felt the kind of drunk you feel when you close your eyes and are lost in your inhibited limbic system, responding only to immediate emotion. Your memory and sense of how time works are disturbed. There was skin and cotton stretching, the blurred muscular fabric of our lips, air exchanged. My eyes opened to see the lights of a passing taxi in my damaged periphery, the streetlight moon falling down on us. I felt the sky take our pulse: heart rates high.

Eventually I walked Josh west along Queen and through the park to his place. We kissed timidly outside his apartment, as if we hadn't just brazenly created our own porn installation.

He didn't invite me in, but I didn't expect him to. If Amy was home, it would be awkward. We hadn't talked about negotiations, the practical elements of respect, honesty, boundaries, making sure everyone felt okay.

I glided home, stopping to take off my impossibly high heels and walk barefoot down Argyle Street. I paused outside my old apartment, the one I had shared with Maria, and noted the new curtains, the toys in the yard. I cut down to Queen Street, and smiled at the guy panhandling outside the bathtub store. I even smiled at the assholes outside the Social and the jerkfaces lined up to get into the Drake—everyone got big grins from me. I stopped to pet small dogs on leashes. I felt light light light.

I woke up the next day with a dry mouth, a scalpel scraping against my skull, inside a coma of fear. I couldn't face the phone or the cursor. Maria texted me again, this time to say she needed space from me, needed to figure things out. I turned the phone off.

"*Hangxiety*," noted Roxy, placing a cup of coffee on my bedside table. "Hangover and anxiety combined. A potent, horrible thing."

[18]

Josh

I tried to kill myself as a teenager. I know: What lonely teen-aged small-town outcast didn't, right? But I didn't really want to die, I wanted to be reborn. My Aunt Lisa understood that, and she's probably the reason I'm still here.

Aunt Lisa was the one person I considered my real family when I was a kid. Sure, my grandmother was pretty amazing, but there were too many years between us. Aunt Lisa was my father's sister. Whereas my dad was self-destructive, Lisa was a gardener, a community activist. She built things everywhere she went. She drove a pickup truck and had once organized a group of women who taught one another how to perform abortions when it was still illegal. She lived on women's land outside town, near Algonquin Park, and she drove to Guelph to help me out when I needed it.

I needed it a lot.

Aunt Lisa was the first person to call me Josh after I changed my name. She said that from the age of four onwards, "I always thought you should've been born a boy." She never, ever called me by my birth name. Instead, I was always Tiger or Captain or Son or Darling Little Shit-Disturber.

Aunt Lisa died of breast cancer in 1999. About a year before she died, she drove to Guelph to visit me because she knew I was in rough shape. I'd taken a bottle of pills, and was basically waiting to die, one way or another. She said, "This isn't gonna kill you, kid. Just you wait until later. There's worse stuff to come, but you'll be able to hack it. I can tell."

"How?"

I expected her to offer me some sage advice. Instead she lit a smoke and said, "Move to Toronto, there's lots of other folks like you."

She gave me a pamphlet about a youth group in Toronto for people who wanted to transition. At first I would call the number and hang up. Eventually I went online and met other kids on the discussion boards. It saved me.

I think about Lisa almost every day. My first tattoo says her name across my chest, a banner flapping over a fresh red heart.

The last time I saw my father was at my aunt's funeral. He was out on parole, and when I saw his tattooed face I felt a lurch of nausea. My mother sat on one side of the church and he sat on the other, and my sister and I hovered in between, like bouncers.

"Does that mean he killed someone?" I asked my sister during the hymns. She was a hundred times more "street" than I would ever be.

"Sometimes it just means you've been in jail. Sometimes it means you've killed people in jail, or lost someone while you were in jail."

"Well, which one is it, for him?"

"Fucked if I know."

My father left before the mingling, telling my sister it was because of his curfew at the halfway house in Toronto.

"He's in Toronto?"

"I didn't want to tell you about that. Apparently he wanted to be closer to Grandma in Guelph. She comes to visit."

Every time we get a call at a rehab centre or a halfway house, I prepare myself to see him. Of course, it usually doesn't occur to me that my father might not recognize me any more. At the funeral, I had been on T for about one year, was still mid-transition. Now, when I run into old classmates or co-workers I know they wouldn't recognize me from a foot away. It's like I've got a free pass and I don't have to deal with those people any more. I like it that way.

My dad may be only half dead to most people, but he's completely dead to me.

[19]

Billy

Something is wrong. My face rested against a bare chest. Inhaling sharply — a mixture of rye, sandalwood soap, and a peppery cologne — I identified Josh. I moved my drool-heavy mouth from his skin, eyes adjusting. I could see his chest in the grey-blue light of the window. My window. Josh and I had been going out a lot since our first date two weeks ago. Starting the nights out slowly, shyly, mumbling polite things and small-talking until we'd had enough drinks to exclaim, ask probing questions and kiss without worrying about our breath.

Josh had a tattoo on his chest that said *Lisa* inside a heart. Who was Lisa? I asked this question the first time I took off Josh's shirt. No answer. Shrug. I concluded Lisa must be dead. I stared at his tattoo and then at the clock that read 4 a.m. The room smelled funny. Like gas. The room had a pre-sunrise glow, as if it were the moment in a movie before the cavalry arrived to save the heroine. My skin was beaded, my throat was dry. I was suddenly sure I'd woken up in the middle of an emergency.

I sat up, making out the shapes of the room vaguely. I smelled the cup of mould that was last week's double latte on the bedside table. Josh snored lightly, his hand inside his boxers. I stood up and wobbled over to him, my foot pressing into a pink high-heeled boot turned on its side. *Fuck.* He didn't wake up.

I pushed open my door, passing Roxy's empty room. Her TV was paused on a scene from *The Goonies*. I could still smell the chemical, or gas, something foreign and frightening. Sliding open the patio door, I could hear sirens screaming close by. A raccoon wandered away from the recycling bin like a drunken homeless dude, turning back as if to shrug.

Inside, I checked the pilot light on the gas stove. I opened the fridge and inhaled. Bloated tofu, batteries, egg tray full of nail polish. Joan Nestle chased a piece of dust across the kitchen floor. I glimpsed the sink, full of dirty dishes. I was still drunk. I'd been asleep for maybe an hour.

The sink definitely smelled of rotting something, and I felt briefly thankful there was no gas leak. I walked around the corner to the bathroom, knelt on the floor tiles, and violently threw up chicken wings (honey garlic!), beer (two at last call!), six shots of Jäger (one more can't hurt! It's medicinal!). There was a delay between my thoughts and actions, as if a little man in my brain was sleeping on the job. And there was a new tic under my eye. It spasmed every few seconds.

After rinsing my mouth in a clumsy waterfall of blue Listerine, I walked down the hall, bracing myself with a fluttering right arm against the wall. The obsessive voices in my head started up. What if I screamed bloody murder? Started kicking everyone in sight? What if I jumped out the window? I needed to be alone. I had to be sure I wouldn't hurt anyone. Hurting myself was less important, but I wanted to make sure no one else was involved. I knew it was irrational, but in the middle of an attack, rational thought didn't matter. I had to be careful. Check the stove. Count my steps. Make sure I didn't lose it. Get anyone I loved out of the way.

I turned on my bedroom light with an emphatic slap. "Baby, you should probably get going."

Josh moaned. "What?"

"I was just saying that you should leave. Amy is probably super pissed." I wished I could tell him the truth, that a panic attack was about to eat my normal brain. I was about to be zombified, I could feel it.

His eyes adjusted. He picked up a roach from the side table and sparked it. "Let's get pizza!"

"Josh. Did you hear what I said?"

"Amy and I broke up." Josh looked at me and shrugged.

"Until you move out, I don't think words like *together* or *apart* really mean anything."

I was trying hard to sound like I actually gave a shit about his breakup. Perhaps I should tell him what was really going on, but I didn't want to fuck things up. It would happen eventually, but for now he still thought I was alluring. I liked that. My stomach lurched. I scratched at my elbow.

Josh was hunched over, wrapped in my bright pink quilt.

"Okay, no problem, Billy. You're probably right." He got up and started putting on his clothes, slowly.

As I watched him, I heard the click and chime of the front door swinging open downstairs. Then came Roxy's trademark heavy thumps, followed by the click tap of several pairs of high heels up the cluttered staircase. I was still standing in the bedroom doorway. I leaned back and peered over the banister to see if I could identify Roxy's early-morning crew.

Tina and Amy came into focus behind Roxy, tearing off their pretty pumps triumphantly and pitching them up to the landing as if they were part of a deranged carnival shoe-throw. Tina followed her shoes and slumped at the top of the stairs in a cloud of expensive perfume.

Roxy set glasses on the kitchen table and unscrewed a bottle of whiskey.

Wanting to be alone and having Tina show up at your house instead means you have to either go dig a hole in the backyard and stuff your ears with rocks so you can get some peace, or just give up and join the party. I stood uncertainly in the hallway beside my open bedroom door, a few tiny specks of vomit drying on the bare paunch between my red push-up bra and the little black shorts riding up my ass.

"Hey!" Roxy looked up from the kitchen table. Then she sprinted down the hall to grab me in a bear hug. "Billy, my favourite girl! My favourite poet."

I winced. Roxy was tall and strong enough to pick me up.

Meanwhile, Amy had ducked into the bathroom with Tina, giggling. Josh slipped past me, vaulted over the banister, and ran down the steps and out the front door. I imagined him walking home shirtless.

As if nothing weird had happened, I settled into a drunken game of Scrabble with Roxy and the girls at the kitchen table. Amy was too drunk to notice Josh's jacket slung over the back of her chair.

Twice she asked me, "How was your night?"

I shrugged both times, and answered, "Drunken."

I am the master of two-letter Scrabble wins. I drank coffee while everyone else got sloppier.

Sometime near dawn, when both visitors were lying on the pullout couch in the living room, I Googled Josh on my computer. Nothing much came up: a doctor in Idaho and a kindergarten teacher in B.C. The only substantial entry was the short film Amy had made about his transition, called *Becoming Man*. I decided to write up a list of questions for him. But after I'd done that, I tore up the paper.

I Googled "hate Hilary Stevenson" and got a few blogs complaining about the state of women in rock. I Googled "love Hilary Stevenson" and came up with an online profile of one of the contestants on *Canadian Idol*. "I loved Hilary Stevenson. I listened to her in Grade Seven and that's when I knew who I wanted to be. I wanted to be just like her. I wonder where she is now."

I wrapped myself in my quilt and sat out on the deck to smoke and watch Joan Nestle go wild chasing early-morning shadows on the snow. I left the patio door open so the cat wouldn't get upset by her inability to decide which side of the glass to be on.

Amy appeared, her hair pressed up against the inside. "Can I have a light?" She stood on her tiptoes, stretching her arm out in an arc.

I handed her my lighter. She stepped fully outside, closed the door behind her and leaned down to pet Joan Nestle. Her blue sweater rode up. I saw a tattoo of the word *Hope* on her lower back. Josh had the same tattoo.

Amy lit her cigarette, fingers shaking. "Thanks." She gazed up at the sky behind my head, exhaling. "I love being up when the sun rises," she said.

"Me too."

She looked at me, daring me to make more significant conversation. I stared back.

"I saw your old video on MuchMoreMusic the other day."

I kept staring at her. I wanted to tell her to stop it. *I get it. I'm not fucking cool.*

"It must have been strange, to have all those birds in your hair like that."

"It was uncomfortable, yeah. You know, awkward."

"Like now?"

I laughed. Drunk girl was a smart-ass. "Yeah, kind of like now."

Amy smiled unconvincingly. "Well, Billy. I'm sorry to have invaded your house tonight. We've been on a bit of a tear."

"It's a good place for benders. We thought about calling it the Bender House at one point."

Amy dropped her half-smoked cigarette into the oversized restaurant ashtray Roxy and I had stolen from outside the Gladstone one night. "Benders are good sometimes, I guess. Good night, Billy." She turned, forgetting she'd slid the door closed, and bumped her head on the glass, then stumbled backwards and fell on her ass. She giggled for a long time with both hands on her face. "I'm not going to remember this tomorrow."

Helping her up, I said, "Probably not. Do you want some water? Or for me to call you a cab?"

"Tina's gonna walk with me. We're going to lie in the snow in Trinity Bellwoods Park."

We stood face to face in front of the patio door. Inside, Tina was rooting around in the kitchen cupboards. Joan Nestle pawed the glass.

"You know what, Billy," Amy said suddenly. "Josh wasn't always so remote. He used to be really present. He used to be, I dunno, like this sparkplug."

"Yeah, weren't we all like that once?" Actually, I thought, to me Josh was all lit up. I had no idea what Amy was trying to say.

She continued to stare at me, almost through me, and slurred, "Like, he used to be full of hope, you know, like our tattoos? Now he's so cynical."

"Well, it's not hard to be cynical these days, especially in his line of work, right?"

Amy shrugged and fell into the patio door. Tina opened it, and helped her inside. Under the harsh kitchen light, Tina poured more whiskey into a water bottle she held over the sink.

"You're hard core," I remarked.

"It's my vacation week," Tina explained, as if time off meant you should drink yourself into a comatose state.

I walked her and Amy downstairs and closed the door behind them after two awkward hugs. With Roxy passed out, I was finally alone.

I texted Josh: *I thought things r cool. I thought Amy knew everything.*

It took him until the morning to text back. On the streetcar I took to work at the call centre, I read, *She does know. It's just not...comfortable.*

[20]

Amy

More than two months after our breakup, Josh and I were still living together and things didn't feel all that different. He still worked long hours, and I spent a lot of time with Tina, and when we did speak it was pretty friendly. It was as if breaking up had taken the pressure off and we remembered what we liked about each other.

In March, Josh and I decided to have dinner together once a week. We would spend one evening a week checking in, to keep communicating about the breakup and remain close.

I finally got up the nerve to ask if he and Billy were officially dating.

"I suppose so," he said slowly. "I would like to, I guess, if I'm being totally honest."

I managed to ask what he saw in Billy—hopefully in a way that seemed non-accusatory and friend-like, despite the fact that I knew his answer would make me feel as if I was bleeding out of my ears. Billy seemed so frantic one minute, so sad the next, I told him. We were at Juice For Life, the veggie joint at the end of our street.

When our dosa appetizers arrived, I asked, "What is so intriguing about her? Is it the celebrity thing?"

He looked at me, running his hand through his almost faux-hawk. "I'm not sure. She just seems so alive or something, so much more honest than anyone I've ever met. It totally seems like she's having an identity crisis, but you know what? I think that's brave. She keeps it together, but I just think there's something really commendable about allowing yourself the freedom to unravel and question yourself."

I nodded at Josh, dipping spongy crepe into coconut sauce with my index finger and stuffing it in my mouth so I wouldn't have to speak. Josh never described people as brave. Last week he had said his job made him think the majority of human beings were freeloading dirtbags. He took a long sip from his mug of cider, a blush creeping across his cheeks. He placed the mug down before closing his eyes in a blink.

"Plus, she's beautiful."

"Yes," I agreed. "She is."

I got up, taking extra time to smooth my skirt down as if nothing were at all wrong, trying not to trip on my heels en route to the downstairs bathroom. Whenever someone suggests they wish they were tall and thin like I am, I say, *Well, try tripping over yourself for ten years and see how much you like it.*

I turned the hot water on full blast and sobbed into the rising steam, picking leaves off the plant sitting atop the long white counter. Josh's admission of what he liked about Billy came across to me so clearly: I'm not honest. I have no depth of character. I'm not brave enough to break myself down and ask important questions. I'm just Amy, pretty Amy, with the easy life and tons of options. Obviously, I knew that Josh's feelings about Billy had nothing to do with me. But I couldn't help turning everything inward.

I don't feel so sure! I felt like screaming. In the face of losing Josh I'd never felt so unsure of anything. And ... *beautiful?* I guess I couldn't argue with that. I looked like a boy compared to her — no ass, string-bean arms.

I wished it could be as easy to remake yourself at twenty-five as it seems at fifteen. I imagined how I would shave my head again and perfect a brooding stare. I would look at things from a different angle. Instead, I reapplied my mascara, dabbed my forehead with a tiny square of scented blotting-paper, and walked back up the steep stairway. Josh had a sprout lodged between his front teeth. I didn't tell him.

I suggested espressos in to-go cups, a bike ride by the lake. It was one of those rare dry days, and it felt good to exercise outside again, even if we were still in scarves and wool hats. Everything was normal. We didn't talk much, and after riding for a while, just parked our bikes and sat on the beach at the same spot where we always ended up. I lay back on a picnic table, face to the sky, smoking a bummed cigarette. Occasionally I turned to watch Josh throw stones into the bloated water of Lake Ontario. I felt sorry for myself. I felt ashamed for feeling sorry for myself. I got out my BlackBerry and made a list of things to do in the morning. The list anchored me.

I looked up again and saw Josh with his phone flipped open, madly texting. When he saw me looking, he clipped the phone closed and shoved it in the pocket of his jacket. We had made a rule about not checking messages during these get-togethers. It wasn't working out.

Now I started to feel annoyed at Josh for his comments about Billy. How could he want to see someone so flaky when he'd been on me for years to work harder, go beyond my comfort zone? How could he valorize her anxieties when he was so resentful of the people he encountered at work in a similar state of crisis? How many times had he said *Fucking 211s!* when we walked by muttering homeless people on the street or angry crazy drunks. I bet those people just weren't as hot as Billy, as laissez-faire.

I recalled how she'd been the other night, walking around in her underwear, totally unconcerned that a bunch of drunk girls had taken over her kitchen. Not one punitive stare. Sitting at the table with her stubbly legs outstretched, sex bruises on her neck and arms, chewing her lip. Seemingly unconcerned that I knew she'd just screwed my ex. She reeked of sex. Her posture said, *I don't give a shit. Whatever.*

Sure, I had also appeared unconcerned. But I'd had a country of whiskey in me. I could've taken out my own appendix at that point.

And yeah, I had shown up at Roxy's hoping I'd run into Josh, get a little anger out. When I got home he was eating a bowl of cereal on the couch, glaring at me.

"Where were you, huh? Stay out all night? Sleep with Roxy?"

"No. We just kept going is all."

"Huh. Interesting."

"Not really."

I went to bed. He went to work.

Still, even though I resented Billy, I understood her appeal. She reminded me a lot of Star. Eccentric, but when she looked at you and said something that came right from her heart, you felt like the only person in the room. She didn't ever say anything to seem polite; she didn't bother with small talk. She had a kind of who-cares confidence I found intimidating. Maybe I wasn't jealous of Josh wanting Billy, but of Billy wanting Josh.

Over the past weeks, my e-mails to my old summer-camp boyfriend Jason had been getting intense, with lots of dramatic language. I sensed that the distance between us geographically was making our connection seem stronger than it ever had been. I had bought a ticket to New York and then cancelled it. "Spring," he'd suggested. "I'll come visit in May. Give you a chance to settle things."

Josh and I biked home, getting off to walk over the footpath bridge above Lake Shore Boulevard. On the other side, he biked fast and didn't stop to look back and make sure I was keeping up. I watched him dodge bikes ahead of me and curl dangerously around cars under the Dufferin bridge. He disappeared in front of a streetcar as the sun dropped behind our neighbourhood's ugly new condo developments.

[21]

Billy

At 7:15 a.m., I woke to the double-beep pulse of an incoming text message. *B there in 10. Unlock your front door and turn on CityNews.*

I ran downstairs naked, unlocked the dead bolt, and peered outside. Pouring rain. I curled back under the quilt again, pushing the tiny TV on my dresser alive with my toe. Perky blonde anchor talking about April spring showers and a new hospital super-bug. I fell back to sleep.

When I woke up again, Josh was standing in the doorway of my bedroom, pulling off his uniform. I couldn't have fantasized about it being any sexier than it was. He crawled on top of the bed, pulled back the covers. I bristled from the cold. He spread my legs with his knee. Wrapped his hand in the mess of my hair.

"You wouldn't believe my night."

He looked both tired and commanding, boyish and soft. No matter how anxious I was, I could always have sex. It was the only thing that didn't fill me with fear.

The television showed a blurry story: Man jumped in front of a VIA train from the side of the Gardiner Expressway. I picked Josh out of the crowd of emergency personnel behind the news anchor, watched him placing a pinkish sheet over the body.

"Whoa, there you are! What did the guy look like?"

"He was mangled."

Josh kissed me while one of the anchors talked about how the jump would affect rush-hour traffic. I pushed him gently off to watch the rest of the footage, the pleasant haze of morning sex now too stark a contrast with Josh's last hour of work.

"About, like, twenty-five firemen stood around doing nothing, as usual," he said, kissing my stomach.

"It's so fucking sad," I said. "I wonder who the guy was."

Josh shrugged, ran his hand under my slip, and hiked it above my breasts. He hadn't slept in twenty-four hours, and he fucked as if his life depended on it. He pushed into me fast, sweat dripping from his forehead, hips pounding. Delirious. When at last he fell beside me, we stayed gripped together. He sighed heavily, and for a minute I thought he might be crying. His eyes were washed in red, all pupil.

"Are you okay, baby?"

"Yeah. Tired is all. I should probably go."

I made some coffee to go in a travel mug and walked him out to his car. The sun was just starting to rise. This time, I wanted him to stay but knew that he couldn't. He looked more exhausted than I'd ever been.

"Billy," Josh said. "You wanna be my girlfriend?"

"Like, your only girlfriend? Your one and only?"

"Possibly. Totally."

"Let's just take it as it goes. Okay? Rebound for now, and see what happens."

"Okay." He took a sip of coffee.

I hoped what I had said didn't sound harsh. I didn't mean it to be. "Same time tomorrow?" The post-night-shift booty call was proving to be both a fantastic way to wake up and a good way to end an all-nighter. This was the fourth dawn hook-up in a row, and I was enjoying the oddness of it.

That morning, while Josh slept at home in the bed that was still Amy's, I accomplished 48 sit-ups, 1 thin layer of mango lotion, 1 online Scrabble victory, 31 minutes of cardio, 4 coffees, 1 witty retort, and 8 sexually suggestive text messages for Josh to wake up to. Scattered throughout these activities were thoughts of the jumper and his life. What had he thought after he leapt? I pictured the moment before jumping. I could see myself in a similar spot. I could totally understand it.

What did it do to Josh, I wondered, to be the one covering up the remains of bodies? Did he particularize each body or did he see them all as a sort of General Body? Had it become for him like it had been for me when I had a job at the candle factory? Trays and trays of the same thing had passed by my vision — wax or skin, it hadn't mattered. It all became routine. Mundane. Life and death. Start your shift. End your shift. Go home. Fuck. Eat. Sleep. Start over again. Probably that's the way it was for Josh. Probably it was not as interesting as I thought.

I was still reluctant to nail things down with Josh. It felt so good to be with him. But I ached for Maria sometimes; I missed how familiar she was with me and my anxieties. It was too soon. Maybe I had too much going on in my brain, too much fear, to commit to anything as hopeful as Josh.

I checked the burners on the stove three times—*Good Will*—and went back to sleep.

[22]

Josh

I was having a cigarette outside the Toronto Western Hospital's emergency department and trying not to flirt too much with Deb, the married nurse who'd taken a liking to me. I had a mild hangover. Mandy, my partner for the day, was worse off. She reeked of gin and kept holding her head and moaning. Now she was sleeping in the back of the truck while I babysat the patient.

Deb and I were having a forced conversation about our weekends, about why I never went out to the bars with the other medics. Her flirting was clumsy and coltish, despite her wedding ring, and it made me uncomfortable. I nervously closed my eyes, wishing the conversation would end.

As if I had willed it to happen, I opened my eyes and Billy was there, cutting through the Emerg parking lot towards Kensington, looking down at her phone, almost bumping right into us because she was so intently texting.

"Oh, Josh! Wow. Hi."

"Hi, Billy," I said, giving her a big hug. The nurse scurried off back through the automatic doors. I felt Billy shaking a little, so I put both hands on her shoulders and stared at her curiously. "Are you okay?"

"I'm cold, just came from a doctor's appointment upstairs. How's work going? It's like a little ambulance party around here."

There were six ambulances parked outside the Emerg, lined up in two rows of three under the awning. She leaned against the *Hospital News* newspaper box, pulled at my collar. Billy's red nails looked perfect against the dark blue fabric of my uniform.

"Offload delay. My patient's going to be here for hours. It's good, though, because I'm kind of hungover today."

Billy loved to hear about my work. She was so curious about everything, especially the gross calls. These days I often left her voice messages in the middle of a shift: *You won't believe the call I just had. The house was literally covered in shit. He put his shit in JARS! They were all over the house, labelled, in old pickle jars!* And she'd freak out. I'd picture her picking up the message on the sly at work, phone shoved into her pocket, having to shut her eyes tightly and whisper "EW EW EW" before texting me back, *Tell Me More!*

"What's wrong with your patient?" she asked.

"Eighty-year-old with abdominal pain." I shrugged. "We won't be able to off-load her for hours."

"That sucks."

"Yeah. You look pretty," I said, unable to stop from smiling like a goof.

"You look pretty hot in that uniform, as usual."

Billy was usually tentative or distracted, so I appreciated this comment.

"Are you allowed to go get a coffee with me? Or water?" she asked.

I nodded and walked her to the Tim Hortons in the Atrium. She held my hand while we stood tenth or so in line. For the first time ever, I hoped everyone took a really long time with their orders. Billy was the only person, other than Amy, I'd held hands with in years. She was a lot shorter than Amy and she held my hand firmly. Amy had always rolled her eyes at hand-holding. After a while, she'd say it made her arm hurt, as if I were holding onto her hand while she just *let* it be held— no reciprocal grip. Billy held my hand, rubbing my wrist with her thumb. Her palms were so soft.

"I can't believe how much people stare at you when you're wearing your uniform. It's unreal."

I had become used to it, but watching Billy watch everyone watching us was kind of amusing. I saw how other guys filled out their uniforms, and still they didn't exactly look like the hot catch Billy described me being.

I almost doubted Billy's sincerity when she pushed down the brown lid of her double double and leaned into my ear to whisper quietly, "I can't keep my eyes off you in that uniform. You just look so...*in charge*. Wanna take my pulse?"

After we got our coffees, Billy walked me back to where the trucks were parked outside the entrance. I offered to show her the inside of my truck. Luckily, Mandy was no longer sleeping in there. Billy hopped up on the bench seat and grabbed me by the collar. For a few minutes, we made out like two teenagers in the back of a school bus. As soon as I pulled away, though,

Billy blushed and fumbled with her right hand, trying to locate the side door handle.

"I'd better get going," she said.

I helped her out of the truck and watched her walk away, phone already out of her pocket, madly texting and not paying attention to anything, as if she'd never run into me in the first place. I wondered who she was texting, so focused like that. I felt almost jealous; clearly I was losing my mind.

Mandy came outside. "I'm gonna book off at one, Josh. I just barfed. I'm toast. Sorry, man, I can't handle it today."

"No problem."

Back at the station, Dave was paired up with me for the rest of the shift. "Hey, Hangman."

This was his new moniker for me. There were old guys who'd been on the road for thirty years and only seen two hangings, but me, I'd been on for three years and I'd seen eight. Dave had caught wind of this, and there you go. Hangman. Lovely.

The day felt ominous, and this feeling was cemented inside me by Dave's comment. Sure enough, our second call of the day was an Echo VSA hanging.

"Fuck you, Josh," Dave said, smirking, as we pulled out of the station gate.

Minutes later we pulled up to a duplex near Eglinton. There was steam rising all around us, as though we were in a movie about someone hanging himself.

A man stood in the driveway and pointed at the garage. "The only way in is through the garage door."

He didn't look too shaken up, almost business-as-usual. *Must be shock*, I thought.

The garage door opened slowly, making an arduous buzz as it showcased the feet, legs and torso of a man who must've been six feet tall, about 250 pounds, his arms straight out, his face the kind of white that could erase you. It was one of the eeriest things I'd ever seen. The VSA smell turned my hangover from mild to tragic. I ran behind the truck and threw up. Pieces of peach. Coffee. Ninth hanging, and first time throwing up.

"Fucking Hangman!" I heard Dave mutter as he walked towards the body. "Code 5, baby, Code 5!" He said this as though he were rolling dice in Vegas. "You think you'd be used to it by now, kid."

Two cops stood by their cruiser and laughed.

When we cleared that call it was only 2:15 p.m., and I couldn't fathom the shift being much longer than it already had been. Amy had texted me, *I hate that I sometimes still miss you.*

Back at the station for lunch, I picked up a voice mail from my sister, who'd called to explain how she'd had a revelation about our dad, made peace with his violent past, and was making an effort to reconnect with him. "*You know, I want to talk about it with you when I come to town at the end of summer, because I'm also coming to see him. People can change, Josh. You of all people should know that.*" She had read a book recommended by Oprah, had broken up with her abusive boyfriend, had turned a new leaf.

I loved her for trying, but I didn't think making peace with Dad was on the agenda for me, at least for the next ten to fifty years. When you watch your father try to kill your mother on numerous occasions, and spend a good amount of your job-life dealing with domestic calls and parents just like yours — well, no. Having a heart-to-heart with him was not going to cut it. That's all I would be able to say to my sister.

"It's pretty simple," was how I had once explained it to Amy.

"It sounds really complicated," she replied. "There are so many emotions involved."

"No, there aren't. Maybe there were at one point, but I've seen enough now, and I've realized that it *is* actually quite simple. He's not a good man, he's certainly not a very complicated man, and I really enjoy the quality of my life without him in it."

Amy was silent after that and didn't broach the subject directly again.

I turned off my phone and slept for half an hour on the couch, waking up to our next call. "*Delta fall, male, 55, not alert. Possibly HBD.*"

The call was at the Oak Leaf Steam Baths on Bathurst Street. I'd driven by the sign many times and wondered if it was really a bathhouse, was curious about what it looked like inside. It was so out of place in the neighbourhood. It had clearly been there pre-war and survived the gentrification.

"Is it a real bathhouse, you think?"

"Why you asking me?" Dave winked. "I'm not that kind of guy. I'm more monogamous husband material."

When we walked through the door of the brick building, we were greeted by a huge guy tattooed on just about every inch of skin. He had an oversized ring of keys around his neck.

"There's a guy downstairs, eh, and he fell down. He's been drinking, right, so he's really starting to piss people off. Won't shut up with his wailing. I think he might have broken his wrist."

The tattooed guy led us along a narrow hallway, and then down two flights of stairs. I felt as if we might be descending into hell, or at least a weird underground zombie world. In my imagination, bathhouses conjured up gay guys having hot anonymous sex, white towels and bleach and cum, and all sorts of reasons for me to keep my gloves on.

Though it smelled overly clean, this place looked more like a shelter, and when we got to the room with the patient, it may as well have been one. There were rows of dark brown beds, looking like tacky '70s psychiatrist couches, about ten to each row. Five middle-aged men were either sleeping or sitting up staring at our patient. I recognized the patient immediately as a regular rubbie, Al-with-the-One-Foot. I kind of liked Al when he wasn't too drunk. He told funny stories.

He recognized us, and so stopped wailing and slurring, and said, "Hey guys, nice to see you again." He smiled with his awful teeth. "My wrist, it's broken, right? I fell."

"Did you hit your head, Al?" I asked, as we got out the equipment to check his vitals. "How many drinks have you had today, Al? What's the drink of choice?"

Al told us his story, admitting that he had indeed been "having a little champagne with the King of France" at the time of his fall, and we suggested he come for a ride with us up the street. He agreed. Dave helped him to his feet.

Most of the other guys on the beds got back into passed-out position, except for one. He was staring straight at me. I stared back, and felt a hard punch in the gut. My father? Possibly. I kept staring. He'd aged a lot, if this was him. He wasn't wearing a black T-shirt, or a lumberjack jacket, or the ratty suede pouch around his neck like he did in my childhood memories. He wore mismatched shelter-clothes, a shirt that said *Rogers Cares About Homelessness!* His hair was white, and he was balding, and half his face was bruised up, so I couldn't see if there was a tattoo. He had the same build as my dad.

"Josh, buddy, you coming?"

I turned to look at Dave, halfway up the stairs, supporting Al as he hopped. "Sorry, man."

I put the bag around my shoulder and turned back once more to scan the possible-father guy.

"What the *fuck* are you *fucking* looking at, *faggot?*" the guy roared.

Without cops or backup, and with Dave holding onto Al, there wasn't much I could say to this asshole. He horked and spit on the ground, and lay back on his couch. I helped Dave and Al up the stairs.

"That fucking little bitch," Dave swore. "I wish I coulda kicked him."

When we got out to the truck, I breathed in the non-chlorinated, non-rubby air. Chances were fifty-fifty, I thought calmly, that the guy really was my father.

And I really, *really* tried not to give a fuck.

[23]

Billy

Hey! Amy! How are ya?

Or: *Hey…Amy, hello, so, how's it going? You look great. I just wanted to chat with you so we would both feel comfortable, you know, in case you are feeling awkward. I want you to know I respect you and…* that's where my thoughts broke.

Shouldn't it be obvious that I respected her? Was I stupid for wanting to make it clear? I felt like one of those people who write personal ads and say they want to meet someone who *likes to laugh*. Who doesn't like to laugh?

I was standing by the bar at Ciao Edie, a tiny club on College Street, rehearsing possible ridiculous monologues. Amy and Josh had walked in together a while ago, and I was trying not to stare at them, even though Roxy and I had come with a group of friends to meet up with them. Since it was the first time we'd all hung out as a group, Josh and I decided to play the night by ear, see if things felt comfortable. If not, one of us would find an excuse to bail. The game plan was to have a quick drink, and then possibly go to an art show.

My reverie was interrupted by Roxy, who was returning from the bathroom with Tina in tow.

"We've decided," she said. "I'm going to have a birthday party at the Red Room this Saturday night. You game?"

"Sure."

I tried to pay attention to Roxy while she talked quickly. But I seemed to have become one of those morons who wonders why the person they're dating doesn't see them right away, ignoring everyone else in the room.

I had spent the day trying to go places. I went halfway to school, got off the Dufferin bus and walked down into the subway. I stood by the tracks and the closer I got to them, the more I became certain I would jump in front of the train as soon as it pulled into the station. I turned and ran up the escalator, then ran all the way south on Dufferin, past the mall, in tears. When I got home, I pulled off my clothes and climbed under the covers, my heart still pounding. I had cancer. I was going crazy. I was about to be felled by an impending aneurism, that old standby.

Eventually, I slept again. I woke up to Roxy knocking gently, offering me soup, urging me to go out for some drinks.

I always found it easier to go outside when I was with someone else. For some reason, my anxiety wasn't as pronounced when someone else was with me. I felt safer. We got on our bikes, and it felt good to move, the air against my face washing away another day of failed life.

Now I retreated to the men's washroom, which was quieter than the women's, to apply lipstick while I tried to decide whether or not to split. I contemplated calling Maria, hooking up for coffee. I texted her: *I miss you.* In that moment, it was the only thing I was certain about. Maria was a solid while everyone else appeared to be made of water or fire, hard to hold onto.

Josh opened the door and jumped, literally, at the sight of me. He probably hadn't been expecting to see anyone because he was one of the few guys in the bar besides the DJ. I put my phone in my pocket, swivelled down the cap on my lipstick and slid it into my purse, turned, and smiled. *Hey.*

"Hey, baby, you surprised me."

"A good surprise, I hope."

Without further discussion, I kicked open a stall door and pulled him in by his shirt collar. I was too preoccupied to feel fear. He bit my neck. I dug my nails into his back.

When we were interrupted, it was with a sense of relief that I disengaged. Something was happening between us that I didn't understand. I straightened my dress. My cheek lingered against his for a few seconds. I loved the smell of him. Once identified and adored, the smell of a face is hard to give up.

We left the bathroom separately, with a purposeful thirty-second delay between us. Roxy, Amy, and Tina had gathered at a table together by the dance floor. Josh went to get some drinks at the bar, and I joined the group.

"Hey, Amy. How's it going?"

Tina smirked a little, and looked towards the dance floor.

"Great, Billy. Things are good. You?"

"Not bad."

"I guess you're in exams and stuff right now, right?"

"Well, I'm supposed to be. I haven't done so well this term." And Amy went mute until Josh put drinks down in front of us.

"Thanks," we said in unison.

Tina checked her phone. "Amy, we'd better get going. It's almost ten."

The two of them stood up and put on their jackets.

"Sure you guys don't want to come see some video art with us? There's free wine," Amy asked.

"Sorry, I feel like dancing!" Roxy exclaimed.

"We've still got drinks and stuff..." Josh said. Josh and I had talked earlier about hopefully avoiding the video-art screening part of the night. Amy looked more relieved than disappointed.

Walking down College Street, Josh and I stopped to make out against the front window of Soundscapes, a record store. Our kisses were clumsy and some sixth sense made me open my eyes. The abandoned street revealed Maria's unmistakable walk, hurried and purposeful. She was towing a bike. My heart sank.

I pushed Josh's hand away, saying, "There are people coming. We should stop."

Maria walked straight past me, stone-faced, like someone passing strangers in a mall.

"So, who was that guy you were kissing on the street?"

I was crouched in the bathroom, looking for a new roll of toilet paper under the sink, wondering why Maria was calling me at 4:30 a.m.

"Did you really call to ask me that?"

"Well, it looked pretty serious. I didn't know you were dating anyone. I thought you weren't ready to date. Besides, you'd *just* texted me. Did you text me while you were on a date?"

"His name is Josh. We're not dating—at least, not officially. Is that what you wanted to know?"

"Well, of all people I never expected *you* to go straight."

"*Go straight.* God, Maria, did we go back in time? Who cares if I date a boy?"

"Is he at least a nice guy? Is he a musician? You always used to have crushes on musicians, if I remember correctly."

"He's a medic, actually."

"A medic? Really. Like, he drives an ambulance?"

"Like, he saves lives, asshole."

"I know, I have to deal with paramedics all the time at work. Brave job."

Josh poked his head into the bathroom. "Are you okay, Billy?"

I cupped the phone. "Yeah."

He mouthed, *Oops, sorry, didn't know you were on the phone*, and shut the door.

"Well, I want to make sure you're okay. I know how rough it's been for you lately. I wouldn't want you to get into anything you couldn't handle."

I was perversely annoyed at Maria's maternal-sounding concern, despite the fact that I longed for it. I located a single roll behind the spray-bottles of cleansers, and lifted my head too fast, banging it on the top of the cupboard.

"So, you're not serious about this Josh guy?"

"What does 'serious' mean?" I rubbed the rising bump on my head and slumped against the side of the claw-footed tub. "And what the fuck are you doing calling me at 4:30 a.m.? Are you drunk?"

"Yeah," Maria admitted.

"Do you miss me?"

"Yeah."

"Good."

"Billy, you don't understand, it's hard to be around someone constantly who's afraid of everything. It starts to grate, you know? I felt so helpless and unable to help you."

Oh, fuck you, I thought.

"Besides, Hilary, I asked you to get back together two months ago and you didn't even call me to talk about it. You just let it drop."

"I didn't think you were serious. It was just a text message."

I could feel the dramatic drunk talk escaping me, those words that in the moment feel so honest but are invariably just heightened lies. I decided to change the subject. "How's work, Maria? What's it like finally to become what you've been working so hard to become all these years?"

"I dunno, Billy. Sometimes when I'm listening to clients talk, especially the ones I know are never going to get it together, I contemplate telling them to just give up. You know, just do all the crack you want to do until you die. It doesn't mean anything anyway!"

I laughed. "That doesn't sound like you. But it's kind of hilarious."

"I wonder why I ever decided to do this. Sometimes I look at the clients and think, it must feel really good. It must be the best feeling in the world if you truly want to walk around with piss-soaked pants yelling out indecipherable things and losing everything. Like, what could make me want to lose everything?"

"That's a pretty big question," I said. I heard Maria take a long sip and light a cigarette. "You're probably just overwhelmed with the reality of how sad people are when you meet them at their lowest point," I continued. "I'm sure, eventually, you'll get used to it. And you really will see how you've helped them."

Maria snorted. "Aw shit, Billy. I've got to go to sleep. Sorry about being jealous and stuff."

"No problem," I said.

And with that, we hung up. A conversation that might have ended in a fight three months ago was now ending harmoniously. I felt oddly reassured; a friendship with Maria might be possible after all.

I stumbled down the hall towards my bedroom, where Josh was leaning out the window. I stood silently in the doorway, watching him smoke. His phone, sitting in an upturned ball cap that also held keys and pocket change, started buzzing. He ignored it. Drunk and curious, I moved towards it and tested the waters. Josh still didn't turn around. I leaned closer. A photo of Amy's face blinked, signalling a text from her.

I handed Josh the phone. He flipped it open quickly, read it and clicked it shut.

"Things okay with you guys?"

"They're starting to shift, you know. She's going to try to date some people. Get out more. She knows what's going on with us. We're all being honest, right?"

"Right," I said.

"I think it would be fine if I stayed over," Josh offered.

It seemed crazy, but I still wasn't ready. I liked the booty calls, the drunken fun, the honeymoon chemistry. I didn't want normalcy to creep into the equation just yet. Plus, I wasn't ready to be up front with Josh about how mentally ill I felt almost constantly. What if I had a panic attack in the middle of the night and he woke up? I would be ashamed.

"It just makes me so happy to be with you, I lose track of time," Josh continued.

I, on the other hand, felt hyper-aware of every moment. "I've got so much homework to do," I said, pointing at the pile of books on my desk, all texts for my Medieval Literary Theory course. I'd read none of them, had attended two of six classes and left both early.

I sat on the edge of the bed and nodded at Josh. He straddled me, kissed my neck. "You're dangerous," I mumbled.

Josh smirked, as if I had meant he was dangerously sexy. But that's not what I meant at all.

[24]

Amy

Tina had become my social panic button, a buffer between me and potential discomfort. We were sitting out on the Drake patio with mugs of green tea, picking at a shared pumpkin muffin. We had the weeklies spread out between us, scanning the live show listings. I was trying to cheer up. Not even work could occupy me the way it used to, and shopping provided no sparkle. I was definitely in a slump. When I was alone, I wanted Josh back so much I felt like my teeth were hurting from the force of my longing. But when I saw him and we slipped back into our routine of bickering and the mundane motions of life, the longing faded.

"So, I can't come to Roxy's birthday party with you," Tina said. "Sorry, babe, but I'm going to Alex's cottage."

"Oh, great," I said. Negotiating the world as a single girl was less and less appealing.

An ambulance pulled into the art-store parking lot across the street. It drew my eye. You didn't really notice ambulances until you met a medic. Then, all of a sudden from six blocks

220

away you'd see a blur of blue and white, and crane your neck. I don't know why that is. Maybe it's like when you think you might be pregnant, and all of a sudden you see pregnant women everywhere.

Tina's hair was newly white-blonde with bits of purple that caught the light. She pushed her sunglasses up to rest on top of her head. I could see some wrinkles forming around her eyes. We were supposed to be having a meeting about our queer youth film outreach project, but so far we'd only gossiped. Last night, Tina had slept with the curly-haired bartender from the little pub down the street. "The girl smoked during sex," Tina had said, loud enough for all the other tables to turn and look. "I mean, seriously. I was doing some of my best work. Still, I kept looking up and she'd light another one."

She turned around now to see what I was looking at and noted the ambulance. "Is Josh working today?"

"Nope. Sleeping off a night shift."

"Huh. When's he moving out?"

"Dunno."

"*Amy.*"

"I know, I know."

"So is he, like, serious about Billy now? Will Roxy's party be weird?"

"I'm not sure what's happening, to be honest."

"Huh. Well, I think you should just go for it with Roxy. She's a nice one, you know, really one-of-a-kind. Minimal bullshit."

"Roxy and I are such good friends, it would be too weird. I'm going to just take things as they come."

"Any other crushes?"

"Well, I got an e-mail from an old lover, actually. A guy I used to date at summer camp. We have this kind of longstanding true-love thing happening."

"Another straight dude?"

Tina wanted me to be a lesbian. She found my lack of gender preference as confounding as the Olsen twins.

"Yup. We might reconnect again. He just got divorced, actually."

"Divorced? How old is he?"

"Twenty-six."

"Kids?"

"Nope."

"Interesting."

"Very," I lied. The truth was, it felt less right than ever.

"You have a backup plan, right?" Tina continued. "A distraction, at the very least. Josh was a good thing, you know, but seriously, that horse was long, long dead and you kept at it."

"That's such a weird expression, 'beating a dead horse.' I wonder where it comes from."

"Tonight I'm taking you out," Tina said. "And you cannot say no. I won't accept it."

I took a sip of my tea. Tina was already on her phone texting someone about a party. She always knew about the parties.

Minutes later, she said, "Okay, we're going to the Beaver tonight. Ten o'clock. It's some sort of Wednesday-night dyke hip-hop or whatever. Wear something totally slutty."

"I don't know." I didn't tell her that my plan for the evening was to continue making a sad experimental film using close-ups of ant farms—the official way I was mourning my relationship—

before smoking pot and watching season two of *Weeds* in six-episode marathons. No, that would sound pathetic.

"We need to get drunk and make bad decisions," Tina said, lighting a cigarette. "It's for your own good."

"Okay, sure. Whatever."

Tina blew smoke in my face. "That's my girl."

At ten, I was sitting on a bar stool watching the three cutest art fags in the world make drinks, wash dishes, and clean up from the dinner rush. Tina was late, as usual. Everyone seemed to know one another in this bar. They walked in and greeted the bartenders, the bus boy, and the waitress, as well as the people sitting at tables. I felt a bit out of it, the way you do when you've been married for years and are suddenly thrust into the scene again.

The bar was pretty small, so I drank my vodka-soda too quickly and popped out to the street to have a cigarette and send Tina irate text messages.

I leaned against the window and watched a cute, blonde, scruffy tomboy lock her bike to the gas line. When she turned, I recognized her as the girl I saw everywhere lately—at the farmers' market, at Starbucks near my work ordering green tea in the mornings, at the art supply store across town, once at the doctor's office. We'd progressed to nodding at each other and smiling, because clearly we were meant to meet somehow. I called her the Everywhere Girl.

She wore a loose white T-shirt, jeans, and a backwards baseball cap, and she was chatting with a skinny guy in purple jeans and a wife-beater holding a crate of records. The guy went inside. I smiled at Everywhere Girl. She nodded, still trying to lock up her bike. It was obvious that her lock was jammed.

"Fuck this piece of shit. Man, if this doesn't work I'm going to have to go all the way back home again."

"Where do you live?"

"Carlton and Yonge."

"Oy."

I picked up her lock and shook it, hearing the telltale click. "The lock is broken inside. It's toast. But if you're going to the Beaver, you can lock it to mine, for a while anyway. I'm planning on hanging out here until at least midnight." Tina had made me swear to stick it out a full two hours.

"Wow, that would be wicked. I'm only having one drink, tops. I have to work early. Are you sure you don't mind?"

"Nope. I mean, I'm bound to run into you in a day or two anyhow." I snapped open my U-lock and attached it to hers.

I introduced myself to her.

"I started calling you the Redheaded Run-In," she told me. "Like, 'I keep running into this redhead,' and that's what my friend started calling you."

She said her name, but I immediately blanked on it. "That's hilarious," I said. "I started calling you Everywhere Girl."

We smiled at each other in that way that acknowledges chemistry.

Everywhere Girl disappeared into the bar and I waited for Tina outside. Eventually she arrived flanked by two girls with similar blunt brunette bangs. They were already drunk, and walking like they were on stage. They carried oversized white purses, just like me. I wanted to go home.

When I ordered us drinks inside, the bartender, a surly-looking indie-rock guy in a cowboy shirt, informed me that all my drinks were going on Everywhere Girl's tab. She lifted her drink from across the room in a toast.

"Are you sure?" I walked over to her table, which was packed with girls in tiny shirts and oversized hoop earrings. "I mean, you don't know me, but I'm a lush. I might order ten shots just for kicks."

"You seem far too nice for that, what with the whole sharing-the-lock thing. Plus, I know you get up early since I always run into you at Starbucks before 8 a.m."

Apparently, Everywhere Girl's version of one drink meant five and my two hours meant six, and even Tina went home before me, leaving the two of us on the patio at 1 a.m., leaning into each other.

Before I realized what was happening, I'd told Everywhere Girl my whole life story. There was something irresistible about the way she asked questions with sincere interest and funny insights.

"Sounds like you have had a monumental year of change," she said.

"What do you do, anyway? I haven't asked you anything!"

"It's a trick," she said. "I'm a social worker. A shy social worker, so, you know, I have ways to make you talk." She winked.

In the bathroom, with my ass in the wall sink and my panties around one ankle, I remembered that it was easy to go out and mess around. I could have many affairs. I could be free.

Everywhere Girl walked me home at 3 a.m., and we pushed our bikes in a weaving line down Argyle Street. We giggled at each other like idiots. I felt the kind of insanity that accompanies a crush out of nowhere, a bomb in the chest.

She gave me her business card: *Maria. Street Outreach Worker.*

"Okay, so I know the world is small, but did you used to date someone named Billy?"

"Yes, for many years, actually." Maria looked at me curiously. "Do you know her?"

"Yes, she's roommates with one of my best friends, and dating my very recent ex."

"Josh?"

"Yeah."

Maria looked at me and grinned. "I feel like I'm on some ridiculous reality show. Or I'm about to get punked."

"Nope. Pure small-world syndrome."

I thought about inviting her in, because Josh was on nights. Then I felt a flash of guilt and decided not to.

"Well, weird meeting or not, I have a feeling we're going to mean something to each other," Maria said from the curb. It didn't sound like a cheesy line, just honest.

"I know. I feel the same way."

I sat on my front stoop and lit a cigarette as I watched Maria bike up the street. The moon was full and I breathed it in. I felt so happy, so...normal. I felt like myself again. Returning-to-normal Amy. I'd fucking missed her.

When I opened the door, I was startled by the blare and glare of the television in the living room. Channels were flipping faster than you could guess what was on them. I steadied myself against the coat rack and looked at Josh on the couch, his uniform shirt unbuttoned.

"Hey, Amy," he said, but he didn't look at me. "Have a good night?" He asked this as if he had to ask but didn't really care about the answer.

"I had a great night, actually." I sat next to him on the couch, pulling off my heels and massaging the balls of my feet. He didn't turn away from the screen.

Josh would never stay in his uniform after work, because it usually got so filthy. I'd never seen him just walk in and sit on the couch, but this was evidently what he'd done. His boots were strewn in front of the coffee table. He flipped through MuchMusic. CityTV. CP24. Infomercial. Infomercial. There was not much on at 4 a.m. I put my hand on the remote, which made him clutch it harder and pull away from me.

"What the fuck, Amy?" he yelled. He had never raised his voice at me before. At anyone, really. "Can't I just watch TV in peace?" He continued to flip.

"Are you jealous? Is that it? Did you look out the window? 'Cause I didn't know you were home. You were supposed to be working. What happened?"

Josh paused for thirty whole seconds. "I booked off early," he said. Flip flip flip.

Whatever, I thought, *I have a right to move on*. I reeled between feeling guilty and feeling entitled and thinking I had completely ruined both our lives. I took a deep breath.

"'Cause I really don't think you have a right to take that tone with me or be jealous. I mean, feel what you want to feel, but seriously, don't take it out on me."

Josh didn't look at me. He paused on figure skating and put the remote down in his lap. "I'm not jealous, Amy. Not everything is about you."

I grabbed the remote and pressed "mute." "Of course not. But why else would you be mad?"

"There's a lot going on that has nothing to do with our breakup. You act like it's all there is."

"Well, maybe it's all there is for me. Maybe it *is* a big deal to me. And I think you're bullshitting. I think you're mad that I met someone tonight."

"Stop telling me how I feel."

"Okay, what do you feel?" I wished I were still in that bathroom with Everywhere Girl, lips mashed together.

Josh picked up the remote, un-muted the television. Flipped through channels again. "Nothing."

The person who had taught me that I could experience a boundless, enthralling sense of intimacy was now this: a clipped responder, avoiding eye contact, angry.

"Why are you still in your uniform?" I asked.

Shrug.

I checked my phone. Seven new texts. Maria? I tried to contain my excitement. Would she be so bold? I stood up and exhaled loudly. "Whatever, Josh."

He snorted without looking at me.

I raced upstairs barefoot, and ran a bath. I poured rosemary oil into the water, lit two candles on the window ledge—creating an oasis far from Josh. I saved the messages until I got into the tub, hair pinned, toes pointed straight, cradled on either side of the tub.

I flipped open my phone. There were sixteen missed calls and seven texts, six from Josh:

1:45 a.m. *Domestic stabbing. VSA kids & mom. Baby alive.*

1:59 a.m. *Baby dead at hosp. Dad tried to kill himself & failed. Weak fucker.*

2:03 a.m. *Freaking out. Booking off on stress. You home? Please be home?*

2:35 a.m. *Home. Where are you?*

2:45 a.m. *I need you. I'm so fucked.*

3:15 a.m. *?????? So this is what you're like now? So much for our friendship, right?*

Then, from Maria:

3:45 a.m. *I had a great time tonight, sexy girl. Reprise?*

I jumped out of the tub and into my robe without towelling off. Josh was still flipping channels downstairs. I sat beside him, put my arm around his shoulders and tried to give him a hug. "I *just* got your texts, babe. I'm so sorry. I didn't know, I swear."

"I don't believe you. You always check your phone. What the fuck were you doing that you didn't hear it go off fifty thousand times?"

He was being so curt, I hardly knew how to respond. He was usually so rational, even when he was upset.

I paused and thought carefully before answering. "I just didn't. Tell me about the call. I'm so sorry you had to witness that."

"Oh, so you met someone, of course. Did you already fuck them? Huh?"

"Um, that's not exactly fair, considering Billy and all."

"Did you?" Josh's voice was rising.

"Josh, you're not being fair. I'm here now, so let's talk about your call."

"Whatever. I need to be alone right now."

"I think you should talk to me about what happened. Let some of it out. Earlier you said you wanted to see me…"

"Never mind."

"Josh…"

"Just go away, please, Amy. You won't get it anyway. And it's not such a big deal, I've seen way worse." He shrugged again.

But I continued to sit beside him. I tried to hold his hand, but he pulled it away. I knew the type of call he'd had to deal with tonight must have triggered thoughts of his father, of his childhood. I wasn't sure whether or not to say anything about that or to just let it sit. I had a lot of assumptions about how Josh might feel, how his dad's violence had affected him, but I didn't know for sure. Despite all our years together, Josh's past was still a big blank for me. That fact made me feel like I'd failed as a supportive partner.

"It's not a big deal, Amy. I was freaking out, but I'm not any more, okay? I'm sorry for yelling at you."

"It's okay."

"No, it's not. I'm sorry."

The doorbell interrupted us. "Who the fuck drops in at 4 a.m.?" I asked.

I pulled back the curtain over the window on the front door. It was a paramedic, some girl I'd never seen before who looked to be about twelve years old. I opened the door.

The girl said hello, and walked right past me into the living room as if to say, *Excuse me, stranger in a towel, I have a job to do in your house.* She sat down beside Josh and opened her arms, and the angry robot on the couch transformed into a sobbing little boy.

I watched for a moment, uncomfortable and hurt. I pressed my fingernails into my palms, angry that I couldn't give Josh the nurturing he needed now. I had always been able to do that before. It was gross to be jealous of a girl who could empathize with Josh better than I could—but I was.

I hung the towel on the banister at the bottom of the stairs and stood naked for a moment, watching Josh and the girl. They didn't talk. Eventually, they both turned to the TV. Josh started flipping again, and the girl pulled a bottle of vodka from her purse and offered it to him. There was a full bar in the kitchen, but he took her cheap brand anyway. The girl looked at me as I stood there naked—although I was partially obscured by the wooden banister—and raised her eyebrows. She blushed, and turned back to Josh.

I walked up the stairs. By the time I was in the bathroom, poking my toe into the lukewarm water, I heard the two of them laughing. I tried not to take it personally. The girl had a cackling laugh with a snort.

I slept for a few hours, and then around 9 a.m. I snuck past Josh and the girl and made a pot of coffee in the kitchen. I brought two mugs into the living room. Josh was asleep on the couch, and the girl was texting on her phone. If she had slept, it must have been in the armchair. I put the coffee down in front of her.

"Do you take milk?" I asked.

"No, this is cool. Thanks."

"I'm Amy."

"I know," the girl said, clicking her phone shut. "I'm Jenny."

She said her name as if I should know who she was, but I had no idea. I knew Mike, Diane, a nurse named Nina, Dave,

Mandy, Mark, and Alisha. I'd never even heard about Jenny in passing. I tried not to assume that this meant something.

Josh rubbed his eyes.

"Do you guys want breakfast?" I asked. "There's oatmeal, fruit." I was acting like a mom. Like my mom. Accommodating. Feeding everyone. Smiling.

"No thanks," said Jenny.

Josh shook his head and stood up. "I'll drive you home, Jenny. Thanks for coming over last night."

The two of them put on their coats. Jenny took a swig of coffee and motioned to it, putting it in my hands. "Thanks, Amy."

She looked like a Girl Guide playing dress-up.

Josh grabbed the car keys from the hook by the door and Jenny followed him. He didn't say goodbye.

[25]

Billy

On the Friday before Roxy's birthday I made it to class, but barely. I had been prepared to tell my professor that I couldn't be there, that it made me too anxious and I couldn't concentrate. But I couldn't make it through the whole class. I dashed out at break, unable to breathe. The lights, the air, everything conspired against me sitting still and understanding.

Outside, the sidewalks tilted, and my legs felt as if they had been switched in my sleep. My head floated above me. The last three days had been the worst to date for my anxiety, and I had no idea what to do.

I walked into Emergency at the Clarke, the building I always avoided walking past because I couldn't admit I was as crazy as everyone else in there. I went into the waiting room and feigned reading a poster on the wall. I could have been a social-work student, a friend visiting someone she knew. I could walk out.

But I left two hours later with a prescription for tranquilizers and a follow-up appointment. I called Maria from a park in Kensington Market. Somehow, simply having the pills calmed me. I could take them if I started to go crazy again. A safety net.

"Billy!" Maria said, before I could even say hello. "Listen, I'm glad you called. I have to tell you something. I met someone, and it turns out you know her. She's invited me to Roxy's birthday party, of all things. Anyway, I hooked up with Amy, Josh's ex. So weird. So small world."

I had no idea what to say. I tried, "That's, uh, pretty awesome. I mean, I feel a bit jealous, sure, but I'll get over it, right?"

Maria was silent. Then she said, "Well, c'mon, you've been dating Josh for a while now."

"Yes, I have. I know. Doesn't mean I can't feel jealous."

"Sure. Anyway, Billy, I have to go. I figured you wouldn't want me around at Roxy's party so I turned Amy down, but I wanted you to hear it from me before it got around."

"Sure, sure." I didn't mention my anxiety attack. When I hung up, I felt more alone than ever. I practically ran home, took two pills, and fell asleep for fourteen hours. When I woke up, I put on my new vintage dress and got ready for Roxy's birthday that evening.

But all I felt was hollow and bone-tired and ready to let everything in the world slip away.

[26]

Amy

I woke up late the day of Roxy's birthday party, the clock on the bedside table (IKEA, the Hemnes, $129 in dark wood) blared a furious orange-red that matched the inside lining of my eyes. I could see them in the bedside mirror. I reached out, clutched the clock and threw it across the room. 12:08 p.m. landed with a thud.

I'm done.

I woke up late and in the same bed with Josh, both our mouths dry and skin tight for lack of water. We shared vague memories of fighting like fiends the night before on a crowded dance floor at the Gladstone. I felt ashamed to have been so public about the fact that our supposed flawless transition from lovers to friends was less and less so.

When we'd first broken up, it had been such a relief that we'd found ourselves being nicer to each other than we had been all year. Just saying the words "breaking up," admitting it could happen, took all the fear out of it. People broke up all the time.

But things hadn't felt so cut-and-dried last night; they'd felt worse and worse, actually, in the few days since I'd met Maria and come home to find Josh in distress. Last night, Josh had had some sort of revelation while sitting at the bar nursing his glass of rye and ginger. He was the kind of drinker who had revelations. It would have been great if he could just chat like a normal guy, then come up with some gradual observations. But, no. He was silent and awkward, refusing to make small talk, until suddenly he was Buddha.

The tiny bartender with long black hair poured me a vodka-soda, flirting expertly. It felt good to be wanted again. Josh laughed to himself, choked a little on the peppery rye, before pronouncing his revelation.

"Our relationship is like a dead baby."

I turned my head towards him, eyebrows raised as if to say, *I'm not amused*, while the bartender took someone else's order.

"Like, we'll be watching TV or chatting over breakfast, totally fine with our decision to break up, when all of a sudden a dead baby appears in front of us."

"What?"

"It's like we try to ignore it but then we're unable to look away. We lose sight of everything except our relationship, clutching its cold body, trying to revive it."

"That's a really sick analogy."

Josh laughed between sips. "It's a metaphor. We can't let go."

I had given him a disapproving stare. I hated the way I knew it looked on my face. I hated the way it felt. But it was involuntary.

The only solace I had felt all night was the vibration of my phone, signalling text messages from Maria. I guess I needed a new crush to get rid of the old one.

The last text message from Maria had said, *I'm here. Playing pool in melody room.*

I texted back: *Stalker?:)*

I told Josh I was going to the bathroom, walked into the adjoining room and caught Maria's eye while she was trying to make a shot. When she pushed up her shirt sleeve, I could see the marks my fingernails had made on her forearms earlier in the week. She blushed and missed, then winked at me.

In the bathroom stall, we made out maniacally, tearing at each other's clothes and laughing.

"I wish we could hang out tonight," she said. "Can you ditch the ex?"

"Sorry, I can't. We're trying to work on our friendship, and I'd be pissed if he ditched me to fuck his new girlfriend."

"Billy," she stated. I scanned her face for signs of annoyance. The last thing I needed was someone else hung up on Billy.

"Yeah, he's dating Billy," I deadpanned.

"This whole thing is pretty bizarre. I don't care, though. I mean, stuff with Billy and me was over a long time ago."

"Yeah, and we'll have plenty of time together later on, right? It's one night, not a big deal."

"Right," Maria said, kissing my neck and kicking open the stall door.

"It would be good, if we're all friends. There's no lack of love, right?"

"Right," Maria said. "Of course not."

I straightened my skirt and applied a new coat of lip gloss.

We staggered out and by the time I got back to the bar, Josh was again looking solemnly into his drink. A cute girl was eyeing him, pointing to him and then talking to her friend.

Every time I looked at Josh, my reflex was still to think: *Mine. Always.*

I had to work on that.

[27]

Josh

Billy would've laughed at the dead baby remark, would have revelled in the gruesome. She'd told me an abortion joke and a rape joke within the first ten minutes of our first date. Of course, she'd apologized and blushed and tried to make it seem as if she didn't normally talk like that, but I soon realized I'd met my cynical and crass match. Paramedics have a specific sense of humour. You have to, or else what else would you do? Probably slit your wrists. Amy's sense of humour wasn't so dark. It bothered me now.

I used to think Amy was a better person than me for not imagining the worst, for not turning everything into a statement about the end of the world. Now she seemed naive.

Last night, four drinks in, Amy and I were straining to have fun together like we used to and our interaction broke down. We fought on the dance floor, arms in motion, eyes wide. The DJ played Justin Timberlake and everyone else rejoiced in a shared ironic love of Top 40. Amy and I stood still among the

239

frenetic motion. The song, like every song, was about love. We stood, finished, while around us everyone danced.

I felt guilty for insisting in my stupor to Amy, "You just don't want me to be happy, do you?" In the heat of my drunk I'd felt vindicated, relieved, almost victorious.

I stood outside the glass doors of the bar, smoking, watching Amy laugh too loudly while the bartender brought her more shots and leaned in close, touching her arm, every once in a while turning to nod at me through the window, then turning back to Amy as if to say, *What's so special about him? You can do better.*

When I returned to the bar, Amy introduced me to the bartender: Sandy. Sandy poured me a shot, slid it across the bar like a symbol of amity, and winked.

"Is this pretty girl your girlfriend?"

Amy rolled her eyes and laughed nervously.

"Nope, not any more."

"You think I gotta shot, then?"

"I don't know. Maybe."

"I think I gotta shot," Sandy said, smiling in a way that was at once challenging to my masculinity and slightly flirtatious. She gave Amy one bravado-laced glance before turning to another customer.

I pictured Sandy and Amy kissing. It made me sick and turned me on, like the first time I saw a porno mag and my face went flush and I thought I might throw up, but it wasn't entirely unpleasant.

You just don't want me to be happy, do you? The words taunted me now as I got out of bed to fill a plastic cup with tap water in the bathroom. I rinsed my sticky garbage mouth, trying in vain to end the gasping hangover. Regret: *You are a fucking idiot. You are a piece of trash.*

The hangover felt like an injury, one obtained from a fall while trying to execute a prank or a fabulous performance. It was not supposed to happen like this. Amy and I had broken up months ago, but still here we were, in the same bed, entwined, like a stubborn stain creeping out towards everything else in our lives, one brave toe or outstretched finger at a time.

"Is *she* going to be at Roxy's party tonight?" Amy asked as I came back into the bedroom. I noted the *she*. Any female person. Third person. Removed.

"Yes, Billy will be there. Roxy is her roommate, remember?"

When Amy got jealous she couldn't stop asking questions she didn't want to know the answer to. It burned her, but she couldn't stop wanting to know. I didn't bother with questions like that. I took a deep breath and pretended jealousy didn't get to me. If you pretended enough, it became true.

I looked frantically through the sock drawer for the perfect pair of green and yellow striped soccer socks. My lust for Billy was so tangible it was something I could hold in my hand. All Billy had to do was say my name — *Hi, Josh. How's it goin'?* — and something in me unravelled. I half expected a cartoon heart to thump out of my chest. This sounds like a fun feeling, but it's not.

In my line of work, I saw people who were so unhinged, so messy with snot and screaming, so desperate. I knew this was likely why I was attracted to contained and forthright people. Like Amy used to be, before confidence turned to arrogance, before independence looked so aloof and cold.

"What about your new crush?" I parried. "Your little clan-destine affair?" The hickey on Amy's neck made me perversely thankful.

"I don't know if it's anything, really."

"But you don't consider my feelings," I said.

"You don't get jealous," she said. "You're like a fucking robot."

I turned away without saying anything.

"So, you're hanging out with that medic Jenny now, as well as Billy?" she persisted.

My attraction to Jenny was this: Jenny never objected to anything. She was so easygoing it was like she was a straight guy. She didn't get jealous. When I told her I had something complicated with Billy, she didn't get upset. She didn't make demands. She was fun to be around. I'm not sure why. It felt good to have an uncomplicated relationship. And she knew exactly what she wanted. Or didn't want. "I don't want a boy-friend," she'd said, the first time we hung out after work. "I'm done with that for a few years. But I want to make out with people."

When I told Jenny I was trans, she asked me questions, mostly medical, and she didn't have any of the transphobic/homophobic assumptions so common at EMS. I felt a little pried apart by her questions, but at the same time I understood and was used to it, somewhat.

Jenny's casual nature was a relief after Amy's erratic blank disregard followed by sudden possessiveness. And lately Billy made me feel too needy. It was as if I had to hang around wait-ing for her to say, *Okay, be my boyfriend already*. I couldn't fake my feelings, though. If Billy wanted to be my girlfriend, I'd say yes with no hesitation. She must have known that. Truth be told, I had spent a lot of time with Jenny talking about Billy, about how to *get* her to be my girlfriend.

"I don't know why I like Jenny," I said to Amy. "I guess because she understands the job, right? She knows."

"What about your life outside the job, huh? Can you actually see her hanging out with, like, me and Roxy and all of us? You think she won't be totally weirded out?"

"She's not like that. She has a great way about her, she listens really well. She's pretty open-minded."

"Huh."

I could see that this was the moment in today's conversation when Amy was going to stop listening to me. She looked at me as if she knew she was smarter than me, as if she couldn't believe she had to explain so many obvious things. When this happened, I found it didn't make sense to keep going. But Amy wouldn't quit.

"Does Jenny even get that you're trans? Does she have any politics? Has she ever even hung out with queer people?"

I didn't want to touch this line of questioning. Amy got all up-in-arms when she thought I might be considered a regular straight guy—as if I were betraying some big ol' revolution should my trans status not be a focal point.

"I should get my own place," I said. "We can't be broken up and living together. It's just not healthy. At first I thought I wouldn't have to move, but now I think it might be a good idea." I leaned against the dresser and pulled on one sock awkwardly.

"I know. I know." Amy's cheeks reddened. She looked at me as if feeling a revulsion she'd never felt before.

I realized neither of us wanted to have a relationship like this. I wanted to tell her: *I'm not who I want to be. I'm not actually this person.* More than anything, I wanted the past to zoom forward, and I wanted the Amy who had changed my world to come back, even if just for an afternoon.

I sat down on the bed next to Amy, put my hand on her naked thigh. I looked closely at her and saw the rage she held in her shoulders, in every muscle.

"Promise me you'll never stop being my best friend," I said gently. I couldn't stop the urge to cry.

Amy placed a hand on each of my shoulders. I thought for a moment about what would happen if she snapped my neck. I felt all the vulnerable points on my body, every artery close to the skin, every possible instant death.

But Amy was looking into my eyes, and the animosity in her own faded. "Josh, you'll always be my family."

She put her hand to my heart and pressed it, and I felt the warmth of skin against bone. She curled her right leg around my torso, lowering her body until she was straddling me. We kissed with open mouths. This was the last time we would have sex. We both knew it.

It was at times mechanical and familiar, and at others filled with a passion we hadn't felt in years. It was monumental and totally normal at the same time.

Amy knew what I needed—for her to grab the back of my neck and look at me in the right way, like: *You fucking worm.* From me, Amy needed more than a regular recipe—she needed ambience and pretense and the right kind of gaze and adoration.

Today, at a certain point, I just stopped trying. She seemed relieved. She slapped my cheek playfully, a little harder than she should have. "You're always so easy," she said. Her words sounded like an accusation, but she said them in a fake, sing-song, nice-girl voice.

"You know I'll always love you, right?"

"Sure, sure," she said.

"Do you want to get back together?" I ventured. In that moment I could see us together a year from now, these last few months an odd blip.

"I don't know. Sometimes. Do you?" she asked softly.

"Yeah."

"Well, for now, I think sleeping together was a huge mistake."

"Maybe."

"And I think you should move out."

This was the first time Amy had said anything so definite, the first time she'd sounded certain.

"Okay."

I fidgeted, turned on my back and stretched out, noting that I'd worn socks the whole time we were having sex. Amy hated sex with socks. She too noted this, and sighed, desire once again thwarted. And once again I was something she didn't really like any more, but was incredibly attached to.

I walked downstairs to the kitchen and selected one of the heavy rock glasses from the drainer. This had always been Amy's house, despite her repeated urging for me to put up posters or photos, make it mine. There were her appliances from Williams-Sonoma, her silver pepper grinder, stone mortar and pestle, careful list of typed emergency numbers on the fridge, fixed with a magnet that read *Art Matters*. I'd arrived in this city in a car I had driven from Guelph, carrying my cat and all of my belongings in four boxes, plus a garbage bag of clothes. The car had died in Amy's driveway and had to be towed away. I had liked Amy's aesthetic, so I hadn't bothered changing anything.

I drank two glasses of filtered water, poured another, and selected a tiny piece of lemon from the saucer of carefully sliced wedges wrapped in cellophane in the fridge. Squeezed and dropped. I watched the lemon slice floating soft and bloated in the glass. Amy's cloudy sophisticated influence embodied. I drank.

There were only three things of mine in the kitchen — a case of Guinness in the fridge, a box of Minute Rice in the cupboard (Amy thought anything other than whole-grain unwise), and a row of chocolate pudding cups.

"Have you always eaten like a teenager?" Amy had asked me the first time we went grocery shopping together. Her green plastic basket had been filled with quinoa, kale, apple-cider vinegar, and rice milk. Mine held canned beef stew, salami, Kraft Dinner, margarine. "I mean, you're studying to become paramedic," Amy had said. "Shouldn't you be conscious of your health?"

"I've noticed the medics I've met on training are notoriously unhealthy." I'd shrugged. "We don't sleep properly. We drink too much coffee."

I walked back into the bedroom and sat on the bed, which Amy had made in my brief absence. She turned to look at me, and I closed my eyes in a long blink, the way I used to. I'd been doing it again lately — the blink — since we'd broken up. I closed my eyes emphatically, hoping the gesture translated to Amy how uncomfortable I was. She didn't appear to notice.

For a few minutes I watched her sitting at her nightstand, applying peach-scented Kiss My Face moisturizer, lining her eyes in black. She pushed two gold hoops into her earlobes.

She had new lines around her eyes. Her arms were so thin. I thought of Billy's curves, how soft her skin was.

"I'm going to Roxy's party tonight by myself," she said, eventually. "You can come if you want to, but I think we should stop habitually moving around the world together. We should be independent." She paused to open her mouth slightly and run a creamy oval of brownish lipstick over her lips. She pursed them together, pressed her pinky into the cupid's bow of her upper lip, and blotted with a tissue. "Change needs to be solid. Certain."

"But I like the time we spend together. Why does everything have to be so regimented and inorganic?"

"Because nothing will change unless we force it to."

"That's a harsh way to look at life."

Amy shrugged as if to say, *I'm tired of your theories.*

"What happened to your camp boyfriend?" I knew his name. Jason. I just liked making him sound like a child.

"Nothing. We decided it's been too long and we live too far apart." Amy shrugged, pulled her red and white socks up to her knees, and stuffed her feet into a pair of red Converse sneakers. "Find somewhere to live, Josh. It's that simple. Look on Craigslist, sleep on Roxy's couch, sleep in Billy's bed for all I care. Just let me have my space."

"You know Billy doesn't want a relationship. She rarely lets me sleep in her bed. You don't have to worry about being replaced in that sort of way."

"You are so arrogant."

Despite these words, Amy looked relieved. I could see through her. I continued reassuring her, as if I hadn't registered the insult. Maybe I *was* arrogant. Maybe I was the most selfish person on earth. "And Jenny, well, you know. She's twenty. She's just a friend, you know? Plus, she's a medic. It could never be anything serious. Medics can't date each other. We're too crazy."

Amy didn't laugh.

"Is Maria coming tonight?" I tried to speak lightly, to not betray more than casual interest.

Amy got up and walked towards the door. "No, Billy and Maria are trying to give each other respectful space in social situations these days." She fidgeted with her socks again.

"Huh. It looks like it could rain. You might want to take your slicker."

Amy's eyes narrowed at my pragmatism. She grabbed her raincoat and left. I could hear that she hadn't locked the door behind her.

I went to the living room and stood at the front window, watching Amy walk down the street. I had a feeling like thirst that I knew wasn't thirst, but I drank another glass of water anyway.

I was looking forward to Roxy's birthday party. I hadn't seen Billy in a few days. I was working 2 p.m. to 2 a.m. tonight, but would likely book off at 1 a.m. so that I could make the last hour of the party. I promised myself: *I will be on my best behaviour. I'll be honest.* Perhaps it would be the night for all of us to shift back into ourselves, to stop freaking out, to realize how lucky we were.

Well, at least I'm not the dog-faced girl. That's what Billy said whenever she had a bad day. She had a photo from a tabloid pasted on her fridge that showed a girl born with a dog-face. It served her as a reminder that things weren't so bad.

At least I'm not the dog-faced boy, I texted her.

That night, I spent the last two hours of my shift at St. Joe's, holding my patient's hand on the stretcher while we waited for a bed. She was 105 years old. If she'd had any kids, they were probably dead by now. I wondered, *What must it feel to be her?* She was lucid until her fever got high. I didn't know why I kept holding her hand. It felt sort of peaceful, watching her breath fog the oxygen mask. She gripped my hand every once in a while, and opened her eyes, startled. Then she calmed down when she looked at me. I smiled, and she faded away again.

When my patient got a bed, I turned on my phone. It was nearly 2 a.m. Dispatch finally said 10-19. I had three texts.

Amy: *Why Aren't You At Roxy's Party? Thought you were booking off early. Come before we run out of tequila.*

Billy: *Amy and I are getting loaded together. Can you believe it? You better show up soon, handsome.*

Amy: *Where are you? I'm sorry about earlier.*

Back at the station, Jenny came out of the change room. "I'm way too hyped to go to bed. Want to hang out?"

"Well, it's my best buddy's birthday. You want to come?" As soon as I said the words I wanted to take them back. Already Billy and Amy were at the party—why add to the drama? But it was too late. Jenny was totally into it.

"I could use a drink," she said.

Our first drink was poured from a flask because we had missed last call. Roxy was loaded, Amy and Billy were nowhere to be seen, and Roxy had no idea where they had gone. Jenny put her hand on my thigh. She had a small, still-healing tattoo of a maple leaf on the inside of her right wrist.

The bar was emptying out, but Roxy knew the bartender. He locked us in, and we kept drinking. Roxy brought three shots of Jägermeister to our table by the front window and suggested we play a game called The Milton Shot.

"Okay, so you take a shot and right after you swallow, the person to the right slaps you hard across the face."

"This is what it's like to hang out with artists," I said to Jenny.

She smiled as if she was game.

Roxy placed her hand lightly under my jaw, stroking it affectionately, and handed me my shot. "Ready? Shoot it!" Roxy slapped me hard.

I felt odd about slapping Jenny when it was her turn, but she laughed, and then she slapped me harder than I'd ever dare reciprocate. We slammed down the glass cylinders still hot from the industrial dishwasher. People stared.

Our faces were like rare steaks. Roxy took a Polaroid. In the photo there was a shadow of someone to the side, spilling a drink. I was grinning, half-lidded. When I looked at the photo, my cheeks burned under their already red and purple flush.

"Why didn't those girls say goodbye?" Roxy asked, swallowing more dark green liquid. "It's my fucking birthday! I'm a quarter of a century! Woo-hoo!" She slammed the shot glass down.

I went to the bathroom and sent Billy a text. *Why didn't you wait for me? I'm here, and I miss you.*

Book Four

[Life 4]

May 16, 2006.

3:06:12 a.m. Delta unconscious, F, 25,
cyclist struck, possible head injury.

3:06:12 a.m. Delta semi-conscious, F, 25,
disoriented, possible leg injury; made call.

You never know how much time you have, right? Think about it now. Feel a little sick? Run your tongue along the roof of your mouth. This is all you are. Cells meeting cells.

Two young women, both twenty-five, bike down Kensington Avenue. One wears a pink vintage cocktail dress and sits astride the gold-glitter banana seat of a child-sized BMX. The other has longer legs, wears slouching red and white striped knee-socks and an over-sized yellow raincoat with the hood pulled up over her helmet. Red curls escape onto her neck.

They both grip the handles of their bicycles. It's raining warm and steady.

Towards the beginning of the night, they'd decided to own up. They were each in love—falling in and falling out—with the same person. They'd done the logical thing, and turned their palms towards each other, danced with stomachs touching, admitted defeat, and in that sweet moment of shared humility, bought each other seven shots of tequila. The seventh on the house. The last three lemon slices poised between their teeth; tributaries of Windsor salt licked along the wrist, then crossing the jugular, and eventually nestling in the valley between their pushed-up breasts.

They had gravitated towards each other slowly. Yellow Raincoat thinking: *Keep your enemies closer.* Pink Dress: *I want to live without fear.* Pink Dress would say it like that. She's not afraid to be earnest, but can always make fun of herself.

Now they yell confessions of affection to each other as they pedal unevenly.

"You're so smart!" one calls out.

"You're so pretty!" is the other's response.

They are both smart and pretty, yet prone to requiring validation. What they really mean is: *It's a relief to know you're a real person and I don't have to hate you.*

They slow approaching Dundas Street, which, for a major street downtown, feels empty. The housing project on the south side of the street appears abandoned, the security lamps blinking a yellow smudge in the stream of rain. Smiling at each other, the young women bike west, fingers curling lightly over their brakes, pumping, pressing.

Normally both girls would hide under an awning in this kind of weather, lock up their bikes and jump in a cab. But the rain is warm and suits the mood. Heat lightning erupts in the distance, brief blankets of chemical-candy blue, as they round the upward curve in front of Toronto Western Hospital. They pause at a red where Dundas meets Bathurst. The streetcar ambling past is a defeated wet insect.

Yellow Raincoat nods at a paramedic who runs across the intersection with a tray of coffees, swearing under his breath. He says her name with a smile of recognition.

Pink Dress sees herself up ahead, body crushed by the transport truck now gaining ground behind them. In a blink, the vision is gone. The truck passes by without incident. This happens a lot to Pink Dress. While biking, she frequently hears an involuntary incantation: *Time's up. Time's up. Time's up.* She has visions of her death: large objects crushing her limbs; two arms flailing as she plummets from the TD Bank Tower, sudden immolation by her own struck match, a knife slicing a check mark across her cheek before the killer plunges it into her rib cage. The images fade but continue to shake her. She blames the meditative state brought on by bicycling, the repetition of pedal up and pedal down, the continuous click and shove. But she is drunk and there is only NOW, and *Now is the fucking thing, man!* In this instance of enhanced lightness, Pink Dress recognizes how ridiculous it is to live anxiously. Her unwillingness to *let go! live a little!* is but one item in a list of many bad habits, appearing after cigarettes but before inappropriate honesty and ill-advised one-night stands.

Yellow Raincoat isn't one to dwell on things she can't control. She pushes her mortality aside like crumbs from a dirty counter, concentrating on the wiped white sparkle, her slight reflection. She has held the hand of a dying person. *So what. We're all going someday*. It's like a hemline around her skirt, unnoticed with no loose threads. She was practically married to a paramedic. You can get used to almost anything if it happens every day.

If you were watching from the air, you might think the two women look like children, aimlessly playing, circling in figure eights, teasing. From the ground you might notice their directionless eyes, gnawed nicotine fingers. If they lifted their arms, you might be tempted to rub your fingers against the soft underarm stubble caused by cheap pink razors bought in haste at the twenty-four-hour Shoppers Drug Mart before a date.

If you looked even closer, you'd see that Yellow Raincoat has softer skin, blemish-free from careful hydration. Pink Dress has overlapping scars on her forearms and a face pursed from years of worry. You might guess by their fashion, the way they articulate sentences, that they each have half a Cultural Studies degree, or maybe they study fine arts. They definitely have the first independently released Arcade Fire CD, a subscription to *Bitch* magazine, and they know the names of all the Broken Social Scene side-project bands. They give almost believable tarot card readings, can shoot whiskey straight without wincing. They believe in ghosts, but consider themselves rational. They own multiple Noam Chomsky books and have read at least one. They are from the generation that had e-mail addresses like PonyGirl85@hotmail.com by Grade Four and took cell phones on their first dates. They aren't used to being unreachable.

If you were close to them, you would smell lemon and tequila, sweat mixed with lavender oil, desperation fading.

The bartender at the Red Room had tried to cut them off after midnight with a good-natured, "Haven't you had enough?"

"Never, ever enough!" Pink Dress had yelled.

They were cute, harmless drunks, so the bartender kept pouring. Pink Dress could stop his breath with a wink. Yellow Raincoat was the kind of girl who wouldn't speak to him if she didn't have to, and there she was. Leaning in, lips pursed with possibility, chewing on her straw in a way she thought was seductive. The look would be pornographically repulsive in a brightly lit room or an afternoon park, but was totally commonplace in the bar, sexy under soft lighting.

Yellow Raincoat pulls her knee-socks up. Gravity and weakening elastic push them towards her ankles. She pulls them up again. Pink Dress runs a finger under her bra strap, which is forming an angry red horizon across the middle of her back. Both women's lips are slick and glossy, both wear mascara that is hardened and purposeful.

Earlier, they were revellers attending their friend Roxy's twenty-fifth birthday party, appreciative drunks in a room dotted with off-duty bartenders and waitresses. Both Pink Dress and Yellow Raincoat were there for Roxy. They loved her. But they were too consumed with themselves to keep their eye on the birthday girl for longer than the requisite drunken singsong while Roxy extinguished a flimsy candle (later used as a projectile) plunged into a Chinese bun from the bakery next door.

Even with the fresh air and the aerobic push and pump of their biking, the girls are last-call dizzy, lemon drop and tequila shooters smearing their glossy red lips. They are singing a song that was playing at the bar. The chorus states emphatically that the singer, like perhaps all women, would be better off without a man.

A man yells, "*Some* people actually want to sleep!" and slams his second-floor window, catching the tip of his baby finger, which swells up, a flower budding. His wife tells him to get back into bed. She had woken with a jolt to a bad premonition.

The young women coast. Their wheels turn and turn, and the low friction propels them forward on their simple machines. They hum. The street remains quiet, the Portuguese cafés, the veterinary office, and trinket shops all locked tight. A guard dog shackled inside the lumberyard at Manning Street barks half-heartedly. The 7-Eleven is swollen with stoned late-night snackers and homeless people camped beside the air pumps.

"I can't believe it took us this long to bond, we are so similar!" says Yellow Raincoat.

"I feel so attached to you right now!" says Pink Dress.

When they kissed earlier in the bar, they were both half-present, well-intentioned, trying to transform absence into substance. They are not compatible kissers — both are used to leading the other participant's tongue. Yellow Raincoat felt Pink Dress's mouth was too small and kept trying to part her lips and get in there. Pink Dress felt Yellow Raincoat was using her tongue too routinely, believes the tongue should be an addition, a timpani drum, not the bassline or the background rhythm. When Pink Dress relented and let Yellow Raincoat direct the kiss, they relaxed into the pattern of lip-to-tongue-to-bite to soft closed-mouth pauses. They were one part enjoying the moment, one part hoping they'd turn their heads and notice someone, a particular someone, walking through the door. Hoping for jealousy, loyalty, sudden rushes of certainty.

"Everybody is only their own," says Pink Dress.

Yellow Coat nods. "What an astute observation."

Pink Dress thinks, *I am so full of shit. That's a song lyric.*

The girls try to hold hands, still biking, drunk to the point of bliss that may soon turn sharply into nausea. Yellow Raincoat closes her eyes, takes a breath from her diaphragm like she used to do during singing lessons. She lets go of Pink Dress's hand and lifts her legs off the pedals, points her toes towards the sky, and screams, "Ahh! I'm *so* tired of relationships!"

"Tell me about it!" says Pink Dress.

One of them doesn't really mean it.

They continue to bike fast along Dundas Street, and make it halfway home before pausing at the north end of Trinity Bell-woods Park. Pink Dress ties the loose string of her strappy sandal while Yellow Raincoat lights a cigarette and stares at Pink Dress, bent over and struggling with gravity. "I can't wait to be out of my twenties. I hear the thirties are where it's at. Everything is supposed to feel like less of an emergency," Yellow Raincoat says.

Pink Dress fears her thirties. "I hope to accomplish some-thing by then," she says. She pushes one pedal ahead slowly, turning to smile.

Pink Dress swerves first. The city is unusually still. Yellow Raincoat doesn't notice the truck as she follows. All she sees is the pink dress, the strip club sign that is supposed to say BABY DOLLS but only says BYLLS. She notices the bright O! of the full moon above Ossington Avenue. She coasts towards Pink Dress, too drunk to notice the signs, to hear anything but her own blissful interior monologue: *I am going to be okay on my own!*

Later, neighbours will describe the sound for weeks: A truck pushing through a yellow light turning west onto Dundas, the girls assuming they are the most visible people on earth, glowing brightly with purpose, turning south on Ossington. A broken bike light, a single helmet, and two heads. A tired driver, pushing limits the way most people do when they assume there is no consequence. More monumental than the mere vibration of matter, the sound erupts from the mouth of bad timing.

Pink Dress hears an extended note veering off key before she blacks out. Nothing could insulate that sound. The sirens.

Back at the bar, a young man touches his wrist discreetly with two fingers and feels his pulse jump. For no reason, a single tear forms in his right eye, and pauses before rolling down his face. He touches the wetness and expects it to be blood. Inspects it closely in the dim candlelight. Presses his finger to the white of the bar napkin, surprised it doesn't rise red.

There is light and sound and then it all stops, like a sudden drop in temperature that freezes the brain. But Yellow Raincoat can't stop it. She has those extra seconds to feel fear. She tries to get off her bike, but it fuses to her. She braces for impact. She thinks of her mother.

Yellow Raincoat and Pink Dress are both knocked down, knocked out. Pink Dress's bike is thrown in front of the TD Bank, red and gold pretzelled, twenty feet from her body.

Yellow Raincoat comes to and touches her helmeted head with the arm she can feel. For a moment, she has no idea where she is. When the sound of the crash stops, before anyone can react, there is a quiet calm in the intersection, the kind of stillness usually felt in the few hours between last call and morning rush hour.

The driver absorbs the scene through the windshield, his body forced forward and then back, his mouth dry. He wills himself to have a heart attack and lie unconscious with the girls, who were only moments ago active agents on bikes and now lie limp on the street, one moving like a broken machine. Then there is the blur of headlights in the rain and the sound of people getting out of cars.

The worst thing is being the only one to see it all from above. The driver feels a sudden empathy for God, an idea he hadn't believed in until he felt the impact of bodies against the grille of his U-Haul. This morning, he had moved his family to the city from Kingsville. He had been given a promotion, bought his first house. He'd made so many choices today—where to get dinner for the kids, to keep the truck for another few hours—all leading up to this moment. Before he left, his wife had kissed him and said, "I'm so proud of us." It was something she had never said before.

Just before the truck struck, Pink Dress's eyes said one thing: *Oh fuck. I had a feeling about tonight.* She was thinking about her earlier vision. In that percentage of a second before the collision, she was resigned to what would happen.

If you were there, you would go to the girls. Press your sweatshirt to wounds. Call 911 on your cell phone. Recall Grade Nine life-saving training. You wouldn't be able to control the volume of your voice.

Two trucks are dispatched to the accident. The medics know this is a shit-hot call. They're not fucking around. This is probably the one call tonight that is a life-or-death emergency.

Diane counts to three before she lifts the stretcher. As her partner, Mike, rolls the patient into the truck, he finally puts his finger on how he knows her. *Fuck.* His heart sinks. The young kid on Blue — Josh. This is his girlfriend.

Mike has a feeling, wheeling her into the ER, that this girl's not going to make it. Uneven pupils. Projectile vomiting. He's seen it a dozen times before. Bad, bad signs.

Afterwards

AMBULANCE CALL REPORT

DATE: 06-05-06

SURNAME: Stevenson   **GIVEN NAME:** Hilary

25, F

PICK-UP LOCATION: Dundas and Ossington, SE Corner

Cyclist struck; unconscious

Pt found lying NE corner of Dundas and Ossington. Pt was travelling through intersection on bike when struck by U-haul truck travelling approx 50 km per hour

HISTORY: Unknown

MEDICATION: Unknown

ALLERGIES: Unknown

TFD, TPD: On scene

MECHANISM OF INJURY / DIRECTION OF FORCE:

GENERAL APPEARANCE: Pt unconscious, GCS 3, S&S of head injury

HEAD/NECK: abrasions to left side of face w bleeding from nose and mouth, no signs of periorbital ecchymosis, possible left side skull fracture at temporal lobe

CHEST: no instability, ribs intact, pt w cheyne-stokes respirations, clr breathing sounds, bilaterally apices to bases

ABDOMEN: bruises and distention, left upper quadrant

BACK/PELVIS: pelvic stable, abrasions present lower back

EXTREMITIES: present, pedal pulse present, good circulation, left wrist with deformity and swelling at joint

[28]

Billy

Billy is mashed up on the stretcher in the back of the sw 8734 truck. The same ambulance in which she made out with Josh only a few weeks back—but no one here knows that. Her faded eyeliner runs like an extra vein under each bruised eye, and her pink dress is a shred. Her brain had rattled inside her skull on impact. The head came to a stop against the Ossington Street pavement, but the brain kept travelling. Go figure—Billy's brain, always going going going. It slammed into the inside of her skull, bounced off, and hit the other side. Like a ping-pong ball. If this had been Josh's call, and he had been driving, he would have sent her a text from the hospital: *Young chick, bike accident, probably not gonna make it. Totally gorked.*

According to Billy's brain, she is sixteen again. Someone is fussing over her terrible style.

"You have terrible style," says the girl with plastic-looking cheeks, picking at the sleeve of Billy's cherished army jacket, with its Jane's Addiction patch stitched onto the breast pocket. "Grunge is over. Did you not get the memo?"

"I was raised to think style was a distraction, a way to pacify the masses."

"That's a tragedy," Plastic Cheeks says, her hands cupping Billy's waist. "At least you are thin. We can work with you. Jason! Run to wardrobe, stat."

A pale and sweating assistant appears clutching a clipboard. Billie is a guest on a breakfast show, and her call was at 4:30 a.m.

When Billy had woken up in the hotel, she had consulted the paper itinerary on the bedside table to remember where she was. Her handler and tutor, Carlie, knocked on the door with two cups of coffee. Carlie hadn't been to bed and smelled like beer.

Now there is a highlighter running over parts of Billy's brain. The brain has separate left and right cerebral hemispheres. Billy experiences semantic memories of her first television appearance. Flashes of Maria walk gently over the outer layer of grey matter, the cerebral cortex. Maria is allergic to shellfish; the seven digits of Maria's home phone number from 1988 to 1998. The scraps of acquired knowledge come in and out like radio waves.

Billy took her mid-term Grade Eleven history exam back-stage before a concert. *When did women get the right to vote in Canada?* asked Carlie, deadpan—*1921, 1901, 1975 or 1936?* She kept picking at her face, saying things such as *Your skin really changes on the road. Fuck. I look fifty. Do I look fifty?* To sixteen-year-old Billy, fifty was a senior citizen. Fifty didn't even make sense. Fifty was: may-as-well-be-dead. Billy took a swig from her bottle of iced tea. She was allowed to pour rum into it after four o'clock. Carlie looked in the back of the textbook and then X-ed in the answer for her.

Neurotransmitters and receptor subtypes: A memory of Maria, Grade Nine, the perfect line of eyeliner, a lesson in the green industrial bathroom. Tube socks. Algebra. Maria's lips, eyes, mouth. How much school will you miss? Can I come with you? Will you still go to prom with me if no one protests? The man who said, You look just like my daughter. Will you meet my daughter in the hospital? The doctors give her less than a year. But oh, what a year we're going to have.

Singing with Sheryl Crow at Lilith Fair, being patted on the head a lot. Backstage at the place in Toronto, near the water: Sarah decorating the ceiling with saris. Prince over by the buffet with his mother. He wouldn't make eye contact. I was born to do this, she thought, looking out over the empty chairs at sound check. *This is my calling.* Maria on the phone later, *You didn't miss anything. Just high school, same old bullshit.*

Everything is just a cell talking to another cell. Consciousness is just this. Beep of a machine. The result of several actions. Her reaction. The harmonies in her brain, the hemispheres in A minor.

Somewhere those cells are chatting it up, have been engaged in debate since Billy was able to decipher death. As a child, she had seen the body of Mrs. Roades in the middle of the street after the snowplow didn't notice her. Billy had asked, after eating one careful bite of casserole at Mrs. Roades' wake, *But where do we go?*

There were answers in Sunday school she found unsatisfying. As she grew, she realized there are people who can live without knowing or understanding their mortality, and people who cannot. Billy could not. "We become worm food!" Billy's mother said. "We go to Heaven," her grandmother said. "As long as we live righteously."

There were people who could have a good time without nagging, useless worries at the edges of all their thoughts. Billy admired them. She felt like she might spend the rest of her days angry at the unknowable, trying to control all she could.

On stage, singing to her first crowd of thousands, she briefly broke through the worry. She was singing six verses and the chorus of a song she'd sung thousands of times, so that she no longer had to be present. Her ribs broke open and she soared above it all, rich with purpose.

Later, she counted, sorted, placed carefully the things that could be contained and understood.

Billy's head aches, but she can't feel it. All around her, hands are wrung, eyes are closed. There is the clicking on and off of lights and the angry beep of monitors. Sirens approach. An intercom voice speaks, disembodied. Memories run through her brain like the soft strokes of a watercolour brush.

[29]

Josh

"Billy's in rough shape." When things happen like this, you report the news to almost everyone in a pragmatic deadpan. I am standing in front of Amy, who closes her eyes in response. Her mother and father are by her bedside in the intensive care unit at St. Michael's Hospital. Amy's face is a puzzle of scrapes and bruising. She's on an IV drip of morphine, her broken leg propped up. Her red hair a shock against the white pillow. "She's in surgery."

We are waiting for Amy's MRI results to come back, but they should be clear. The doctors are just being cautious.

This is all I tell Amy, because she's still pretty banged up. I don't want to worry her with the fact that Billy might not live.

Amy can talk, form sentences, make sense. When they said, over and over, "You've been in an accident," she understood. She has no significant head trauma, just some small fractures and a broken leg. She'll be home tonight or tomorrow morning at the latest. She won't remember this conversation, likely, but she's here now, in front of me. All of her. Not like Billy.

There is almost nothing worse than the feeling of not being able to do something constructive when all you want to do is be useful. "I'm going to check in with Roxy and see if Billy's family is here yet," I tell the O'Haras.

Amy's mother dabs her eyes with a stiff Kleenex she pulls out of the front pocket of her cardigan. Mr. O'Hara pushes Amy's hair out of her eyes. I'm not sure they've heard me.

"What a piece of crap hospital. I want to get Amy transferred to Sunnybrook. It's a better hospital, right, Josh? You would know these things. You would know all the insider secrets."

I nod, though I doubt what I know about the health care system would be at all comforting. I know Mr. O'Hara needs to do something in order to feel valuable. "Amy is going to be fine. She's lucky. You can relax."

It's hard to be sympathetic to Amy's parents, because I know she's going to fine. Of course she would be the one wearing the helmet, even though Billy is usually the most cautious of any of us. I back out slowly and go back to the Quiet Room, where Billy's family is starting to show up and gather.

When I first got to the ER and couldn't find anyone, the bitchy triage nurse with braces tried to give me attitude and I just let her have it. She stopped and stared at me for a minute, like she couldn't believe anyone would dare to yell at her.

"Redhead in Trauma 4," she said. "And the blonde is in the OR already."

Pacing outside the Quiet Room is a tall woman with short blonde-brown hair in dark skinny jeans, a sweatshirt, and orange Converse sneakers. She's pressing madly into a cell phone. When she sees me approach, she reaches out to touch my arm.

"Josh? I'm Maria. Listen." She looks into my eyes. "You need to do something for me. Can you? "

She's using paramedic voice on *me*, speaking in such a way that I can't help but agree to do whatever she says.

"I need you to pick up Billy's mother and sister from the airport. They get in at noon and they'll need someone to get them here fast. They don't know the city. Cabs are expensive. Can you do this for me? I need to be here with Billy when she wakes up, and Roxy is still too drunk to drive anywhere. Plus her father will be arriving any minute and I know him and want to make sure I'm here."

Maria hands me keys to her car and a piece of paper with Billy's mom's name scrawled on it in Sharpie.

She has thought of everything. "Red hatchback parked on Victoria."

"I have my own car." I don't want to leave Billy. I'm the one who can understand the jargon, read between the lines of what the doctors manage to communicate.

"But it's not here, is it?"

Of course, I left my car at the station. I was out drinking. It's almost morning already. How did all this time pass? My cheeks burn. I close my eyes.

"Drive like a fucking maniac, Josh," Maria says. "I mean it. You know how to do that, right—like you're driving the ambulance."

I feel like smacking her when she says this, she is so condescending, but when I look at her I see she's starting to cry. She's doing the best she can. *Stop judging*, I tell myself. *Be still. Be calm. Just start walking.*

"And, Josh, Amy is still stable, right? She's okay?"

"Yes, she's going to be fine. Just a broken leg."

Maria smiles. "At the very least, this is good news."

Walk, I tell myself.

If it were an ordinary day, Billy would be painting a new coat over the chipped polish on her toenails, sitting on the pink yoga mat, feigning a regimen. Billy would be contemplating calling in sick to work again. She'd be wondering if the faint headache were an impending aneurism.

I calculate that I have time to stop at home and get in uniform before coming back to the hospital. They might let me in to see Billy this way. I'm deciding whether or not to do this when I run into Roxy, who is pacing outside the ER doors, smoking and circling, driving herself into the ground. She smells like alcohol. She looks at me like I'm vermin.

"What the fuck, Josh? What the fuck? You should've showed up earlier, when they were still there. Maybe they were fighting. Maybe they were yelling at each other and that's why they didn't see the truck. You could've resolved this."

"It's nobody's fault, Rox. It was an accident."

"This wouldn't be happening if you could just make a fucking decision, man. That's all I'm saying."

"It's not that simple. And there is no decision, Roxy." Roxy doesn't know how much I love Billy, and how much Billy knows it. For some reason, she thinks Billy's the victim of my uncertainty when it's the other way around.

I keep walking towards the car. I hear Roxy yelling after me, but she's really yelling to herself.

"Oh really, it's not that fucking simple, eh? *Look at me, I'm Josh. I'm so calm. I'm so used to this shit.* Billy's going to DIE, you fucking asshole. Fuck you, man. Fuck you."

[30]

Billy

Billy thinks she's sitting in the kitchen at the Parkdale Gem in May 2006. She can really feel the hangover, her head in her hands as she turns to read the words IGGY POP and BOOB, spelled out in rainbow lettering on the fridge.

Her wrist, ribboned in a plastic hospital bracelet, is a limp gift over the metal railing of her bed. She is dimly aware of friends sitting in the waiting area. But it's like an overlapping dream, one where she knows she's in the hospital, and another where she is sitting, hungover, in the Gem kitchen.

She overhears the news that Josh is driving her mother and sister in Maria's car, and she imagines uncomfortable silence and small talk as he zips down the 427, frustrated by his lack of lights or sirens. The white noise of the hospital leaks into Billy's thoughts, but she doesn't wake up. She has a lateral skull fracture with an epidural hematoma. Her brain surgery is over and she is in recovery, but she still needs an MRI. They are prepping her.

Her body is a field of weeds, memories, and imagined present-tense.

Her unconscious vision continues: after two glasses of water, an Advil, she is suddenly at her new job, the tele-research company. At twenty-five, she's the oldest employee. She likes being older because none of the kids recognize her from the Lilith Fair tour or the cheesy CBC Juno Award moment. All night she thinks, *One more call and then I'll quit.* From one call to the next, it's always the last one. The second to last one. She feels lonely in the office, but she's almost comforted by loneliness sometimes. This is fame's biggest consequence.

She thinks, *One more call and then I'll go to the washroom to put on some gloss.* She smiles weakly at Stan, the evening supervisor, as he sits behind his computer desk through the glass doors playing Tetris as if nothing is wrong. Billy knows that Stan has a crush on her. Billy thinks Stan is creepy but pictures having sex with him anyway. Pulling on those cheap ties. Slapping his face. Involuntary two-second daydreams.

She adjusts her headset, runs an index finger over the next typed name on the list and phone number. All Edmonton contacts. It must be dinnertime out West. Perfect time to harass people. *Good Will.*

[31]

Josh

Billy's brain is being drilled into right now. I touch my temples. My fingers are shaking, cold at the tips.

Outside in the parking lot, her father is pacing, talking quietly on the phone. Nobody knows what to do. I check my phone, then go up to the room where we're allowed to gather. Maria comes in with a tray of tea and coffee, a box of mini doughnuts. I take one out of habit; it tastes like paper. I crumble half of it into a ball and shove it in my pocket. I try to delete any visions from my head—the time I witnessed residents basically kill a patient with their incompetence. All those secret moments of incredible lack of judgement that lead to death. It's routine. Instead, I try to envision Billy's operation going smoothly, everyone in the room well slept and concentrating.

I'm repeating myself for the new arrivals among Billy's family and close friends: "We know she has a lateral skull fracture with an epidural hematoma. That means they have to drill a hole in the skull to drain the blood and relieve pressure. If it's caught in time, and the bleeding stops, there's usually no brain injury. They're investigating it now, and the extent of her internal injuries. The best thing to do is stay strong and hope for the best."

"Have you had patients like this who've survived?" Billy's mother asks.

"Yes," I lie. "Absolutely." The truth is, I hardly ever know whether my patients live or die, and often I don't care to think about it.

Now this not knowing, this waiting, is a kind of torture.

In my uniform, I can pretty much walk anywhere in the hospital. A nurse outside the OR is Janie, who just transferred from the ER. Janie likes me, a lot. She dates Jon, a medic on my colour code. She has been keeping me apprised of Billy's status.

When I go over to her, she looks pale. She has on her *tell the family* face.

"What's going on, Janie?"

"They just figured out she has a lacerated spleen, with considerable internal bleeding. They're going to operate now. Her pressure's pretty low."

Dr. Kellerman walks up to Janie, fiddling with his pager. Kellerman happens to be the only surgeon I know in any kind of personal way because of a weird, fluke, nighttime call that happened during SARS. We'd smoked a cigarette together outside the ER and he'd broken down. He always remembered me after that. He loaned me books about atheism.

"Dr. K.," I say, "Hilary is my girlfriend. Can I scrub in and watch? Please. I think it would make a difference if I'm there."

He looks at me for a moment, and then shrugs. "As long as you can handle it."

"Yes, I can. I know I can." I've never been less sure of anything.

"Janie can show you how to scrub in and get sterile. Be quick."

The total number of things I know about spleens: In healthy people, the spleen helps fight against bacterial infections. It is in the uppermost area of the left side of the abdomen, just under the diaphragm. It is attached to the stomach, left kidney, and colon. I run through this while scrubbing in and pulling on my mask. I feel blinded by the whiteness of the room, the weird ET-like quality of everything. I palpate my own spleen area in a nervous unconscious motion. I've never, ever wanted a cigarette more.

I look at people gorked out on stretchers every week, people who sometimes die and sometimes don't. On occasion, I've spent the final few moments of a person's life being annoyed with them, or not believing them. Other times, patients have thanked me for my patience and help during their most traumatic moments. I have to say, for all my cockiness, my apathy, my general sense of having seen it all, nothing has prepared me for this.

Billy is so white wherever she isn't banged up. Even the tattoos on her arms appear to have lost colour. The prepping and mechanical motions around her contribute to this feeling. It's as if she isn't in the room.

I was hoping for laparoscopic surgery, tiny keyhole incisions, but I guess Dr. K. needs to assess all the damage inside, so he goes old-school, cutting into the abdomen, finding the spleen and separating it from the surrounding organs. I'm not fascinated or drawn to each odd shape of the human body like I have been before. I worked on cadavers in college, I've seen other surgeries. This is so different. I cannot be objective or curious. I want it to be over, and I want Billy to sit up and say something rude or dirty or mean. I want to go back in time and do shots with her at the bar.

I can't believe I didn't book off early last night. If I had, Billy might not be here right now. If I hadn't held the hand of 105-year-old Helen Harris for close to two hours, I might not be watching Billy's broken spleen land in a metal tray. All the beeping machines are driving me out of my mind with guilt, and the certainty that I might have prevented Billy's pain. I can't even think about the possibility that she won't make it at all.

[32]

Amy

I remember falling, and staring at car tires passing while I was still on my back. I don't remember the impact, but I do remember seeing Billy in my periphery, landing impossibly hard against the street. Or maybe I just heard the sound of her, a cracking noise, a dividing line drawn with a sudden *thump*. It's hard to know what's a real memory and what I've recreated from what I've been told.

I remember reaching for the cell in my raincoat pocket and dialling 911. The operator tried to keep me on the phone but I hung up when I started seeing white at the edges of my vision. I called Josh instead. I wanted to say goodbye if this was it, because although I was conscious, I had no idea how bad my injuries were. I remembered how Josh used to tell me that dying patients often have no idea, they talk so normally, and then it's lights-fucking-out. I left a message on his voice mail as my vision went completely white.

My sight came back when the medics got there. Two trucks. I was able to talk, to give the attendants all our information, to stay lucid enough until everything was taken care of. I don't even think I felt the pain. The medics who showed up were friends of Josh's. Apparently I tried to joke with them, unaware that the wet I was feeling was blood, unsure why they were moving so fast. *Aren't you supposed to be slow and annoyed all the time?* I'd asked, laughing. No one laughed. I had so many bits. *Don't you like my comedy? I'm a real knee-slapper*, I thought, always a cut-up in an emergency. I got only polite smiles, stern faces. I had broken my right leg and dislocated my shoulder. I had a concussion and bruises from where I'd landed.

I couldn't see Billy any more. She was taken away in another ambulance. But I knew it was bad for her. She was a body, not Billy at all. I tried to yell her name, *Billy! Billy!* But she didn't stir.

"Promise me she's going to be okay, Mark."

"I'm not sure how's she's doing, Amy. I know they're doing all they can. She's with Diane and Mike, and they're good. Don't worry."

That's when my pressure must have dropped. The adrenaline that had been keeping me up subsided, and I passed out. I made Mark tell me this story over and over afterwards, trying in vain to remember anything, to figure out if I could have done anything different to change what happened.

*E*talk came to the hospital. Roxy punched a cameraman. She told me later that when she was on the way to the police station she was wishing that Billy would somehow sense what had happened and wake up to watch the coverage. *You would be so mad, Billy. That glib fucker showing all your old footage. Wake up and tell him to fuck off on air! Tell him to just Come Out!*

My parents took me back to North York to take care of me, set me up in the basement on the pullout couch with the giant TV and my laptop. But I just stared at my phone, waiting for updates about Billy.

[33]

Billy

"Hello, is Mr. Barkley there?"

"There is no Mr. Barkley."

"Mrs. Barkley?"

"No. We don't want to buy anything anyhow."

Click. Next name. Similar conversation. Billy is tired. Next call. This guy is obviously masturbating.

"Are you jerking off, sir?"

"Yes."

"Can you stop?"

"No."

Click. Be polite. Your calls are recorded. Stan will have a laugh at that one.

"Hello, Mr. Chris Cameron?"

"Yes."

"Good evening, sir. My name is Penelope Woodrow, and I'm calling on behalf of Masters Marketing. We are not trying to sell you anything. We're conducting a survey tonight about beer. Are you between the ages of twenty-five and forty-five?"

The name Penelope is really funny when customers get mad and have to yell it. It's immediately funny. Never *not* funny. And it's four syllables. You have to really get mad to yell it. Billy likes it best out of all the names she uses. Sometimes she'll be Lydia Lunch or Nancy Spungeon. Debbie Harry. But Penelope is a polite girl, kind of sweet. Gets the job done.

"Yes."

"Great. The survey only takes approximately seven minutes of your time." (This is a lie. It takes about twelve.)

"I'd answer your survey, Penny, really I would, but you see, I'm dead right now."

"Excuse me, sir?"

"I'm dead. I'm on the other side. I can see the angels, if you get my drift."

"I could call back later if this is a bad time." Billy tries to sound serious, but can't stop herself from laughing.

"Oh, you think it's funny? You think it's funny that I'm dead?"

"No, sir. No, of course not. Death is a very serious thing." Billy doodles *CRAZY* next to Chris Cameron's name but wants to get some commission, so she takes a breath, tries again.

"How about 7 p.m.? Is that a better time to call?"

"Well, I'll still be dead then. But you, you'll be okay. You're going to wake up."

"I'm clearly awake now, sir. Do you drink beer if you're dead?" Billy looks around surreptitiously, makes sure no one heard her go off the script.

"Oh yeah. Hell, yeah."

"Okay, then, Question 1, how many beers would you say you drink on average between Monday and Friday?"

"I can drink five thousand."

"Five thousand?"

"Sure. It doesn't matter, I'm dead."

Standing up with her neck craned low, still attached to the headset, Billy tries to catch the eye of Stan over the row of cubicles. He is usually sitting at his large intimidating desk on the other side of his office window, watching, monitoring calls. But he is gone. Billy's not sure what to do with the dead guy. She wants a cigarette.

"Question 2. Can you describe a recent advertisement on television that you have seen for beer?"

"Sure. There was a white, bright light. You were there." The man's voice sounds bored.

"Can you describe a recent advertisement..." *Just repeat the question*, Billy tells herself. The customer may not have understood the first time.

"This is related to your reticular activating system. Do you know if you're awake right now, Penelope?"

Billy pauses, longer than she's supposed to. *Never let the call get out of your control. You are the one directing the conversation. Don't answer questions.* These directives go through her head and she puts her shaking hand on her head. Grabs a pile of hair.

"It's okay, Penelope. It's you we're worrying about. Do you ever feel as if you're just totally out of control?"

Billy sits on her knees, perched on the rolling grey office chair, and leans into the cubicle, fists grabbing at the edge of the desk, faux fetal.

"Penelope, you asked me questions. Now I have one for you. Have you been experiencing fluctuating disturbances in cognition? Attention? Self-awareness? Memory function?"

"Sir. Please understand I am trying to complete my assigned task, which is what I get paid for. If you will take a moment to consider your beer-buying habits. When was…" *Don't lose control of the call*. Billy pictures the three-dimensional brain Josh gave her that floats in water and grows. Her brain feels like a grey ineffective sponge. She holds her head in sweaty palms. The voice on the other end of the phone says, "Now you are trying to decide if you will live or die, right? You have a choice. Me, I think you are young and you should choose life."

Billy pushes her finger into the off button, keeps pushing long after the call hangs up. *Good Will*. She looks around. *Good Will*. It's not working.

Natasha, the shiny-faced teen in the Tupac T-shirt in the cubicle beside her, asks, "Pervert call?"

"Yeah. Real asshole." Billy scribbles down the dead guy's phone number on the back of a debit receipt from her wallet, grabs her purse, and walks towards the door, running straight into Stan's ample sweatered chest.

"And where are we heading?" Stan always spoke in "we."

"We're going to go kill ourselves." Billy pulls her pink shawl tight around her neck and pushes past him, marching purposefully towards the stairwell.

Stan stands with eyebrows raised and arms outstretched.

"Do you know what I realized today, Billy?"

"What?"

"You're Hilary Stevenson. You used to be a well-known musician."

"Nope."

"Yes, for sure. I looked at my sister's CD yesterday and there's no way it's not you."

Billy continues to walk, but she calls back from the elevator. "Well, I wouldn't say *well-known*. I would say *briefly radio-friendly*. I'm going to visit my friend in a coma. Mail me my last cheque, okay?"

Stan shrugs. There's always one quitter a day.

In the elevator, Billy holds her breath as if it's an accessory. *Good Will.*

When she gets home, she takes her guitar out of the hallway closet and tunes it. Hums a few bars of a cover tune. Then proceeds to sing as if she'd never stopped. She sings loud and then quiet, and she writes the best lyrics of her life, singing them over and over and over until she commits them to memory. She feels her heart getting strong and a calmness taking over.

If she wakes up, she will hear the song in her head.

She will sing it every day afterwards, for at least a year.

She will sell it to a young singer, the winner from *Canadian Idol*, and live on the royalties for years.

If.

I think: *I'm paralyzed. I might be asleep. I might be having one of those dreams where I know I'm asleep but I can't wake up.* I can feel my eyes. I try to make them open, but I can't. I can feel the sheet, the hard mattress, bodies shifting around me. I feel a primal urge to call for my mother, but I know this is ridiculous. I am in my bed, in Parkdale, Roxy a few feet down the hall. I try HELP. Try ROXY. "*Raaa. Raaa.*" That's all I can manage.

Nothing. Soon Roxy will shake me, offer me an inappropriate-for-the-time-of-day beverage.

My mouth moves, opens slightly. I manage to lift one eyelid slightly. I can see the side of my pillow. Light. My pillow is not the worn-in Strawberry Shortcake pattern I'm used to. This confuses me. *I must still be dreaming.* I try to open both my eyes.

I am stuck in sleep and can hear the sounds of what I believe to be Parkdale ambient clatter through an open window. I am awake enough now to know I am asleep. I count to ten, hoping the lucid dream will abate and I can wake up normally, all my motor skills intact.

It occurs to me that this might be what dying feels like.

Okay.

Here we are, brain. You're still with me.

This is the part where I'm supposed to accept it, right? As soon as I think this, I start to calm down. *Well, there's nothing I can do about it now.* With this realization, I'm able to float above my body, see myself asleep. I am surrounded by white. How can my death be so *All My Children*? Why a white room? I'm a talentless hack, even as I'm dying.

With this thought, I am suddenly back in my body. I feel my fingers! Each digit a triumph! I still can't move, though I feel the blood moving in my hands. WAKE UP WAKE UP WAKE THE FUCK UP. I'd only meant to nap. Just a little avoidance nap. Roxy said she'd wake me. She said she would call if she left.

I hear Josh's voice, and Roxy's laugh. I hear my mother's voice. My sister Rebecca. I smell Dad's tea-tree soap. Maria's sandalwood oil. When my eyes finally stop betraying me, the first thing I see is white. A line of fluorescent lights on a ceiling.

"Billy, you've been in an accident. You were hit by a truck on your bicycle and you broke a few bones, but you're waking up now. You had surgery, so your confusion is normal."

I try to move my lips as the words I hear start to make sense. It takes a long time. Where am I? A hospital? Bikes.

Streetcar tracks, laughing. Tequila. Stomachs touching. Legs in a V.

I pull things into focus, see a chorus of people around the bed. Dad, Mom, Rebecca, Josh, Roxy, Maria closest to me, holding my hand.

"I don't understand," I manage.

An unfamiliar man appears. "Billy, I'm Dr. Cameron."

Dr. Cameron—the dead guy from Edmonton! He leans over me.

"Can you feel this?"

When you're having a panic attack the one thing you're certain of—besides your own death—is that the attack will never end. Even when it does stop, there's always a sense that another one is on the horizon, and it's a self-fulfilling prophecy. But I know when mine ended. With the sound of Dr. Cameron's voice. On Saturday, May 23, 2006, in the afternoon. Over. Forever.

Epilogue

September 2006

Josh and I are sitting across from each other at a table by the window at the Beaver Café. We've ordered matching breakfasts—tiny cups of fruit and granola, lattes, greens and eggs. I'm able to walk around now, after weeks in hospital and recovering at home, and it's a freedom I can't speak about without crying. I'm sure I'm embarrassing to be around, but I don't care. Josh doesn't seem to, either.

I'm thankful for fall and winter coming soon, so I can cover up the scarring on my arms and legs. I'm battling my memory, willing it to return full force. I have all my childhood memories, and my short-term is just fine. It's the weeks leading up to the accident that are blurry. Roxy assures me that they weren't wonderful weeks, not for me anyway.

I'm so grateful to be here. It sounds cornball, but now I've got a straightforward second chance. I spent so much time afraid to live; maybe this shock was all I needed. All I needed to be okay. Roxy keeps leaving drawings of the Buddha on my bedroom door to bug me. She thinks I'm going to write a self-help book or something.

Josh and Roxy moved all his stuff into our apartment. Amy decided to sell her house, get a condo instead. There was a lot of room for Josh in my room since I threw out almost everything the day before the accident in a manic fit of purging. Apparently. The day Josh moved in, I watched as he got sweat across his brow, his eye twitching from the stress of hauling boxes all day. I felt so lazy, watching, wiping the surfaces clean in my room, trying to organize, but was winded after the smallest amount of activity. These days his hair is shaved close to his skull, the faux-hawk too much to keep up with.

We chew in silence, looking up at each other once in a while.

I wonder what he thinks, really, of the injured me—the slow-moving Billy, calm but not entirely the same girl he got involved with.

Last night on the porch, he said, "You seem so much more grounded than you used to."

"Ironic, huh? The secret to renewed mental health: head injury! Fly through space! Irresponsible drunk cycling! I can see the Oprah show now."

Now, through the window of the Beaver Café, I notice Amy, coming up the walk with her new dog.

Josh jumps up, runs outside to greet her. They hug. Their hug brings tears to my eyes. That's another thing that has been happening to me since the accident—random bursts into tears. Amy waves at me through the window, gives Josh the leash to hold, and walks inside to see me. We are, as always, awkward.

And although we are unmistakably bonded through the collision, there is another gap now. The Josh and Maria gap. I'm confident this will cease to matter after a while.

Because at first, nothing mattered. Crisis does this. Josh and Amy and Maria and I were all suddenly in love with one another. We had survived! We were okay. As things return to normal, it is easier to feel the complications again.

Still, it gets better between me and Amy every time we see each other.

She grabs my hand when she notices my tears.

"I can't stop crying. I don't know why," I explain. "I'm happier than I have been in years, I think."

"No more panic, eh?"

"No, it's like the anxiety got squished out of me by that fucking truck. My therapist says she can't believe how much I've changed."

"I feel the total opposite. I can't even ride my bike without breaking out into a sweat. I tried riding on the sidewalk like an old lady, and freaked out. I put an ad up on Craigslist to sell my bike." She laughs.

We hold each other's hands, skin against the crumbs of toast on the wooden table. We don't do anything, just look at each other. It's only been a few months, but both of us are changed. I have my heart back, and a brain on regular speed.

I appreciate you, I whisper to almost anything these days — the aloe plant, the cat, Roxy, Maria, and especially Josh.

He smiles and blinks at me. "Please promise me I'm not going to come home and find you watching evangelical TV shows, baby."

"I promise, no money to God."

Now I show Amy my new tattoo. It runs across my chest, covering some of the scarring. It says, *Good Will Trucking*.

"I don't get it," she says. "But it's pretty."

"Maybe you and Maria can come over for dinner sometime."

"Yeah, totally. We should."

The offer is genuine, but I'm not sure it will happen anytime soon.

Amy goes back outside, and she and Josh stand facing each other, holding hands, as though about to break into a dance. When I look up from my breakfast, Amy is walking away with the dog, and Josh's face is pressed against the glass, making a monster face at me.

You already know all my fucking secrets, don't you? I took you to therapy, for God's sake. What do you want? But okay, I'm a joiner. I was raised by hippies. So I'll *co-operate*.

I'd like to do nothing for as long as possible, just sit in those moments in between, with no expectations of the world or my place in it. Sometimes I watch Josh from the window of our bedroom as he pulls up in the ambulance after an overnight shift. Running the siren in a brief *hello* so I can hobble downstairs to kiss him. The absence of fear is an opiate.

That's my secret. Holding still, thinking nothing at all, is my biggest accomplishment.

Glossary of Toronto Emergency
Medical Services Terminology

Alpha low-priority call, nursing home transfer, falls, inter-facility transfer calls

ALS Level 3 medics trained in Advanced Life Saving; ALS medics are able to perform intubation, needle thoracostomy, and all drug administration

BLS Level 1 medics trained in Basic Life Saving; able to administer five drugs

Bravo assaults, third party unknowns, domestics, psych, suicide, MVC, personal injury

Charlie abdomen pain above the navel; stroke/CVA

Code 5 dead/VSA

Colour code each shift rotation of paramedics is designated a colour and has its own supervisor and schedule

CTAS Canadian Triage Acuity Scale

CTAS 1 acute, have to resuscitate

CTAS 2 requires spinal board

CTAS 3 abdomen pain, ankle fracture, less life-threatening

CTAS 5 patient can walk

Delta	short of breath, chest pain, unconscious, shootings, stabbings
Dispatch	emergency services phone dispatcher
DNR	do not resuscitate
Echo	cardiac arrest, choking
EDP	emotionally disturbed person
Fire	short form for *firefighters*
HBD	has been drinking
Medic	short form for *paramedic*
Offload delay	a delay in the ability to off-load patient from stretcher due to ER over-crowding and lack of ER physicians; medics sit with patients "on offload delay" until they can be admitted and seen
OLD	acronym/sarcastic term for offload delay
10-2s	the police
211	psych patient
Truck	another word for *ambulance*
VSA	vital signs absent

Radio Codes Between Dispatch and Medics

10-7	We arrived. ("We're 10-7 at scene")
10-9	We're en route from scene to hospital ("We're 10-9 to Toronto Western on a CTAS 3")
10-2000	danger, need cops immediately
10-8	going to a call or to standby ("We're 10-8 to call at College & Shaw")
10-90	lunch

10-33	emergency, require assistance
20	your location ("What's your 20?")
10-20	exact location
10-4	copy, okay
10-19	go to your station/home
10-26	cancelled, off call, or standby

Acknowledgements

I'm forever indebted to the "Blue Shirts" of Toronto Emergency Services for their invaluable and often hilarious insight into downtown paramedic life: Deb Bisztriczky, Fabio Bosagri, Charles Brotherston, Marcilyn Cianfarani, Mark Harpur, Trish Heinbuch, Joel Johnson, Aelish McCreary, Laura Taylor, and Billy Young. Thanks to Lyla Miller, Coordinator of Communications and Media Relations at TEMS, for arranging the ride-outs.

Anansi—you're all stars. Lynn Henry, Laura Repas, Julie Wilson, Sarah MacLachlan, et al.—thank you for believing in this book.

For always being in my corner, I owe many thanks to Samantha Haywood at Transatlantic Literary Agency. Thank you to the Ontario Arts Council for funding through the Writers' Reserve program, and to everyone I worked with through the University of Guelph's MFA program: Catherine Bush, Meaghan Strimas, Susan Swan, and Michael Winter.

Extra special thanks to Lynn Crosbie for the summer '08 mentorship.

I am so grateful to Robin Pacific for creating the Dayne Ogilvie Grant and Don Oravec at the Writers' Trust of Canada for administering the prize, which allowed me the time and support to finish the book on time.

For editorial feedback along the way: Gavin Downie, Dave Brock, Lisa Foad, Ange Holmes, Jessica Lyons, Lara Karaian, Mitzi Reinsilber, and my LJ nerds. Thank you to Heather and Luke Whittall and my parents for being so supportive. For faux sister-in-law literary cheerleading and spa dates, hugs to Christyn Cianfarani.

Marcilyn: I couldn't have done this without you. xo.

For research into COHERT, I consulted the Public Health Agency of Canada's web site and the NOHERT program's mission statement. The tone and phrasing of the fictional mission statement was inspired by the real NOHERT mission statement at http://www.phac-aspc.gc.ca/cepr-cmiu/ophs-bssp/nohert-eng.php.

AUTHOR PHOTO © KELLY CLIPPERTON

ZOE WHITTALL's first novel, *Bottle Rocket Hearts*, was named one of the best books of 2007 by *The Globe and Mail* and one of the best ten books of the year by *Quill & Quire* magazine. *NOW* magazine awarded her the title of Best Emerging Author of 2007. She is the author of three poetry books, *Precordial Thump* (2008), *The Emily Valentine Poems* (2006), and *The Best Ten Minutes of Your Life* (2001). In 2008, she won the Writers' Trust of Canada's Dayne Ogilvie Grant for best emerging gay writer in Canada. *The Globe and Mail* called her "the funniest, toughest, most life-affirming, elegant, no-holds-barred writer to emerge from Montreal since Mordecai Richler." Born in South Durham, Quebec, she has lived in Toronto since 1997.

Anansi offers complimentary reading guides that can be used with this work of fiction and others.

Ideal for people who love talking about books as much as they love reading them, each reading guide contains in-depth questions about the book that you can use to stimulate interesting discussion at your reading group gathering.

Visit www.anansi.ca to download guides for the following titles: